Beast of Ephesus

Elisabeth Greaves

In memory of my brother David, who pointed me to the heavenly gates just before he entered them.

To Joan, love from Elisabeth

Prologue

A priest cowers on the marble steps of Artemis' temple before his master, and stutters in fear; "Your Reverence... We...."

The chief priest is unusually snappy. "If it's not about the games, I don't want to hear it. One of the gladiators has already been killed, in practice!"

"Your Reverence, er... the girl we chose for a sacrifice to Artemis... She... She's a Roman citizen!"

"Jupiter! How is a High Priest supposed to put on a good show with this chaos? You have two days, find a new sacrifice. Make it a slave, they've got no rights, nobody will miss a dead slave."

Chapter 1

All the slaves in the kitchen are working quietly as we should. So all the rest get to hear me curse. "Oh, Vesta!"

A bowl has slipped out of my fingers. I watch in horror as it falls, spilling garum sauce across the earth floor. I grab out for it, too late. It smashes in seven pieces; I count them as I stare in horrified silence, knowing what'll come next.

Little Mir jumps into Aunt Yildiz' arms.

"Aysel, careful!" She yells; she sounds angry but she's stroking Mir's hair to calm him down. I try saying I'm sorry; that's not enough, Mum's watching me quietly. As she looks down at the pot her shoulders shrug, as if she can feel the mistress' birch broom on her back already. I used to break pots a lot, and Mistress Lucina always beats Mum for it. That's if Mum's lucky. If not, Lucina beats her first, then has her tied up in the peristyle garden at the back of the house, and forgets about her. She'd never hit me, maybe because I'm a child.

Once the master and mistress have been put to bed I can squeeze out of the kitchen window, scramble over the wall and let Mum loose before the cold of night gets to her, and help her back over the wall to her bed in the kitchen. Sometimes we sit for a while and whisper. Lately she's talked about men, how you can't trust any of them. She says now I'm fourteen I'm an adult and need to watch out even more...

"Maybe they won't notice," Aunt Yildiz hisses softly. She's passing the shards to Naasir; he stoops under the door to the wood pile. I've lived with his quiet ways long enough to know he's unhappy about deception; the mistress probably heard the thud anyway. I rush to take the evidence from him.

"Well, she won't beat Mum this time. I'm going to tell her I did it. On my own!" I add, as Naasir shuffles up beside me. As if a slave thousands of miles from home and nearly forty could help me! "Mum, I'm fourteen, she's got to treat me as an adult." I can imagine the broom on my own back now; Aunt Yildiz thwacked me often enough when I was small and clumsy. Mum can't get the pieces out of my hands which are young and strong from untying ropes and fixing nets. There's a tear in the corner of her eye as she reaches for the camomile cream I hid away to treat her bruises. Aunt Yildiz nods at me, proudly; Naasir creeps off to his old man's corner to pray, that's how much faith he has in me!

Mistress Lucina's in the atrium. She spends most of her time there, sitting on the edge of the central pool where the rainwater gathers, hair perfectly piled and balanced on her head and a bowl of expensive powder beside her. She stares vaguely up through the gap in the roof to the sky with huge, dark eyes, as if she were as much a prisoner as the rest of us in the Celerus household.

As I stand quietly at the door, she dips one hand in the cool water. She has a streak of mascara on her cheek- I think she's been crying, but she hasn't thrown the usual temper. By her side there's a little shrine to the goddess Artemis, the one from beside her bed upstairs. Artemis and her little bow are bent over as if they're bowing to us instead of the other way round. "I heard a noise," she murmurs.

"Mistress, I broke a pot," I tell her in a frightened whisper. "Mistress, please could you whip me instead of my mother?" She stands up in front of me, her hands trembling the same as mine.

"Well then, er…Aysel." By Jupiter, she knows my name! "You must go and buy a new one." I can't answer. I never speak to her, I wouldn't dare. She stares back for a moment, glancing at the red front door as if wondering whether the master will come home. Then she hands me a drachma.

"Er… Aysel, take this shrine to the silversmith's shop and have it fixed." I manage to nod, holding the silver thing in both hands. I daren't imagine the consequences if I let that get damaged even more! "You'd better go at once." She's hurrying to the door, and of course I follow. Naasir swings open the door without a word, and closes it quietly behind me.

Instead of that beating, I feel the sun warm on my back. I have a rough idea where the agora is, along to Curetes Street, past the gods and up the hill. If I waste time peeping between the rows of terraced houses I can glimpse the sea; everything at home smells of it. And if my rough wool tunic were slightly longer I could pretend I was one of those rich Roman women in a flowing stola, free to wander where she likes. The slap of my bare feet on sun-warmed stone could be the sound of fine leather sandals.

A soldier stands beside the road, with a spear much taller than his head. I catch my breath;   he's looking at me suspiciously. Why should he? I'm only a slave going about her mistress' business. Maybe I should pray for some god to keep his eyes off me.

Here are the gods now, on top of pillars lining the wide road to the upper town that climbs the side of the mountain. There's one for Jupiter, king of the gods, Bacchus, god of wine, Vesta, goddess of the household- Mum's top favourite- and a dozen more, lovingly carved by artists in the city. There they tower, high above me, looking down on us the way Lucina looks down her nose at me. According to Mum, the gods made me a slave, so why look down on me as if it's my fault?

I'm nearly at the agora, the grand arches Mum described are just above me, as high as the Celerus house, but completely shaped of stone. It's odd being here alone. Once or twice I've come to town with Mum, but usually it's Naasir's job.

Naasir! Is that who Mum's warning me about when she begged me not to trust any man? I know she finds him scary-looking, with his dark African face, and that scar which runs from his forehead right down his neck. But appearances can fool you; he's not scary at all. When I was little I used to pretend he was the father I longed for; I wouldn't listen to the other children telling me my skin would be much darker if he was, I only stopped playing when my Mum set me straight.

"I'd never be interested in a sap like him," was how she put it. But I'd swap our master for Naasir, I've never heard an angry word from him. I know he's old, but I couldn't keep quiet if I had the beatings he gets.

The gate of the agora's filled with men in flowing woollen togas, talking louder than anyone ought to. I don't feel safe trying to cut through them, but if I don't I'll never get to the potter's, and I'll be in such trouble I'll never be let out again. They're shouting something about gods and shrines; I don't really care, I just wish they'd move.

In the middle of the crowd there's a short man, half-bald, holding up his hands in silence, waiting for the rest of them to listen. But his voice cuts above them all soon enough, when he looks in my direction.

Why me? I'm hardly a grown woman, in the tunic and collar of a slave, as plain tanned and brown-haired as anyone on the quayside, far beneath the notice of a Roman Citizen.

"Men, stand aside for a moment, this young lady needs to get past." I can't believe it. The crowd parts at once, and I walk through, hoping I'm using the elegant walk of a Roman lady. The little man turns his wispy head and his funny nose to me, and sends me on my way with a friendly smile.

For a second there I was someone! I want to stop and breathe in that feeling of importance...

No time; the soldier's there again, in his red tunic and polished breastplate. No, maybe it's another one, they all look the same. There's no need for me to be as alarmed as I am, no need for my heart to beat faster. If I stare straight back, he might go away, but I'm a slave, we don't tend to look freemen in the eye.

Stallholders throng the agora, selling everything you could ever wish for, crying their wares;

"Come and taste our fresh lamb!"

7

"Get your sauces here!"

"Olives, ladies, lovely, shiny olives!"

There's cloth enough to clothe the legions, red wool like the soldiers' cloaks, glinting brass plates- wouldn't they be harder to break than pot?   Crowds of regular people throng the baker's, buying their daily bread- no chance for me to stop and fill my rumbling stomach.

Once I admit to being hungry, the smells of food are all around me, sausages dangle, live turkeys cackle in pens, sheep are bleating, even sacrificial doves look tasty. At home I'm always hungry and I hardly notice, but I pass so close to a fruit stall here, I hardly think they'd notice if I helped myself to an apple, or even a fig.

I'm carrying a very expensive bundle under my arm, so I'd better hurry on my mistress' business. I'm nobody again; I'm not allowed to have money, so I close my eyes to all the bright colours and hurry to the potter's, easy to pick out by the whirring sound of his wheel as he spins it with a pole.

Again I'm in luck. He has just the sort of pot I broke. I've seen him sometimes when he delivers to the house, and it's good to see a familiar face. "Morning, Master Potter!"

"Morning, Aysel! Out on your own today? You broke another pot?" He passes me a new one, I hand over the money, and he fixes me with a frown. "So you had to come alone? How's your mother?"

"Fine." I don't know what he means, or how much I dare say to anyone outside the household. He knows it, and explains what he already understands.

"Usually your mistress beats her. She must be strong..."

Yes, she's my mum! I don't think it's any of his business! I stick to answering him simply; "Not today. She's fine." And now I have my pot I need to find the silversmith's.

He's at his shop door. He has a fierce stare, and mutters; "Don't get many of your sort up here!" He means my collar; if I was a higher-class slave in a richer household I probably wouldn't wear one. All I can do is push the bundle at him and stretch out my hand, where I've clasped the money tightly all the way from home. I wish I was back there now, where everyone knows who I am. Maybe I can leave the broken shrine with him for my master to pick up later.

Or maybe my mistress doesn't want him to know it's broken. "Can you fix it?" I whisper. He stares in disgust at the statue.

"Juno! What happened to that? Did it fall on the floor? Artemis won't be pleased!" I can't answer, and he soon realises that. "Yes, I can fix it. Give me a few minutes. Go and get something to eat." I nod at him, but I don't move away. What's the point? I've got nothing to buy food with.

"Go on!" His fierce stare deepens. I'm starting to feel even worse about people in Ephesus I don't know, when he picks up a little coin and throws it to me. I'm so delighted I forget to say thanks.

What should I eat? Suddenly there's such a choice. Barley porridge doesn't appeal. Fish? I could taste it hot for once.

My legs are leading me, my stomach's already chosen; I'm back at the fruit stall. Now I can pick a fig for myself, hold it in my hand with its soft skin tickling my fingers. Close by is an empty pillar; probably one of the gods got knocked off in a drunken fight. With the fig in my mouth I scramble up above everyone's head. Those men from the arch are still arguing, some are even shouting. There's likely to be some drama, and since I can't get away, I'm in a good place to watch.

If that soldier up there on the wall would stop watching me…

Chapter 2

The short, friendly man who let me pass is still in the middle of the crowd. The men in togas throw so many questions at him, he scarcely has time to answer them. They keep laughing as if they know better than a stranger. I hear them crying out stuff about Artemis, swearing by Jupiter and Juno. The taste of my fig's more interesting than that.

It tastes as sweet as Ephesus town looks right now. It's so busy and full of life; there are children running, playing with toys- I don't remember ever having one of those- bone dolls and wooden swords. Why didn't I? Of course, because I'm property. And there are young ladies in long stolas which fall to their feet, not just tunics that make your ankles stick out. Some are talking freely to a group of young men. Will I ever get to know any men outside our household? No, of course not, because I'm just property.

"There is neither Jew nor Greek, neither slave nor free!" What? That smiling man's got my attention now. What kind of world does he come from, if he believes that? Jew? The province of Judea, maybe? Wherever that might be. *Of course* we're slaves; we have no rights at all, we could starve and die and no real person would care!

Ah, no, once I listen properly I understand a bit. He says it's not fair, all men and women are equal, Africans, Asians, Romans, just everybody! Seriously? Even the gods don't believe that, or they'd do something about it.

The gods! My mistress' shrine must be fixed, and if I get stuck here with it in a riot, it'll definitely be me tied up in the peristyle this time instead of my Mum. I slide down off the tall pillar and sneak between people towards the silversmith's. At least my pathetic diet means I'm skinny enough to get through little gaps. The shrine is fixed; the silversmith has stood Artemis back up again, now she can stand back beside my mistress' bed to help her get through each day.

Why does she need help? She's rich enough, I wouldn't have thought she had much to complain about. I bet she never has strange soldiers staring at her across the market when she's going innocently about her business! There he is again, definitely the same soldier. I'd better find a safe way home. Behind a fish stall there's a small arch, a back way out of the agora. I follow it; with a pot under one arm and a silver shrine under the other, I can't afford to take chances. I'm in a street on the side of the mountain; the houses are taller here, the stone's cut flatter, there are plants outside the doors.

The air tastes sweet, the view out to sea is amazing, but I have no idea where I am. Some soldier will catch me, read my collar and drag me home with a story about my running away. Still, it's easy enough to head down towards the sea. The lower we get, the tighter the houses are packed, and the louder that voice rattles in my head.

"Neither slave nor free." If only.

I'm walking just above the stadium, where I've been once or twice before. It's not so far from home; the master goes there a lot, to watch the entertainments. I hear they have musicians there, and races with horses and chariots, and strange sacrifices. Mum said they sometimes show animals there, animals they trapped in distant countries and brought here for the people to stare at. I didn't believe her, until one night I was woken by a roar which made my stomach churn. Naasir whispered that it was a lion from Africa; I suppose he ought to know. But he isn't allowed to go to the stadium and can't tell me anything about the thrills of the circus.

Beside the stadium is a gymnasium where men go to exercise, and do even more discussing. I'm there right now. Inside I can see a wide patch of clipped grass, and men play-fighting, tumbling all over the grass, laughing out silly battle-cries. I have to stand and watch for a moment; I didn't know they wear nothing to train in, absolutely nothing!

11

A young man in a tunic comes out from the arch. I don't know whether he's looking at my collar or my bundles. "Hello, little one."

"I'm not little," I snap back, walking on. Two of his friends join him behind me; one's in a toga, wrapped all round his body and over his arm. All three are on the pavement a few steps away, walking the same way as me. I hope that's just coincidence.

"How old are you, then?" one of them calls. My Mum's endless warnings about men flash through my head. I walk faster, and turn down a side-street to let them pass. They are following me, closing in on me. I daren't run, in case I damage the shrine under my arm, but my heart starts to pump harder all the same.

"Answer me!" He grabs my collar, his fingers squash it against my neck. I can't answer; he's a free citizen, I can't talk to them. One of them reaches to take my pot away.

Silently, a dark figure steps out behind them. Is it someone come to rescue me? No, it's only Naasir, wandering back from buying some fish. These trained, athletic boys will have him tied up in a moment. In my head I'm laughing bitterly that the only decent person around to help me is a weak-willed slave with an ugly scar.

But the young men aren't laughing. Naasir isn't running. He steps up beside me, takes the bundle of silver from me, and tells the three of them; "Masters, go home. Your parents would be ashamed."

"What are you going to do about it, slave?" jeers the man in the toga. His friend leans over, and whispers in his ear. His face twists, and he growls;

"Naasir, is it? You'll be sorry you crossed me, when I tell my dad!" He picks up a stone and throws it at my head. We quicken our pace as the others pick up stones too. Up the alley, past a warehouse, back into the street. I can hear stones falling behind me, bouncing, they're throwing them so hard. I hope Naasir's following me as I round a corner to the red

12

front door. Peeping back up the street, I can see him trying to hurry with the shrine cradled in front of him.

"Go in the back way," Naasir reminds me. As I follow him I notice red flecks all over his tunic. He's bleeding badly. I've only got one sore patch from a stone on my head, but he's been behind me all the way home, and all the other stones hit him.

Mum's treats Naasir with cream, but he can't stand straight enough to carry the plates into the triclinium for the master's evening meal. So Mum has to serve; she needs to borrow a clean tunic from Aunt Yildiz to go to the front part of the house in. She walks slowly, trembling at every moment, but determined not to break anything.

I open the triclinium door for her, and she carries in a dish of meat and sauce. Mum comes back for the next dish, and carries it with less of a tremble, while I take the first dish back to the kitchen, running my fingers round it before my aunt can scrape it. I scrounge a few blobs of meat and tangy sauce.

Then, as the master's mood improves, he looks about and demands; "Where's the African?" The mistress doesn't know, and my Mum says nothing. "I don't feed and clothe him so he can shirk his duty, however you favour him!"

"I don't." The mistress answered so quietly I scarcely caught that. But as Mum steps out again, with the door open, I hear her add; "Not like you favoured that woman!" We don't often hear that much gossip. And that's all; Mistress Lucina grows very quiet, as quiet as Mum, more food comes back to the kitchen than usual. Soon the meal's over, and she takes up her lyre to help Master Panaius relax.

We wash up, then I wonder whether it's worth asking Mum about soldiers and how they behave. No, it won't be worth it. Instead I take my spindle and a tube of clean wool. Spinning calms me, and I settle for asking;

"Mum, is that true? Is the master fond of other women?"

"No." She says that so firmly, I have to believe her. And her tone makes it clear the conversation's already over. I draw the wool through my fingers, twist the spindle and drop it; it draws out a satisfying thin thread. In an hour I have a little ball, enough for a few rows of weaving. No harm has come from that staring soldier in the agora. Naasir has dozed off in a warm corner near the stove, safe from the threats of rich boys, the sun has set and the excitement of my day's faded back into grim normality.

Morning begins just the same; more stoking of the stove, washing of clothes, spinning in brief moments when we need rest from other tasks. In the alley I can hear the clank of an axe, rhythmically chopping wood; injured or not, Naasir's up and doing what he does best. After we serve the master with bread and cheese, he sets off to work, up in town as a clerk. He won't ride, he likes walking as much as I do.

Little Mir scrubs the tiles round the pond in Naasir's place, giving him a chance to catch up on his wood-chopping   All is calm, it's business as usual, no news, no talk, just constant work.

A knock at the back door breaks the calm. Before Aunt Yildiz can reach it, it bursts open and two soldiers march in. The brightness of them in our plain wool-and-soot kitchen is startling- I stare at waxed leather breastplates, red tunics, proper sandals, and worst, gleaming swords.

"Where's the trouble-maker?" they want to know. Auntie shakes her head; none of us ever cause trouble. A soldier grabs her by front of her tunic and carries on; "We're here to take the troublemaker away. The circus is on tomorrow."

"There must be a mistake," Auntie begins, but they shake their heads, and he tosses her away, to the ground.

"There's no mistake!" I recognise him, and he recognises me, I can tell by his stare of surprise.

"We could take them all..." the other soldier suggests. I think I must be exhausted from yesterday's drama and I've fallen into a strange dream, standing up.   It grows more unreal when quiet, injured Naasir creeps out of his corner to stand between us women and the soldiers. I've never heard him speak so clearly.

"You must mean me." Troublemaker? The old slave who wouldn't say 'boo' to a goose, who put up with being stoned by boys, because he couldn't run as fast as me? The soldiers think he looks trouble enough; they grab an arm each, nearly lifting him off the ground.

"You're wrong! He's not trouble! You've come to the wrong house! Let him go!"

"Aysel!" Mum gasps. She means, 'Why are you talking back? Don't risk that!'

I don't know why I'm still talking, I've just seen red; not the red of those soldiers' tunics, but the red on Naasir's back. He was protecting me in the street, from those boys, and now he's protecting us all.

"This isn't fair! Let him go, I'll tell my master. He's Panaius, the town clerk!"

"We know," one of the soldiers laughs. Auntie's edging towards the door to the triclinium. With a prayer to Fortuna she listens for our mistress- but what would she do to help us?

A soldier grabs my collar, pulling my face so close he spits in my eye as he speaks; "Rude little slave, aren't you? I think we'll take both of you."

"To the circus?" Naasir cries out. "A girl?"

"A little prize for the gladiators?" the other soldier cackles. "The other one went missing, but look at the face on this one! String her up in the middle of the arena, they'll love that!" I've heard enough from Mum and the children in the street about the circuses they hold in the stadium just a few streets away, executions of anyone the Romans don't like, people sacrificed to animals, with no escape because the place is ringed with soldiers. They're both leering at me now, their breath smells of decay, as if I'm already dead.

Somehow I manage to gulp; "I caused the trouble. He's nobody." I'm tied up, and terrified. But they don't swallow my story. Naasir hasn't had the sense to run away, so they're tying him up too. Mum slaps one of the soldiers; he puts his sword to her neck. Auntie yanks little Mir back, to stop him thwacking the soldiers' knees. Who knows what they'll do, in this temper?

Naasir and I are marched into the alley, past his abandoned woodpile and his un-mended fishing nets, out into the street. Yesterday I thought being a slave was a miserable life, but compared to being a prisoner of the Romans that was life in the Elysian Fields.

Chapter 3.

I get to watch my friends' faces grow pale in front of me, as they salute us with horrified silence; they know when anyone from our neighbourhood's taken away by soldiers they very rarely come back. I know it too; I'm struggling to make my feet work, I'm so full of fear. The little girl from down the street is crying into her father's apron.

We're into the street where the fishermen's huts are. They're called free men, but that doesn't seem to mean much. They still fear the soldiers, but instead of silence they dare to blow me kisses, shout thanks to Naasir for various little kind deeds, and call out blessings to us both. I bet some of these will be at the circus tomorrow, eating and drinking, and calling for our deaths in the name of entertainment.

We walk up the wide Curetes Street, where I swung my legs so freely yesterday. As well as the slap of my bare feet I hear a dozen curious strangers pattering around us. The scent of the sea, which I've smelt all my life, is fading, now it just clings to me and my clothes, and my tight bun of greasy hair. I gaze up to the elegant statue of Jupiter, and joke with him; "Send a thunderbolt, please!" He wouldn't send one for a slave, we don't count as people in their eyes. Maybe I should try another god, there are lots to choose from, all brilliant white in the unstoppable sunshine.

Maybe I'll choose Vesta, Mum's prayed to her often enough; her marble eyes stare vacantly, way above mine. Naasir isn't looking at any of the statues, but he's not stumbling either, so he must have had a word with one of them. I wonder which one he picked; he must have thought a lot about death at his age, few slaves seem to make it to forty.

We're back in the agora. The market bustles the same as yesterday. As we march by between soldiers, people ignore us until one soldier decides to do some advertising on the chief priest's behalf. "Here comes some entertainment for the circus tomorrow!" Some stallholders laugh obediently, afraid of the legionaries turning over their stalls. Naasir jumps to feel a sword prodding his back.

"Come and watch the new gladiator!" the soldier yells.

Passing the silversmith's, I throw him a glance that definitely begs him to help us. He points at our collars, jokes to a customer, and follows us, probably to buy his tickets to the holiday event. But the woman on the fruit stall throws us each an apricot. One of the soldiers catches the first, and bites straight into it, spilling juice onto his stubble and tunic. The other is squished beneath a Roman foot and bleeds into the dusty floor of the agora.

I look for the short man and his hopeful smile, for another suggestion that somewhere in the world someone believes in equality and kindness. He's not out orating in the agora today. There are two more. They sound even louder than the little one, and they have the free men listening. One of them's stood beside that empty pillar I was lounging on, not even a full day ago.

"This is what I'm talking about! All these gods, you carved them by yourselves! Do you assign power to your tools, made by men's hands? Or even to your children, who you brought into being? Your children don't have power over you! There is only one God, and He looks like this!" Even Naasir lifts his head and looks back to see what the orator means. Of course it's an empty pillar.

The discussion I found dull yesterday is suddenly interesting, I want to stay and listen, so I don't keep walking to whatever prison they've planned for us. I want to hear anyone who talks about life going on and on and never stopping. I want to know why that orator cares so much that he'll stand in front of so many people to preach something so controversial. But the soldiers force me on, and I miss everything, except for the silversmith turning back to the man at the pillar with an angry hiss of; "I make the gods!"

They're not taking us to the stadium in the lower town; I don't know where we are exactly, but we're passing a temple.

Like everything on the side of the mountain, it's built of stone, hewn in the quarry where so many ordinary men work and die.

Smoke is rising from the temple, as it does every day, I can see it any time in the evening if I climb our back wall to look for the moon. Close up, the stink of burning flesh is awful. I don't want to think of burning flesh, or sacrifices; is that what I am now?

I'm getting used to walking in fear, or my legs have decided to keep working without me. I'm surprised they've brought us to the theatre. That's not far from where my master works. If only we could get word to him, we've always served him faithfully, he can't wish us dead. But I can't write, even if I had something to write on, and as I think of him and his grim face I have yet another sickening feeling. Panaius Celerus sent us here.

He must have! He works near the barracks in town, he thinks his wife treats Naasir too well. So he's had him taken away. And he's not even aware that I exist, so he'll never miss me.

The gladiators are training in the theatre, where businessmen can watch them and place bets on who'll live and who'll die. We're shoved in front of their trainer, who looks us over critically, and clearly doesn't like what he sees. "Well, well! You don't see a scar that size every day! You should've died from that! Yes, he'll do fine, he'll give them something to get started on. But what were you thinking for the girl?"

"Didn't you hear about the Artemis girl who got away?" the soldier chuckles. "The little prize for the winning gladiator?"

"This scrawny girl, a prize?"

"An honouring of the goddess," the soldier leers.

"They'll fight over her," the trainer observes, over my head. "They'll probably kill her too." In answer, the soldier rattles my collar. Who cares if a slave dies? The trainer

19

doesn't seem to. He points a fat thumb at a row of arches in the theatre wall; they're where the gladiators shelter from the weather, and change out of their armour, and this is where we'll stay, tied together, until the trainer decides what else to do with us.

At last, of all the strange places in the world, I have a private place to talk to Naasir. And what's the first thing I say? Thank you? Good fortune? No. "We're going to die."

"Maybe."

"Certainly! Look at us! Look at them!" He is, he's watching the gladiators more closely than I dare to. They're all bare-chested, but like everywhere else in life they seem to be unfairly matched. Some have short Roman swords made of razor-sharp iron, and strong helmets, while others only have tall forked tridents like Neptune's statue, and are flailing nets about like fishermen. Well, not like the fishermen in our part of town; they can all spread nets out over the water with a quick flick of their wrists, their sons used to show me when I was little, in snatched minutes while my Mum bought fish. The swordsmen are chopping up the nets with an abandon that would drive the fishermen crazy; they depend on their nets, while these men are playing with their tools, and tomorrow they'll be playing with their own lives. "Naasir, I don't want to die."

"No. Who does?" he asks. He doesn't want any reply, he's too keen on watching the fighting. I watch a muscular long-haired man chopping his sword down on a little shield, trying to cut it in two. He's thrown his opponent's shoulder out of joint and he's wriggling like a fish, struggling to click it back in again. But the swordsman's oblivious, he chops on, over and over, as if it's real already. He's a ginger-haired barbarian from the north. Barbarian's the right word, he has a thick ginger beard which hides half his face; if he was afraid, no-one could ever tell.

There's another man wielding a hammer, battering it into a large pillar of sailcloth. As he hammers harder and swings further, his blows break the stitching and straw spills out of it. Just straw today, no blood, no guts. Naasir looks riveted.

"You're a man of peace, how can you watch this?"

"Everyone has his flaws," he hisses back. I'm going to get no comfort from him. "Learn a man's flaws, and you can use them to your advantage." All right, now he's said more words in one conversation than he's ever said to me before, in the 'prison' of Celerus.

Half my mind's still on our horrible abduction, the other half's distracted by another man with a net. He's being beaten almost to the ground by a gladiator as big as a bear, and probably as heavy. He's a good-looking young man to be thrashed like that; I have to face the facts, his looks don't matter at all. If he's going to face that bear-size man again tomorrow he'll be cut to ribbons in the first few minutes of his bout. And I doubt I'll be conscious to see it.

"I am so scared, if I'd eaten I would have brought it up," I observe to Naasir, in desperation. Maybe talking will help me feel less sick. "Why aren't you afraid?"

"I am. I'd be a fool not to be. But I need to get you out of here."

"Me? Both of us!"

"I've seen plenty of this life. You're just a girl."

"A grown adult," I protest. "And you'll do no better than me against that lot!"

"I might." He's got to be joking! This isn't a situation for false hope. The only bright spark here's that blazing sun frazzling my bare feet that stick outside the arch. If he's going to be driven mad by fear, it's up to me to do something useful.

"Heh, what are you doing?" Naasir hisses. He fights against my hands behind our backs; he can feel I'm pulling at the knots. I've freed Mum plenty of times before, I've unpicked the knots, we both figured out how to twist your wrists so they can't tie you so tightly. I can nearly slide one hand out of the ring of rope.

"Shh. Almost free."

"And what then? Are you going to run away across a field of gladiators in broad daylight?" I stare at him, straight into his large brown eyes, stupidly steady. I wonder if my father was calm like that, or was he grimly determined like my Mum? Suddenly I don't like Naasir any more. I had a little glimmer of hope, and behind our backs he's winding us together again.

"Be patient," he whispers, rationally. "Wait until you have the advantage."

Before I can argue, I'm distracted by a cry from one of the gladiators, the young one who looked like the worst from my point of view. It's a yowl of pain. The bear has caught him by surprise, thwacking his sword. He skids along the orchestra floor and skins his chin on the ground at my feet. Hmm. Under different circumstances I would have been amused.

He looks up, wiping his chin with his wrist. He jumps to his feet and grins; "Hello, I'm Secundus! Who are…?" His question dies on his lips; he's seen our collars. You don't talk to dogs, so why talk to slaves? Without another word he grabs his tunic off the stone bench beside us, a plain wool tunic just like ours, and strides away to his comrades in arms.

Naasir's almost smiling at the sight he made. "If you'd been a Patrician lady he would have wrapped you round his finger!" I don't know what he's implying, but I do know what gladiators are like. I've heard them paraded through town sometimes, with women screaming their names. They're treated like heroes, and think they really are.

This one hasn't gone far, he's still a distance from the rest of them. He stopped to pull on his tunic. Now he's turned back to ask his trainer a question, and the trainer's marching straight up to me.

He grabs my chin in his hand and scrutinises my face and hair. Hopefully if I avoid looking him in the eye he won't notice my terror and command that Secundus to run me through at once- although that could be a blessing in a very heavy disguise.

"Escort her to the temple priest," he tells the gladiator, but it's too late. A crowd has gathered at the theatre entrance, loads of those rich men in togas, fired up and angry about something. It doesn't look as if anybody could squeeze out through that arch between them.

At their head, being pushed along and jostled by forceful arms, come those two men we heard speaking in the agora when we passed by before, the ones who were preaching equality. I wondered why their talk hadn't driven the Ephesians mad; I suppose now it has. The silversmith's leading them; that's not surprising, he sounded deeply offended an hour ago. Now he's not just muttering, he's brandishing his tools and yelling at the top of his voice;

"I make the gods! We make the gods!" Tradesmen around him join him in his shout, slapping their tools on their leather aprons, or against each other's tools.

"They insult our goddess!" he carries on. "Artemis is the Mother of Ephesus, Ephesus is Artemis' home!"

The mob are surging into the orchestra, piling round the wide semi-circle of seats, some knocking others out of the way and down over the stone without any care. They all take up the chant;

"Artemis is great! Artemis is great!" There are women waving kitchen tools, pans, brooms and rolling pins. One or two of them are carrying small children; their baby cries cut sharply through the chants. And the two men who dared to preach freedom are trapped, while people of all races are demanding their blood.

Chapter 4

"Artemis is great! Artemis of Ephesus!" The chanting's filling my ears. The theatre's filling with white-robed bodies, forcing, crushing. Even though I'm a prisoner, I'm relatively safe within my cool stone arch, with two gladiators directly in front of me. If I turn my face to the wall it blocks out most of the chaos and I can almost think clearly. Maybe when the gladiators move, Naasir and I could squeeze out into the crush. I could shake off the ropes and we could disappear. With our collars proclaiming who we belong to?

That Secundus and his trainer watch the crush closely. Wooden benches are pushed over, the clatters echo out over the valley. "You see how men can get swept away?" the trainer observes. "The theatre's a good place to learn to play your audience."

"Sir, they're going to lynch those men."

"It looks that way," sighs the trainer, briefly, with a shrug. He must have seen much more death than most people, in his profession.

"Should we do something?"

"Against that mob? It's none of our business." The gladiator shrugs in agreement, and they both move back to shelter under our arch, so I can't talk privately to Naasir any longer.

"Who are they?" Secundus wonders aloud.

"Followers of that man from Judea, I heard. The pint-sized fool who keeps speaking in the market and the lecture hall and so on."

"The one who says gods can't be made by men? No wonder the tradesmen are angry. Go on, get them!" he laughs. It seems that's what the crowd's about to do, take hold of them and throw them down somewhere. "So, where's the Judean today? Hiding from this lot?"

"Probably. The Jews are a rotten bunch." That gives them both cause for a sneering laugh. The crowd's seething; all types of race are there, do the gladiators have a grudge against them all? I don't want to watch these two men torn to pieces like birds in front of the temple.

"Is that Judean the one they call the miracle man?" Secundus recalls from some gossip about town.

"Yes, they do. They're saying he heals the sick and brings the dead to life. It's ridiculous, the stories people make up. Wait till they bring out Artemis' statue tomorrow morning, she'll do just the same miracles!"

I try to focus my mind on Artemis, the beautiful goddess with a silver circlet on her brow, and flowing hair. She carries a silver bow to defend her city, and rests her hand on the head of a crouching lion, knowing it can cause her no harm. I was born in Ephesus, under the shadow of her temple, so surely she could save me, and take me back to the Celerus house, the closest place to Elysium I can think of right now.

But I keep picturing her bent over before me, toppling dangerously down onto the lion's mane. The silversmith fixed her up with a few blobs of solder, while he let me eat. What's turned him from that decent, considerate craftsman to the fierce rampager inciting a riot in front of our eyes? I could easily believe the heat's the cause of these people's boiling blood; I don't remember it being this hot in years. Plus, the silversmith will lose money if people stop buying his rich shrines and gods.

Somebody's climbing up to the stage, and not someone in the garb of an actor. I look up, expecting to see the fiery Judean speaker, come to save his friends. Will he strike the rioters down with flames, or will they lynch him too? No, the man approaching the stage is flanked by Roman guards carrying tall spears. I recognise him at once, and Naasir looks up from whatever dream of death was absorbing him. It's Panaius Celerus, our master.

As he walks up the stone steps, he's trying to mutter something to the other soldiers he's brought with him. They're waiting below, and by the time he's raised his voice enough to be heard over the incessant chanting, he's talking loudly enough for me to hear it all. "Tell him I can see him from here, and he must leave at once."

Peering carefully between the tightly-packed bobbing heads to the entrance arch. I can just make out a wispy head, lit by the roasting sun so his face seems to shine. No friendly smile for anyone today. Soldiers have taken him by the shoulder. "Naasir, I can see the Judean."

"Paul."

"Excuse me?"

He hisses back quickly; "His name is Paul." Then he shuts his mouth firmly. Our master's making progress on the stage, still giving orders as he has to us since I was born.

"Don't let that man in here! See to it! He's well-known here, if he dies in a riot, we'll be blamed, and he'll become a martyr. That will cause a stink across the whole Empire. Look at the trouble that other Jew caused, the one they crucified! So keep him away!" As I stare up at my master, surprised by his insistence, I notice Naasir's usual frown-line has gone from his nose; something's roused him.

Panaius at work is so different to the master we know. He shows his authority just as strongly, yet here, in the heart of a riot, he's unusually calm. He watches as the soldiers he's commandeered pick out the victims in the chaos, and bring up the ringleaders of the riot. They're not stupid; one caution from a fully-armed legionary and a quick poke with a sharp spear is all they need to calm them.

Panaius' poise and control astonish me. He actually commands the silversmith to raise his hands in a request for peace from his mob. He waits, with a faint tapping of his foot, until quiet descends on the whole theatre. I wait to hear the fate of the two orators who stand, helplessly waiting. So does the crowd. Only when he has silence does Panaius speak.

"Do you dare cause riot in one of the Roman Empire's greatest cities? And do you expect me to blame these men, who are virtually strangers to us? NO, I WILL NOT! They know little of our ways. But you, be rational, and remember we are the guardians of great Artemis' temple. Her image fell from heaven to US, in Ephesus..."

Of course my master's been educated in the Roman way. He's lived his life in public, rising to be the city clerk; he understands how to speak well to a crowd and how to sway people.

"These men have not robbed our temples, nor blasphemed our goddess. If you feel they have wronged you personally," and he glares at the sheepish silversmith, "Take the matter to the courts in a civilised fashion. Or will you see our city defamed because of this commotion? I WILL NOT!" he repeats. At once the crowd begins to cheer.

"We will not! We will not!" Sheep! I have to admire Panaius' calm in the face of chaos. He's content to perform for his audience. I'm sure that he could get me and Naasir out of our mess.

"Then go home," my master orders the people. "Save your cheers for the circus!"

That remark churns my stomach. I have one brief moment to decide; he may help us, or condemn us again, but only if I give him the chance to choose. The crowd's murmuring instead of chanting, the soldiers are gesturing with their spears towards the gate. People start to wander away, now the excitement's gone out of them. Panaius is coming down from the stage with the two orators, who are thanking him, and sweating, either with relief or just with this crazy August heat. He passes within feet of us.

"Master, Panaius!" I scream out from under the arch. Naasir glares at me, and shakes his head. Does he think he has a plan, because I don't see him trying anything to free us!

Secundus jumps back with a clank of the metal greaves on his legs. His trainer clamps his hand over my mouth, waving away two soldiers who've turned their spears in the direction of my cry.

Panaius Celerus walks on, deep in conversation with the Romans protecting him. He probably hasn't even heard me. He's gone past us, and would never see us in the arch if he looked back now. Of course he wouldn't notice me. Can the sand on the Mediterranean shore turn the tide? A slave's as powerless and as worthless as a grain of sand.

The drama's over, for today. Some of the people rioting a just minute ago are chatting in cheerful groups, arranging to meet at tomorrow's circus, laughing over a list of the entertainments to be shown on the holy day. Two boys, swept along in the action, are playing with their dogs where the gladiators have been fighting. One woman's sat down quietly to feed her baby on a wooden bench. As it suckles she's singing softly; I know the song, a song of Artemis, one my Mum used to sing to me.

"Run with my deer, my arrows will guard you;
Sleep without fear, no lions will harm you.
I'll keep you safe, whatever may come;
Sleep without fear, and dream."

The gladiators have all gone, except that Secundus, who's ordered to untie Naasir. He doesn't notice our ropes are loose, and doesn't care that he's taking away the one familiar person I have left in the world. Naasir was only ever a gentle fellow-slave to me, a distant dreamer, someone who didn't affect my life in any way. Now being taken from him floods me with a new despair.

"Naasir!" I sound nearly as hysterical as our mistress. "Don't leave me!" Tears are filling my eyes, tears which have been waiting hours to fall. The world around me turns to fuzz through the mask of my tears, and my legs give way.

The trainer's dragging me up from the ground. Who knows how long I've lain there? Not long, if he has anything to do with it. He studies me curiously, but not unkindly. "You must have been a very bad girl, to be sent here," is all he can say, although he offers me his arm to lean on while my eyes refocus. I step out of his way, dash away my tears with a work-callused thumb, and snap back;

"I'm a woman! An *innocent* woman!"

"Finding a bit of spirit now?" he retorts. "You'll need it!" Now he takes a firm hold of my wrist, clearly confident that I could never escape from him. I'm marched out of the theatre and along the side of the mountain. I never realised the city was so big; I bet a hundred thousand people could live here, in these houses packed close together, spreading out between the mountain and the sea. And the temples tower up, set high up on the mountain as the gods are far above us- there are plenty, all ornate, pillared, cold and forbidding.

At first the street up here is quiet, as if all the energy of the city is suddenly spent. But quickly we reach the temple of Artemis, the Artemision. It's marked out by the frequent ching of coins in a box, the moans of people praying aloud and the unending trail of acrid smoke from the sacrifices free men and women make whenever they're in the mood, to bribe the stone gods to forget how bad they sometimes are. Mum taught me not to worry too much about sin; our master and mistress are like our gods. The rest is their responsibility.

A scruffy woman is perched on the edge of the steps, listening with her head on one side as my bare feet slap the stone. She must be a soothsayer, waiting to tell people their futures, for a fee.

"You're joking!" The chief priest stands over me, on the step of the temple. "This is what you bring me to tempt those gladiators? They're a fine-looking set of men, we could dress them as Mars or Jupiter and they'd carry it off. But what were you thinking with this? She's filthy! She doesn't look like a proper woman! *And* she's got the collar!"

"You're known for performing miracles," the trainer tries, to flatter the priest into agreement.

"I'll need a miracle," agrees the priest. "You know well enough, these are my games and my reputation hangs on this. You realise one of the Senators from Rome is coming tomorrow?" The trainer nods slightly, hesitant at the reminder of his students performing in the arena before such an important guest. "We need a big fight, and the best show!"

I want to plead with him there and then, tell him I'll never provide decent entertainment, so he may as well let me go. But it's so long since I tasted a drop of water, my tongue sticks in my mouth, and my fear keeps me silent.

The soothsayer on the temple steps has been foretelling the fall of the world to a wide-eyed girl my age. In an instant she pushes the girl away, draws a dagger from her threadbare tunic, and squeals as she waves it;

"Hail Artemis of the Ephesians, fallen to Earth in a beam of moonlight!"

The priest turns to me with one bushy eyebrow raised, and asks a question I've been dreading; "What did they say your name was?"

"Aysel," I whisper.

"Moonlight," he translates. "Interesting."

I'm dragged inside the temple, and into a room behind the hall where the sacred flame is burning. It's the most luxurious room I've ever seen; the stone walls are covered with warm tapestries in brightly contrasting colours, showing images of the gods. I see Artemis stroking deer and a lion in a dazzling green forest, and Jupiter carrying off a maiden, and other stories I was never told.

There are three long couches, covered with deep, embroidered cushions for the priests and priestesses to lounge on. Large bunches of grapes and bowls of nuts are displayed in the centre of the room on a rug woven with an intricate pattern which leaves my hungry brain dizzy. I'm hardly even looking at the nuts when the chief priest shakes his head, wobbling his ceremonial hat, and snaps;

"They're not for you!"

I know, I'm not stupid, what's the point in false hope?

Another huge man is here with the priest, a thickly-bearded man in a wide leather apron dusted with soot and flecked with burn-marks. Like one of the gladiators, he wields a hammer. I'm told to lie down with my neck across his blacksmith's anvil. I'd prefer not to, but I'm not allowed a choice. The metal is pleasantly cool, reminding me how thirsty I am.

The blacksmith comes at me with a long pick and the hammer. To deal me a merciful death blow? No. He gives two strikes with that hammer, and I'm ordered to stand up again. My head feels ridiculously light, and my collar's still lying on the anvil. He picks it up, mutters; "Handy piece of metal!" then takes his tools and leaves.

For the first time in my life I'm free of my collar. And it doesn't mean a thing.

Chapter 5

I'm still running my fingers round my neck in unhidden amazement, when another stranger arrives, in those bright colours I'm so unused to. At last, it's another woman. She looks a few years older than me, from what I've glimpsed now and again in the kitchen water bucket, but a hundred times more beautiful. Her hair is glossy, almost shining, and her cheeks are full of colour. She walks in with a swing to her step, showing off new leather sandals with some marks of the carving tools still on them, and asks the chief priest without any hint of shyness;

"What do you want me to do with this one? Oh, Artemis!" The blue powder on her eyelids makes her eyes look bigger, but not as wide as they grow when she looks at me. I thought she must be an educated lady, but she obviously doesn't know it's rude to stare. "Call in the other girls, I can't manage this on my own. To Hades with that Senator, coming at this time of year. She's ten times worse than last year's girl!"

She doesn't care that she's insulting a slave to her face, but grins at me and introduces herself; "I'm Drusa, I serve here in the temple. Don't worry, by the time I've finished with you, you'll be the most beautiful sacrifice Ephesus has ever seen! What's your name?"

I can't seem to open my mouth. We both just walked past the altar on the front porch, the heat of the flames and the stench of burning cow-flesh are filling the air as she speaks. And she thinks it's funny to joke about being a sacrifice? At any rate, she chats on, oblivious. "Is there something wrong? What's your name, girl?"

"Aysel." It comes out as a croak. "Please... please could I have a drink of water?"

"Of course! Your skin's very dry, you should drink a lot more! I'll give you a pot, though; you're trembling a bit, and I wouldn't like you to break a glass." I try to stop it, pushing my body down against the tremor, while she stares. "Are you cold? How could you be? It's roasting out there. Do you have some sort of condition?" I shake my head and grit my teeth. It doesn't matter what I do, I'm still trembling. Wouldn't she?

"How about some wine?" Drusa suggests. I shake my head; I've never tasted it, but I've seen what happens to my master when he drinks wine, and I'd rather be in my right mind. "Grape juice?" I nod; I suppose I could try it, if she thinks I'm allowed it, anything to soothe my throat and help me speak. I've a tiny idea I might gather some useful information from her if I let her chat, something that might help me escape.

The grape juice tastes sour. She promises me that's because it's from the sacred spring up on the mountain. It's too full of flavour, I only wanted fresh, simple water, but I can't refuse. And it has an instant effect; almost at once it relaxes me, the trembling stops and the thought of death seems further away than before. The two girls sent by the high priest come with a large copper tub and jugs of water. One of them turns her head away from me, the other pulls a face, and tries to hurry with the jug so she can get out of my sight.

"Iris!" Drusa snaps at her, and she nearly drops the jug.

I've caught it just in time; broken pots are a very bad thing in my experience. I don't know why she couldn't manage it; it's no weight or size, compared to the amphorae we store wine in at home. I slosh the water into the tub as carefully as I would in Mistress Lucina's bedroom on bath day.

And it's worth helping out the girl when she comes back with another jug; she mutters a few quick words of thanks, and passes me a sweet cake from the central table. It's in my mouth whole, and half swallowed, before Drusa can do anything about it. It's drenched in honey; everything here's sickly sweet!

That's the only food they let me touch. Now I have to bathe. They make me strip and sit down in it like a noblewoman. Drusa hasn't bothered warming the water as we have to for our mistress, but I'm glad. The instant cold of the bath chills my fears, cools my cheeks and takes away the sting where they're scrubbing my skin. Any water's welcome in this heat. But sitting still is horrible. I'm trained to serve, not to be served, to do, not to watch.

As I sit, trying not to cry out at the violent scrubbing on the body I've never shown to anyone, I can't help thinking. My Mum will be worked to the bone without me. Little Mir will chop off his foot if they try to make him chop the wood as Naasir usually does. Naasir must be a plain slave sacrifice, abandoned at the stadium, ready to be thrown away tomorrow at our goddess' request. At least I might escape some pain, he won't. I hope they send me back to him, wherever they've taken him, so I can comfort him, at least. I wish I knew how to be comforting.

One of the girls throws the rich cushions off a couch onto the floor, and throws me at the bare wooden slats. They rub me with oil, the same way I'd rub oil into a piece of meat for the master's table. I suppose I am just a piece of meat to them. Drusa doesn't notice the similarity, or how she throws up my arms the way she'd throw a puppy onto the altar.

"You are so privileged," she sighs, "being chosen for Artemis' festival. In front of a Senator, too! For a slave to rise so high, you must be so honoured! The girl we had last week didn't measure up, she kept screaming, and then her grandfather bought her Roman citizenship, so we had to send her away. That must be why they've agreed to using a slave now, nobody will care where you are. Except your household, I bet they'll feel the honour. Let's start on her hair, girls."

Wrapped in an impossibly soft towel, I grit my teeth tighter than before. I'm lucky if I tidy my hair once a week, so I expect it to be uncomfortable, but they're interested in speed, and Drusa actually seems a bit jealous of me, so they drag a bone comb through my taggles until the teeth start to break off. A plain wooden comb's even less use, pulls more and takes longer. I can hardly think of anything while they're pulling my head every way and cursing like men. So I reach for another sip of that grape juice and try to keep them talking.

"Has any girl ever done this twice?" That raises a laugh. Drusa takes out a large pair of shears, and squeezes out a compliment.

"You've got good hair. The gladiators like a girl with plenty of hair. Don't they, Iris?" The older girl blushes and frowns, taking up iron curlers and pins. There's clearly a story there that she's not going to tell. Curling my hair hurts, I'm glad I don't have to have it done every day. "Well, there was that girl a few years ago, that a gladiator took a fancy to. I'd rather be a dead sacrifice than a gladiator's wife. Heh, Iris?" The girl nods, stabbing my scalp with a long pin.

"So, when the girls die, Artemis drops in to say thank you, does she?" I don't know where these questions are coming from, I seldom talk much at all, though somewhere deep inside I realise I've always wondered about things. "You've seen her do miracles, haven't you? That's why you work for her?"

Suddenly, finally, I have a moment of peace from the girls' chatter. There's total silence. They're thinking, all right; they're sure they ought to know the answer. The younger girl points at a picture on a tapestry, waving a finger and trying to think what point she wants to make. Drusa opens her mouth to give me a sharp put-down, then shakes her head. Iris scratches her cheek, which fills her nails with whitening powder, then she battles to scrape the nails clean again.

The peace doesn't last long. "This is working," Drusa proclaims. "Let's do your nails while we're here." As the fox-hairs of her paint brush tickle my fingers, she smiles at me forgivingly. "This is my own nail colour, you may as well go down in style." She wants me to die. I bet she'll be in the stalls of the arena tomorrow, watching and cheering.

"Iris, massage her shoulders, she's tense." Yes, I am, and I want to rub in her confusion about her gruesome sacred job.

"That Paul the orator does miracles. All of the town's talking about it!"

She sighs as if I'm a total fool. "He's a Jew! They're nothing but trouble. They have meetings *inside* their temple. Imagine, all crowded in, in the heat, women and children too! The gods would be stifled!" She dips her fingers in a bowl of water and shakes away the water angrily. Her perfect eyebrows rise higher. "Those Jews are always praying, they bother their god with all their little troubles, instead of saving him for things that really matter. One god, for all their complaints! If he managed to listen to them all, *that* would be a miracle!"

"But they say he heals the sick and makes lame people walk." I've found a pressure point that really winds her up, and despite the danger I can't stop poking it.

"They'll make up anything to get attention. At least we don't bother our gods unless we need something, or they'd get into our whole lives!" She has to stop ranting while she paints my nails bright scarlet like the women who work in the Roman bathhouse. It's a tricky job, and they're all scandalised by the condition of my nails, amazed that I never oil them or clean the cuticles or anything.

"I heard Paul say all people are equal, and there aren't really any slaves at all." That's too much for Drusa. She raises a hand to slap me, only she doesn't want to mess up the cream the young girl's slavered all over my face. So she points a finger and growls;

"He's a weak-minded fool! You're a slave, nothing more. Remember your place. Just because you're chosen by the priest, it doesn't make you someone! You're nobody! Get the dress, girls."

I can't agree with her, I saw the man in the market, not afraid of speaking his mind, even though his height's against him and people think he's crazy. He's a trier, a fighter, all my only friend Naasir is not. Still I wish I was back with him, wherever they've put him, to try and give him some hope if I can. I long to be back with my own scruffy tunic, spun and woven by my Mum, mended in my own careful stitches, with my own hair-ties, with people who don't ply me with wine, passing it off as fruit juice! I don't care about some dress; I want my old life back desperately.

I can't argue back, either, because the transformation of my face has begun. The wine makes me wonder playfully if it wouldn't be less painful just to cut my head off and sew on a posh one. They're shaping my eyebrows with tweezers, squinting at me between bouts of plucking. This is as much pain as my mistress can ever stand, according to Mum. Next they cover my face with chalk, dry and scratchy, and paint my cheeks with a fake pink.

Colouring my eyelids just like Drusa's is tricky, since I can't stop blinking, so they hold me down and pull my eyes taut until they're satisfied. A thick coating of greasy red lipstick… Oops, I'm so hungry I had to taste it; I just licked it off, and it tasted disgusting. The girls curse again, by Artemis and Jupiter, and give my lips another coat. I still have just enough inbred obedience to leave it, and let them back off.

In silence I'm given soft, spotless underwear and a white tunic, made from the finest linen. The younger girl's rigged up a screen for me to change behind; they've had enough of staring at a slave. The linen's very soft on my skin, softer and less scratchy then my woollen tunic that they're throwing away with the skins of sacrificial animals. In fact, my skin is much softer too. Another scrubbing like that and it might be as soft as my mistress' delicate hands.

Drusa passes me a stola without a word. I know how to put them on other people, not on myself, but it's not too hard to slide on; I smooth the stitched folds of fabric onto each shoulder, heavier than my old tunic on my sore neck. I gather the loose folds round my waist, which is even smaller than usual today, and kick out the hem where it's catching round my feet. With my hair piled up in curls on my head so I have to balance it as I walk, and with linen skirts brushing my ankles, I long to relax and imagine I'm a free woman. I can't.

The chief priest has returned. He's worried.

"What's taking so long?" he asks Drusa fiercely. In his hands he's twisting a pile of scrolls, and his cheeks are red like my master's when he comes home from the tavern. "We need to get her under lock and key!" Drusa calms down at once, while the other girls bow to him and scurry off for the dress she demanded. He looks at the curls on my head, the odd stray one on my cheek, the whitening paint, the black lashes the girls have painted on me, and smiles suddenly. "Sandals?"

Drusa pushes a pair of sandals at me so moodily the priest asks why she's grumpy. She shrugs.

"Isn't cleaning up a slave bad enough? And she's been going on about that preacher." No need to name the man in front of the priest; his beard creases in a frown instantly, while she adds to explain her temper; "You're getting poorer every day he's in the city! Have you seen them burning prayer scrolls? And heard them saying they might not come to make offerings again…"

The priest has a finger on his lips, and points at me, trying not to wriggle my tough heels on the smooth leather of the sandals. Drusa goes quiet again. She hardly wants to finish her task transforming me, but the priest's drumming his hand on his arm, so she picks up a circlet from a cushioned alcove in the wall. It's battered in places, with a small lump of solder at the back; I can sensibly assume it's seen more heavy treatment than hair accessories usually do, if it's been into the Ephesian arena. But it's made in the same style as my mistress' shrine, probably by the same man. It's pure silver.

When Drusa places it on my head, the priest's eyebrows raise, and he nods in appreciation of something I can't

38

understand. "I see. Send a gift to the soldier who picked her up. He has a very good eye for detail." In a painted panel on the far wall is a mirror of polished brass; the girls have strangely stepped away from me, and their clenched fists are now open hands, gesturing in the same way they gesture to the altar. So I can step back fraction to peep in the mirror.

I stagger away at once, in shock. I wonder if I dare hold out my palms as they do; am I allowed to? Am I worthy? In the mirror, looking straight at me, I have seen a vision of Artemis herself, identical to the statue they parade in the street on her feast day- tomorrow! The finely painted girls are staring at the mirror too. Their hands have lowered again, and they're slightly, though when they look back at me they're not looking down their noses any more. Is it possible that the goddess Artemis has revealed herself to me, a humble slave, when these girls who serve her temple can't name me one thing she's done for them?

They allow me to look in the mirror again, standing straight in front of it this time. The image is still there, it's not Artemis, it's me, a false, glowing, idealised version of me. I am nothing but her sacrifice. She demands that I die tomorrow.

NO, I WILL NOT!

Chapter 6

The priest's girls are uncomfortable about walking me down to the stadium to put me under lock and key. They naturally prefer the fine houses and the mass of temples on the hillside. As we leave behind the milled marble pillars and reach rougher-carved porches topped with wood, they walk slower and crowd closer to me. I know they find spending time with a slave pretty repulsive, so I suppose they're hoping I can offer them protection from the rougher end of the city. That's ridiculous; all I can do is lift amphorae, make cream for bruises and spin wool!

When we were still high up on the hill near the temples, the youngest girl thought it was funny to borrow the silver circlet back from me and wear it herself. She said I might break it or steal it. Now she's taken it off, and hides it under the folds of her palla, her rich shawl she put on before. It's a good idea, since the sun's going down over the ocean. And she's wise enough to hide the circlet to avoid the attention of thieves.

Once we're in smelling range of the sea and the fish market we're much closer to the home I'm supposed to live in. I'll never see that house again, my master clearly wants me out of his way permanently. There is a faint chance I could overpower these three ornamental dolls and be back with my Mum and aunt before the girls could scramble up and check their make-up, but I'd rather see Naasir.

After a short walk along the sea-front, where the girls raise their colourful pallas across their noses to mask the fresh smell, we pass the gymnasium in quiet and reach the stadium. It's so tall I can see it from home. Up close it towers over me, and I feel incredibly small again, despite the fine appearance the girls have given me. They dither by the arched gateway, unwilling to go in. Iris huddles back against me when she sees a leather-clad man coming our way. Once the gladiator's trainer has me by the arm, the girls turn at once, and scurry back to the temple in alarm.

He's a good deal stronger than my master, with a stern face any girl would naturally be afraid of, but he seems to be in a decent mood, and listens when I beg him; "Please put me in with Naasir!" I know he may be squashed in a cell with a load of other male slaves waiting to be killed, but he's never laid a finger on me, so I can probably trust him to keep me safe from them. I've never needed a friend so much, so I'll even trust someone my Mum says is a sap.

I'm led into a stony courtyard where weapons are stored in a corner- nets, tridents, swords and spears, hammers and axes. Ringing the courtyard are cells full of resting gladiators, bare-chested and hairy.

"No, please put me in with Naasir! In Vesta's name, please!" He opens up a cell, and I nearly get my head knocked off. Naasir is swinging a sword, with an eerie swish, right above my head.

"I'll have that now," the trainer growls, taking back the weapon. He locks us in, locks the courtyard gate, and vanishes with a little whistle of a chirpy folk tune. In sheer relief I close the African in a tight hug; he seems taller than before, even now I have sandals on.

"Naasir, why have they put you in here with the gladiators?" He pushes me away gently, without replying, only asking in a whisper;

"Let me look at you. Yes, that's much better."

"What is? This isn't me, this is…"

"They were bound to remove the collar, but they've done a lot more. Now you look like a lady. Can you walk like a lady?" I shrug, uncertain what he's on about, and my stomach rumbles loudly. "Oh, here." Under a cloth on his camp bed he's hidden a small, round loaf, *and* a piece of cheese. The crazy lipstick disappears the instant I grab the bread and sink my teeth into it. It's good, solid bread, the sort Aunt Yildiz makes for us slaves in the kitchen, chewy and

41

filling. It helps dull the effect of the wine, and shuts me up long enough for Naasir to speak without interruption.

"Hairpins? Good. Don't eat too much, you've got a window to squeeze out of." I squeak in surprise through my giant mouthful. Action? I like it! "Over there you'll see Ampyx the Greek. Behind his cell is a tree which should disguise you; he'll let you through in exchange for a hairpin to pick locks; I hear he's got some business in the city, I didn't ask what. Go straight to the lecture hall, up Curetes Street, third on the left. Use back streets so you're not seen. Ask for Paul. Failing that, go home, round the back way, climb the wall and see the mistress. Plead with her, for my sake."

I'm trembling again, this time with a glimmer of hope. I can surely manage all that, since my life depends on it. "I'll stay there till you arrive," I assume.

"No, I can't get through the window, and my collar will give me away. I have another plan that doesn't involve you," Naasir insists.

"Oh, thanks!" What do I expect? Just because we were in the same household, doesn't mean he's stuck to me like glue. He's not my father. He takes the last crust from me, and yanks out the biggest and longest hairpin. I don't want to know where he learned to pick locks, and what he uses that skill for, but it works, the door opens and I'm out into the courtyard in a moment. Naasir sets to work on the door of the cell opposite. Inside, a man with a straight, striking Greek nose rises to meet him, his bare chest full of muscles and his tight stomach well-fed.

"She cleaned up pretty," he growls, with a wonky grin that I'm instantly suspicious of. "Thought so!" I flatten myself against his damp cell wall, but the second I'm in reach he grabs me and kisses me so tightly I'm likely to suffocate. Yesterday I was imagining what I'd do if ever a young man takes an interest in me, but this is wet and disgusting. Naasir tuts at the gladiator.

"I warned you, don't defile your goddess' sacrifice."

"You don't believe in Artemis," snorts the gladiator, holding me still tighter because I dare to struggle. If these muscles come at Naasir tomorrow he won't last more than a minute. Still he dares to talk back to the Greek;

"I respect your beliefs, so you respect my friend!" Ampyx lets me go with a grunt, takes my hairpin as payment, and gives me a leg up to the window. I can just squeeze through, although the long stola causes me more trouble than it's worth. The stench of sweating men and unwashed feet fades in the evening breeze; I can climb quietly down the tree, fluff out my skirts and concentrate on walking like a lady.

Nobody's about close by, which gives me the chance to get more used to walking in sandals. Finding my way up the town without using the main road is confusing, I try to follow it through an alley strung with washing and littered with children and their games; the little ones stare at me until I realise I look high-born and out-of-place. I pick up my pace, through wandering alleys and closely-packed streets, but my progress is slow with the heavy skirt and the sandals. I think I'm mastering the walk; hold your head so high it feels stupid, swing your hips slightly like you think you're really someone, and keep looking towards your goal, don't care too much about other people coming at you.

So many people are walking the same way, all busily absorbed in their own business, that I suck in a deep breath and step out onto the main street. No-one notices me, most people are heading home from work and trading, some are heading to the temples carrying small animals, others are walking along with me the way Naasir directed, to the lecture hall.

I've heard my master and mistress discussing visits to the lecture hall with guests before, and it looks like I've made it there in one piece. The building's more enclosed than others, with a large door, painted as pink as the sunset. It's locked. I suppose I have to knock; I begin softly, then, when nobody comes and a few passers-by have glanced curiously at me, I hammer louder, in rhythm with my heart pounding. I must finish my errand quickly, someone here must help me. Still there's nothing. Trying not to appear suspicious, I wander down the side of the building; I can't hear a sound, nor see any sign of movement, the place is deserted.

My heart has sunk in an instant, then started to beat faster again. So close to getting help, now I'm just a girl in the street without the cover of crowds. Go home, Naasir said. Can I make it that far? And if I do, how will my mistress ever be able to help? My master won't listen to her, even if she cares enough to listen to me. From up here it's a long way to go.

I need to find Paul, if I can recognise him. I have to believe he'll care, it's the only chance I really have, short of heading into the hills and trying to live as best I can. I'm close to a building which stands out from the rest. It has less columns, it's more enclosed, carved with six-pointed stars. The tail-end of a small crowd's heading in there now, women in tight headdresses, men in little caps. At the Artemision Drusa mentioned the Jews gather in their own temple for group worship, and Paul is a Jew.

I sway towards them, and creep in last in the line. The curly-haired man on the door gives me a suspicious look, and dithers about letting me in. I look him in the eye, trying my mistress' firm stare; he lets me through unwillingly. I'm driven on by old, bearded men, into a room with wooden pews. At the front, another old man's begun a song in a foreign language, but not Latin. He's clearly a leader, he must know Paul.

The men are mumbling as I walk; they've sat down, and I'm in the middle of them, with my fancy Roman hair, a curl down my neck where I'm missing a pin, and bright white clothes. Behind me I can hear whispered women's voices; I look round, to see them all hiding on a balcony, heads primly covered, not a hair out of place.

Jeers have begun. I must block them out, my purpose is clear, and Naasir may die a captive if I let the noise distract me. Stopping just below the singer's platform, I call up to him;

"I'm looking for Paul. Please, do you know where he is?" He doesn't want to stop his song, and others are coming to get me, so he can ignore me. Unless I shout louder. "Where is Paul? Please help me!" I recall an old story I heard on my mother's knee, and plead straight at the singer's face; "I claim sanctuary! Help me!"

The name of Paul is thrown around the congregation. They seem surprisingly ambiguous in their opinions of him. Isn't he making them famous in Ephesus? A lot of the men are virtually spitting at the sound of his name, and the women don't even get to express an opinion, stuck up on that balcony.

"She defiles our synagogue," a man in a big headdress growls in my ear. I'm surrounded, with no way out. What will these people do to me?

"I'll talk to her," the singing man offers. He grabs my arm, pulls me through the crush and out of a back door into another, smaller room. "There's a mood of riot here today. Alexander and his men think you were sent here on purpose by the Romans, to defile our worship." I'm shaking my head so much my curls are wobbling. Why would I defile something? By being a slave, or just by being female? These people wouldn't like Paul's talk of equality at all.

Except for this man; he's not ashamed of talking to me. "They say the same about Paul of Tarsus, that he defiles our old traditions. His followers were hurt today, and he's taken them home. Why did you want him?" It's no good, however benign this man looks, with curls to match my own, I can't tell him my story. He doesn't mind.

"We must not have blood in our synagogue. Can you climb through a window?" he asks.

"I can."

45

"Go quickly, my daughter, and God be with you." He throws open the curtain and hurries me to climb on a chair and out of the high gap. He looks away from my bare legs as I scramble, then glances down, waiting to see me land.

I've gone up, onto the roof. Below I can see Jewish men coming out of the front door, searching for me. Their hunt is limited by their belief that I'm a Roman lady. With no proper zeal for it, they quickly return indoors. I can only spare a moment to catch my breath before I head home.

From up here the city *is* great. It's organised, temples high up, businesses close to each other, homes ranging right out to the sea in descending order of rank. Trails of smoke rise from many of the houses; the townsfolk are cooking, eating, the city is prosperous. The stadium stands in a key position, bloodthirsty entertainment's very important to the citizens. Right below me I can see one old Jew heading out of the synagogue towards the legionaries' barracks. And, heading home from the city hall, I can see my master.

He looks up. I must keep calm; he won't see me from there, and he surely wouldn't recognise me. He'll be waiting for the joyful news at home that he can go and shop for new slaves. I slide foot by foot down the roof tiles, all nailed in tightly. There's another roof opposite, the corner of it's only a small jump away.

I have to jump. I grab at the apex tiles, and I can scramble up, over and out of sight. But now I'm in sight of a soldier guarding the city. And now, hiding on a roof, I look highly suspicious. My blood's pumping in my ears like a drum. All I can do after all this is head out of town. Over rooftops I scramble; the soldier seems to look my way, then vanishes, a bad omen.

Not too far away lie the city walls, and beyond them a few random houses and then the mountainside, Mount Pion which towers over us all our lives. There are some bushes I could maybe hide behind, and some may bear fruit I can eat while I look for a road to a new city, Pergamum, perhaps. Below is a

46

long channel of terracotta, on tall pillars, running up onto the mountain, part of the aqueduct system bringing water into the city.

There are three soldiers down below me now, one is pointing up. They come round a corner and in full view of me. Make that four soldiers, casting long shadows down the wide street in the dusk. I don't even stop to think; I'm on the aqueduct. It's well-built, and I'm not. I'm full of such desperation I've convinced myself it must hold my weight till I'm over the city wall.

A soldier's walking below me, another's taking out his sword. Another on the watch-tower is stringing his crossbow. The thought of Naasir in his cell drives me to hurry. One uncomfortable, wet sandal slips; forget the city walls, I'm falling down onto the street.

First a shop awning breaks my fall, then the arm of a soldier. I've survived death on the stone, and I'm being marched back to the stadium to await my death tomorrow. The gladiator trainer shakes his head at me.

"You couldn't keep away, could you? You won't provide much entertainment if common legionaries can catch you this easily!" As he herds me along, he digs at my bowed head with his fat fingers, pulling out all my hairpins, gathering them in his leather pouch, scratching my scalp in case any are hidden. "You needn't think I'm putting you in with your friend again!"

So Naasir is still here too? I'm shoved into the cell beside him; we can talk, but I can't see him. If he hasn't even been anywhere, what was his wonderful plan for his own escape?

Chapter 7

"Naasir, you said you were going to get out. What happened?"

"I told you I had a plan," he corrects me in a whisper, from the cell beside me.

"What plan was it, then?"

"I spoke to the gladiators, and told them I have no intention of killing any of them."

I can't help laughing. They must have laughed too, hearing an old slave say that! I'm surprised he's even been brave enough to speak to them at all. "I bet hearing that cheered them up!"

"I've never known you to be cheeky, Aysel."

"I'm sorry," I concede, "but I'll never get the chance again, so I may as well say what I think for a change. Anyway, what else?"

He seems unwilling to say any more now, yet he does. "In the arena I'll do my best to protect you for as long as I can. Afterwards, I told the gladiators I'll go to a place of peace and pray to God for all their souls."

A nice dream, but he's ignoring the obvious. It won't be some children's play-fight, they won't all finish up shaking hands and going away. We all know death is everywhere around us, and even the snores of the men in the other cells are brutal. I can see the rich red of blood behind my eyelids every time I blink. I hate to tell him; "Naasir, you're going to die!"

"Yes, of course," is his smooth reply. "Didn't I say that? I'll protect you until I die, then I'll go to a place of peace and pray to God for your souls. That's my plan." It doesn't strike me as a good one. He must be joking.

"God?" I echo, copying the mood of the rioters. "Which one?"

"There is only one."

"You sound like that Paul," I observe. "What makes you think there's only one?"

"Hmm!" Though I can't see him, I know by that tone that he's smiling; smiling in jail the day before your death, well done! His reply surprises me, until I realise it's what I'm coming to expect; "I know because I've met Him."

"Seriously like Paul!" But how? An apparition like I saw of Artemis in the mirror?

"I don't know if you've ever noticed, but I have a scar."

Haven't noticed? It's the first thing anyone sees of Naasir, a raised mark going from his dark forehead right down his neck.

"I was hit by a sword which nearly knocked my head off. It should have killed me. But Paul was visiting Ephesus at the time. He says he was sent to me; to me, a slave! I'm no-one!" Telling the tale is making him chuckle. From my point of view it's hard to take in, and I don't share his amusement. "I don't know how it happened, but I when I came back to consciousness a doctor was sewing my skin back together. I hear it had healed so quickly his stitching wasn't really needed."

He's talking rubbish, the gods aren't real- what, aren't they? Why am I thinking that right now, when I desperately need someone to trust? And yet there's the scar. He's right, Aunt Yildiz has often said he's lucky to be alive. He's served in the Celerus house all my life, but of course he must have had a life before that.

"Tell me about this God," I whisper, picturing the empty pillar where this morning's riot must have begun. It doesn't help me imagine a human face, only a vastness like the night sky in my window.

"Gladly. But we have all night. First, I need to tell you about the gladiators. I've been observing them and talking to them. You'll need to know their weaknesses if you want to survive. And I think you could; you weren't allowed to escape, so we're clearly here for a purpose."

49

He has hope, at least for me? I've never hoped much, I've always just worked, one day at a time, without any need for a purpose. Hope is a good feeling, and Naasir's assurance lets me grab hold of his hope. He begins to drill me in the gladiators' names and appearances, telling me all he quietly observed during their morning's practice and this evening's meal, which I missed!

"Next to you is Crispus. You'll know him because he's blond. The lanista's made him a retiarius for this fight, but he's uncomfortable with a net. I need you to repeat that to me, so you learn the details."

"Fine, but that's too fast for me. What's a lanista, and how am I supposed to know what a reti..." I can't even say it, so I have to give up.

Naasir explains that the lanista is the gladiator trainer, and a retiarius fights with a net and a trident. All right, I remember seeing them fight this morning. Crispus, blond, net, trident... And the detail- he's not used to it. A fisherman could handle a net better.

"Then there's Aetius, the man with the brown beard. " I have a vague memory of seeing him, too. "He's also a retiarius, and the trident is just too tall for him, it makes him slightly unbalanced." I repeat, Aetius, brown beard, retiari-thingy, wobbly. Naasir persists until I get it right. "Next to him is Ismet. He's a local, left-handed, and a murmillo."

"A what?" Where has he picked up all this stuff? Of course, our master is a big fan of the games, and bookmakers come to the house regularly to take his bets. Panaius might well be studying the odds right now, at home in his cosy study.

"A murmillo is armoured, he carries a large shield so he's hard for others to target, and he has a fish on his helmet. Remember the fish, Ismet's is painted green." Why should I remember him, is he particularly dangerous? "No, I'll come to those. Ismet has no interest in women, he doesn't want to win

50

you, and admitted freely that he doesn't intend to kill you either. He's on your side."

Ismet, green fish, friend! But the list goes on. "Ennius and Florus are Romans, brothers. They're built like marble statues, and they fight consistently. But both are easily distracted. You might be able to put that to your advantage."

He knows so much, I can't help observing that he'll be there, too, fighting near wherever they tie me up. He answers simply;

"Don't count on it. Now, tell me what you've learned so far."

Carefully I repeat all he's told me, retiarius, murmillo and all. He's pleased that I've remembered, and promises we'll go through all the details again in the morning. That'll rub my face in my fate, won't it?

"You've got an ear for detail, Aysel, you're your fath..." Suddenly he slams his mouth shut tightly, then coughs.

"What? You were going to say I'm my father's daughter, weren't you?" He can't deny it. "It *is* you, isn't it? Come on!" Before we die, it would be decent if he finally told the truth. And he does.

"What kind of man do you think I am? If I had children, it would be in a marriage!" He sounds embarrassed, so am I, I can only whisper an apology and beg him to go on.

Now I learn about Kiral, the man who lost an eye in a fight, and can't see you unless you move into a certain range; apparently I have a knack of creeping about quietly at home, that's going to help. But in Naasir's humble opinion he's very dangerous, more than most, and very keen on carting off women. Then there's Ampyx, the one who let me out last night. He's a vicious fighter, which is bad for Naasir, if he gets that far, but apparently good for me, because after one-horrible- kiss he wants to win me and marry me! I can't help thinking that would be a fate worse than death.

Ampyx the Greek was paired this morning against Secundus, the one who skidded at the theatre. He'll be easy

51

to spot because of the scratch on his chin. Apparently the younger man will be in trouble, because Naasir's noticed he's a bit of a dreamer. He's always a step behind, just as he was in the theatre; that's why he was trapped with us and the trainer- the lanista, I mean; I'm starting to learn the jargon.

The gladiators have been ordered not to kill when they fight in pairs through the day, but to hold back a little until the final bout when it's every man for himself. But Naasir's convinced Ampyx will kill Secundus accidentally, without realising how weak the boy is. He rants about his dainty sword-thrusts and insists that the boy has too much of an urge to entertain, and loves nothing better than an audience. If I happen to free myself, on no account am I to try siding with him under any circumstance.

I learn about the hoplomachus, a gladiator who fights with a short sword and a little round shield, and the provocator, dressed in the armour of regular legionary soldiers. Ennius and Florus, the Romans, are provocatores, and Balbus is a hoplomachus. I can't see any of the gladiators in the dark, but I'm told Balbus is named for his big, bald head, and he's trouble. He's very superstitious, and thinks catching me and then killing me is what Artemis wants on her feast day. So Naasir won't let me put him out of my mind. There are others to learn about, but two of them have daughters, and one has a new wife, so he doesn't think I need to be so concerned about them, except that I may get caught up in their cross-fire. But in a few minutes of stomach-churning talk, I feel I know all I ever want to hear about Balbus and half-blind Kiral.

Again Naasir makes me repeat what I know, in a detached, business-like way. I try to picture the men at the theatre and fit names to faces, and I recall one he hasn't mentioned yet.

"What about the big, huge one? The one as big as a bear?" There's no response from Naasir's cell at first. Then he grunts.

"He's a dimachaerus."

"A what?"

"He fights with a sword in each hand. And each one looks equally deadly. Don't get in his way."

"I was hoping not to. What else do you know? Does he have family?"

"He wouldn't talk to me. At the meal he just stood and ate. I didn't manage to catch his name."

"So, what are his flaws?" I wonder. There's no answer. "Naasir?"

"He doesn't have any. Don't get in his way, and pray that he comes nowhere near you." That really doesn't comfort me. The Bear is the tallest gladiator by far, the one with most muscles, and he must be the most likely to win the contest. That means he'll win me, if I'm still alive. I must not think about that, I dare not. I know enough about life for that to fill me with enormous fear, so much that I'm almost back to the idea of stealing someone's knife and plunging it quickly into myself.

Is there any way I can find a grain of hope? I need to distract us both from staring into the dark courtyard in the direction of the Bear's cell. "Are we done?" I whisper. Naasir agrees, as long as we do it all again in the morning. "So, now will you tell me about your God?"

I'm forced to wait again, in eerie silence, while he thinks what to say. It must be taxing for someone of his age to talk so much, teach so quickly out of desperation, when all my life he's said so little and seldom had to think for himself.

One of the gladiators, possibly superstitious Balbus, begins a droning prayer, reeling out a list of family names, repeating a Latin word over and over, maybe the word for victory. It's the last thing we can do before morning, our fears are greatest in the dark and we'll cry out to anyone, take any company we can. Naasir apologises that he can't explain things as Paul does, and tries his best anyway.

"I can't describe God, except to say that he's nothing like the statues you see everywhere. They're statues of men and women, but God isn't human, how could He be? He made us

53

in his image, not the other way round. He doesn't need to be seen, His presence can be felt. Trying to make images of Him would only confuse us, and distract us from what He really is."

"And what's that?" I ask, sleepily. I won't sleep, of course, how could I?

"Something bigger than the sky, higher than the stars, powerful enough to heal a man whose head was nearly severed. Aysel, He made us all, every one equal, men, women, slaves. We took the world He created and corrupted it. Nothing stays pure in human hands, nothing at all. Long ago the people used to pray to Him, but they corrupted their worship, built idols, followed their own desires. These games are our evil interpretation of an offering to make the gods pleased with us. That's corrupted. It's wrong." His words are calm and reverent, soft and sad. He conjures up an immense greatness in my head, I dream I'm looking down on the world from higher than the synagogue roof, from somewhere in the distant clouds. From there people all look the same, and they're so small.

"God gave simple us rules to live by. For example, 'don't be jealous of other people's possessions, because I've given you all you need, and the strength to deal with it.'"

"Seriously? Naasir, you mean we're slaves on purpose?" By corruption of men, he prefers to say. But the strength to deal with our circumstances comes from his God.

"I mean it. Are you afraid, Aysel? Look." He sticks an arm out between the bars of his cell. I have to squint to see the dark flesh in the dimming light of a single candle, but I see what he's saying; his hand's perfectly still, not a tremor.

"That's why you deal so well with slavery. Your God helps you. Don't you wonder why you're a slave, then, when the mistress screams at you like you're a dog?"

"She's not like that any more." True, I hadn't noticed. She still complains, not as much as she used to, but the beatings have tailed off... "And it's not about this life, this is only a preparation for the next one. There, I'll meet God in person."

"By Vesta, you sound convinced!" I try to keep my tone respectful, and to hide a yawn. "You must be a *really* good person!" I'm starting to see that he is. Maybe his subservience isn't weakness, as I thought, maybe he isn't the sap Mum always says he is.

"I'm certainly not good. I've broken the simple rules many times. God says you must not lie, you must not steal, and you must not kill. He made us, so we have no right to destroy each other... Aysel?"

I grunt back an answer from where I've sat down in my little bed. My head won't lift off the wall, I'm so tired. The grunt didn't reach him, he thinks I'm already asleep, and the lullaby of his words has stopped part way through his tale. Great, so we two innocent slaves have to face the gladiators, and Naasir's God says you must not kill!

It's quiet, as still as an ordinary summer's night after everyone's gone about their ordinary business and nothing unusual has happened. Surprisingly, I don't mind my eyes shutting; the red of blood has become the black of a starry sky. The vision of Artemis bent over her lions in her shrine has faded, while the vastness of the stars cradles me. The bed is comfortable, the cell is locked and private. Mum's lullaby drifts through my head;

"Run with my deer, my arrows will guard you,
Sleep without fear, no lions will harm you..."
Yet in my dreams I still hear the growl of a lion.

Chapter 8

I woke at the crack of dawn, as always. I jumped up, ready to stoke the fire and start gutting the fish delivered fresh from the sea, for my master's table in the evening. But I wasn't at home, there was nothing to do but worry, so I lay down on my camp bed in a gladiator's cell to worry until my stomach hurt. Sleep came too easily. Now the sun's well and truly up, I wake again, feeling more rested than ever before.

The girls from the temple are back, and Drusa's cursing as much as the gladiators sparring in the courtyard in front of me. I've let my hair be pulled about, and squashed it by lying down to sleep. My dress is marked with red lines from roof tiles and smudges of moss. And my nails are ruined. Fortunately she doesn't want to hear how I've got myself in such a state; her job is to smarten me up for the procession, if she can keep the other two girls away from their flirting with the gladiators.

We skirt round the courtyard to use the lanista's room while he's busy with some last-minute training. I can now identify Secundus, the play-actor, and Finian, the British soldier with ginger hair; he's slightly slower than other swordsmen. Then I pick out Aetius with his beard and trident, blond Crispus…

Iris has stopped in her tracks, gaping shamelessly at two tall Romans. "Ennius and Florus," I inform her, as if I know them all personally. She's jealous, pouts, and waves at one of them. Both men turn, bow briefly, and wave; then they fall back into a fight over which one she was interested in. A sharp word from Drusa brings Iris back to attention, and she drags the young girl away from Secundus, who's already stopped training and crossed the courtyard to talk to her. Several gladiators have turned their practice bouts towards their audience, keen to impress the impressionable girls.

We pass Demir, and Ampyx, who raises his sword to me with a wink. Then we have to dodge round the most dangerous ones; Kiral and Balbus look jumpy and aggressive even as they take some rest, and the Bear only has to stand there, towering, in frowning silence, for me to gulp down a wave of fear. While the girls chatter, I do my loyal best to remember the facts Naasir taught me; I can't recall which one was Talos, and whether it's Galyn or Pollo who has the dented shoulder... It must be Galyn, because he's a murmillo and they carry large, heavy shields. The dent shows he's been fighting a long time, so he must be good.

"*You* have not taken care of *your* hair!" Drusa hisses, and the girls get to work like yesterday; they brush my skin again, with hard, dry brushes, so vigorously I'm surprised at their energy, and more surprised that I don't bleed. I'm covered with oil again, and they promise, ever so kindly, to put more on this afternoon, when I'm due to face the crowd. This morning I'm only being forced into a procession, the raucous kind I'm never usually allowed out to watch.

While they pull and scratch, I concentrate on picturing the gladiators with families. Pollo has a young wife, Demir with the sickle-shaped sword has a daughter, and so does someone else... There are so many names, I can't remember. Why didn't Naasir just give me the name of the one who'd run me straight through and put me out of my misery? I suppose life isn't that simple, nobody knows what will happen, they might not even know how they feel until the battle begins. I might not.

I have to change my dress. They've brought me a new one to die in. I recognise the fabric from one of my mistress' favourite cushions, it's silk. Through clothes and make-up they're turning me into a Patrician lady of the very highest class, for one day only. After Drusa's retouched my nails, cursing all slaves for being so scruffy, she puts on the silver circlet again. "At least we saved this from your messing around!"

I can tell they've painted me up properly, when they step back in reverence. They don't hold out their palms like I'm a goddess this time, but a moment's peace is enough of a compliment. And even better news, it's time for breakfast!

The gladiators eat outdoors, from a table at the side of the courtyard. It's basic food that I'm used to, plenty of barley porridge and bread, meat left from their feast last night, fruit, juices, weak ale... I grab a chunk of bread first, remembering to bite carefully so the lipstick stays on. Someone has cut open a pomegranate with his sword, and left half of it on the table; it looks tempting, with its red juice and seeds swimming in pink flesh.

I feel sick. Suddenly that crust in my mouth is all I can swallow. I gulp down a whole pint of water, pure and life-giving, but I have to leave the breakfast. The gladiators eat plenty; all of them have a healthy stomach full of last night's feast, except Naasir.

He's dressed in a clean, new tunic, and his collar is brightly polished. He's permitted to walk beside me to the temple for some blessing or other, though it's difficult for us to talk. His presence is comforting after my nightmares last night, and sometime I might get the rest of his story out of him.

On the steps of the Artemision temple the gladiators are made to stop; Iris has draped me with a red palla over my head, either to protect my hairdo or to disguise me before the procession. I wonder if the high priest will approve, but anything to do with me and my attempted escape is far from his mind. He stands by the stone altar with a grim face, and whispers to Drusa in a loud croak;

"The hens aren't eating." Poor hens, whichever hens they are! They're most likely better fed than we usually are, if they belong to that chubby high priest. And yet Drusa thinks that's a real problem, if the grimace on her face is anything to go by. She tries, and fails, to be sympathetic.

"So the gods are angry? Haven't you prepared properly for the festival? I did say you should think about giving the job to a lay person, like that Panaius, he's calm in a crisis."

The high priest is far from calm. He's holding a hen, staring fiercely at it as if he can scare it into eating. "Next time I will. Ask Panaius to take over the Volturnalia festival."

"That's in two weeks!"

"Tell him to think of it as a challenge," the priest commands. "And now, let us examine a liver, to see how the day will proceed." He hands the hen to another priest to be dispatched and disembowelled. While we wait for the chicken liver to be brought, with my nerves growing and my legs starting to weaken, Naasir asks me to go over the gladiators' skills and flaws in my head. It does help keep my mind off other things.

The condition of the hen's liver doesn't please the priest, but a horn is blowing, calling the people out into the streets to watch the procession; nothing can stop Artemis' festival, not even the wrath of Artemis. I have a hot, hurried walk in the hood made from my palla to the start of the procession. In front walks a boy with purple stripes on his tunic and a bunch of sticks in his hand. Behind him come the priests and priestesses, some walking with hands folded into their robes and heads bowed in quiet prayer, others waving and calling out blessings on the good, and curses on anyone they don't like.

On Curetes Street, heading down from the mountain towards the sea, a noisy pattering greets us, and crowds of boys run to join the priests, banging shields and helmets, pots and pans. Women and girls line the street, hammering on any metal household tool that will clang. All of it's done to remember the Curetes, some soldiers in the old Greek tales. When the god Zeus was born, his father Cronos wanted to kill him. The Curetes made a racket by banging their shields and spears together to mask the cries of the baby Zeus, so Cronos didn't know his son had been born. I've heard that noise so many times in my life; this is the first time I've been in the centre of it. Did my father never hear I was born? Well, who cares right now?

Behind the screaming boys come musicians, warming up to play in the arena as the crowds assemble and start their picnics. There are shining horns made of brass, and reeded wooden shawms blaring out. They're backed by the driving beat of drums, quickening the hearts that listen and keeping everyone marching together. Dancers follow them, dressed in greens and reds and yellows, with wide strips of other colours waving everywhere as they twirl and drum on tambourines.

After the dancers, in a heavier step, march the gladiators. Some of them are very popular. Everywhere there are posters announcing their appearance, with their victories listed. Half the city must have studied their odds and made bets on who'll be the winner, the survivor. Girls begin to crowd round them, even muscling into the parade to grab their arms. Some believe the touch of a gladiator can cure things, like cowardice. The procession swells with as their followers join it.

I'm right behind them, on the platform beside the statue of the goddess. They've tied me by my waist so my hands are free to wave. I'm really not in the mood for that. Naasir stands beside me as a fake guard- the gladiators in front of us are enough of a deterrent. Now the doting girls have lengthened the distance between us and the Curetes, I can hear my own voice again. "So, tell me the rest."

"When you've told me what I taught you."

"All right!" I'm getting impatient with all that now, I don't want to be reminded, so I fire it all off as fast as I can. "Crispus, blond, retiarius, net. Aetius, brown beard, trident. Ismet, local, left-handed murmillo, green fish, friend. Ennius and Florus, provocatores, distracted. Ampyx, sloppy kisser..."

"Aysel!"

"All right, all right, Ampyx, hoplomachus, big shield, friend. Talos, can't turn well. Narkis, Demir and Ambrus, daughters; Demir, curvy sword, get on his left. Galyn, murmillo, bad shoulder. Pollo, blond, young wife, friend. Oknus, black beard, awkward with women. Finian, ginger, slow. Mars, laquearius, has a lasso, useful."

"Why's that?"

"You know I always use a rope to get Mum out of the garden when Lucina ties her up there."

"You mean our mistress?"

"Not much point worrying about titles now, is it?" I finish off with the most important gladiators. "Mars is dangerous. So is Balbus, big head, superstitious. Kiral, one eye, dangerous. The Bear, extra-dangerous, no flaws. If I cross him, I'm dead."

"Good," Naasir agrees.

"Hang on!" a gladiator chimes in. It's Secundus, he must have the ears of a fox, and he's actually thrown two pretty girls off his arms to sidle near to the cart and hear my rundown of his opponents. "What about me? What are my flaws?"

"Secundus, dreaming play-actor," I rattle off, without looking at him. I don't mention that Naasir thinks he'll be dead very soon. Naasir adds, in a fatherly way aimed at cheering him up;

"You need to spend more time fighting, and less playing your audience." The young man isn't at all offended. He takes the criticism with a laugh, explaining;

"That'll be my dad's fault. He's a playwright. My brother Primus is an actor, and I ran off to join the circus! Would you mind telling me those details again?" Naasir's not keen, but I can spare a moment to whisper them to Secundus; we need all the friends we can get.

And then, to business. "Naasir, tell me about this God you were brought up with. Quickly!"

"I wasn't brought up with it, I only heard of it all when I met a friend of Paul's," he corrects me. "Paul could express it much better. He follows a man from Judea, Jesus. They called him the Christ, the Chosen One. He was the Son of God, the one God. The Romans crucified him- nailed him up on a wooden cross and left ..."

"I've seen crucifixions," I observe, softly. They're horrific. Death can take days to come. People go to stare at the victims hanging from the crosses because they think it's entertaining. "That's a miserable story."

"Then, because He'd lived a perfect life, Jesus became a sacrifice, the only perfect one. We never have to make sacrifices again, only trust in what He did." Now, that sounds too simple! "After He completed the sacrifice, God brought Him back to life, and then He went straight into Heaven. If I'm given the chance, I'll tell you more; I'll try and tell you how Paul tells it. Time's short now."

Yes, I can see the stadium close by.

"It's He who gives me strength, and hope. Because of Him I *know* I will soon be in Heaven; that's similar to the best afterlife the Romans have dreamed up. That's where I'll pray for the gladiators."

"That's different to anything I've ever heard!" I whisper, in a hiss, to be heard through the rising shouts of the crowd. "But why doesn't everyone know?"

"Because their hearts are hard."

"What if you told them about it, right here, like Paul did?"

"They won't listen to a common slave, if they wouldn't listen to Paul; he's a Roman citizen."

"So why do you believe?"

"Because I'm alive."

Standing on a platform beside the goddess all the people around me worship, I know it's good to be alive. I want to stay alive as long as possible. I don't want to be here, talking about the afterlife as if that's my only option. Naasir has faced death before, that scar beneath his collar tells another tale I want to hear.

"Naasir?" He's gone deep into thought, but he raises an eyebrow at me. "Can it really be that simple? One perfect sacrifice?"

"Yes." For some inexplicable reason I don't want to believe him. The gods have always seemed complicated, demanding sacrifices for everything, whether you can afford them or not, revelling in death and hatred. I hate the gods, especially this one next to me, Great Artemis, crafted from cold stone with a stern, unmoving face, accompanying me on the march for the gate to the arena of death. I feel anger growing in my stomach-

Before I have a moment to think, I'm jolted almost off my feet. A girl has thrown herself at the cart, screaming;

"Artemis! Help my sick mother!" Everyone knows there have been miracles in Ephesus lately, so it shouldn't be a surprise that she's appealing to the city's most popular goddess. But she hasn't grabbed the statue's feet, she's grabbed mine. Only the rope round my waist keeps me from falling over; the girl clings on, dragged along behind the pair of cows pulling the cart. Her dress is nearly catching in the wheels. People are laughing, others are pointing and cheering.

Drusa steps in, but not to help. "Raise your hands," she orders. "Give her a blessing!" What in the name of all the gods... Naasir thinks that's disrespectful, maybe I shouldn't be swearing by the gods... That hardly compares to what I'm doing now, though. To save the girl from being rolled under the cart, I place a carefully-painted hand on her head and mouth a kiss of blessing- best not to use words, I suppose. She falls away, to safety, with amazement on her face. Her friends surround her, pointing and shouting at the tops of their voices;

"She is the image of Artemis! Artemis in the flesh! Hail Artemis!" I raise my hands to them, Drusa smiles and basks in the reflected glory; Naasir stands motionless, I don't need him to tell me what he's thinking.   People are reaching out, hailing me, throwing flowers and palm fronds, praying to the goddess.   I turn my hand to an old lady hobbling dangerously by the cart.   She thinks I'm magic; the moment I touch her she faints in the street.   Hysterical onlookers leave her lying and flood after me under the Roman arches into the arena.

Chapter 9.

The Romans and freemen of Ephesus rejoice, the day of the circus is here and the games are about to begin. Marching before everyone, musicians play a bright tune, welcoming the audience to the arena. They sit on a raised wooden platform in the centre of the oval, above the sand where the gladiators will fight. The audience can't come near them, a ring of water protects the seating from whatever chaos may come later. They stream in from a dozen entrances, past the main arch or the shops beneath the stands where food and drink and souvenirs are sold. There must be many thousands of people, clothed in all the colours cloth can be dyed, some with their children at their sides, in the same clothes as their parents, and just as excited. All are coming for the spectacle of men murdering each other for no reason other than the command of Rome.

Singers mount the platform, singing tales of love, love returned, love spurned, love and death. The stadium has been designed so that everyone can hear the voices in the centre. Even locked up back in a cell, I can hear it. I've heard music played in the Celerus house before, when the master has guests and they recline on their covered couches feasting on the delicacies we've cooked them. Sometimes the mistress is his musician. But I've never witnessed such songs before, with different parts, accompanied by lots of different instruments. I need a few minutes to take in the mellow beauty of it before I can concentrate on the words. They're clever, they cast up images of romance, filling the young with hope of love and reminding the old of love they have, and once had.

Next comes a whole play. I can't see it, my cell turns away from the arena, there are guards outside, and they're instructed to keep me awake so I don't mess up my appearance. But I can hear a lot of the words, and I saw the characters in the procession, dressed in their garish costumes with eerie-looking comic masks, whirling in weird dances. It's another love story, with a bit of fake fighting, something about a noble lady who runs off with a gladiator. It's appropriate for the games, and the action has the crowd chuckling. One chuckle would hardly be heard, but tens of thousands echoing across the arena all at once is as loud as a storm wind off the sea. It must be a fine sound for the performers. It seems that the more laughter they hear, the better they perform, to win more laughs.

Close by, a soldier rattles the bars of my cell. "Grapes," he snaps. I could have guessed that by looking at them. "From Drusa."

So Drusa's pleased with my behaviour in the procession; she's sent me a bunch of black grapes, straight from the high priest's seat in the best part of the audience, close to the action. They'll be watching anxiously, to make sure the entertainment is of good quality; if the citizens are unhappy they have a great deal to lose. And I suppose the Roman Senator who's visiting will be sat with them, showing off one of those white senatorial togas with the purple stripes that my master dreams of. I don't want any gifts from Drusa, and I couldn't stomach the sweet grapes, so the guards munch through them happily enough; I may as well let them like me, it may do some good.

Some time around noon the gladiator fights begin. I know now that they've been warned to hold back from killing if they can, to save up the drama for a final bout later on, when the sun falls a little and the unusual heat is more bearable. It's some idea of the chief priest's, to spice up an otherwise routine event. They'll be fighting for me, over me, over my body, and I have ten bouts of fighting to listen to first, hours in which to dwell on the horrors I can't see.

Secundus is called out, the dreamer; they've set him against Mars, the mighty warrior named after the god of war. My heart sinks just to hear that; he seemed like a decent man, for a gladiator, and it makes me sad to think I'll never see him again. Cheers rise and fall in the audience, they groan and heckle, as if they were only two boys in a toy street fight. And yet it's the clash of iron ringing hard in our ears, not the bash of wooden practice swords. I wonder whether I should pray for the young man, or how to, or to whom. Aren't I the goddess just now, according to the people? He had a cute smile; has Mars the gladiator wiped the smile from his face once and for all?

Applause and cheering tell me it's the end of their bout. Mars has kept to his lanista's agreement, and let the young man away with his life. While Mars returns with a swaggering walk to rest in the courtyard, swigging from a huge tankard of beer, a doctor tends to Secundus in grim silence. At first his head drips with so much blood I can't make out his face, but once they've cleaned him up I can see a gashing knife-wound to his scalp which has taken off part of his hair.

He's brave enough, swigging his own drink and gritting his teeth against a piece of wood while they sew the flap back on. Then the mark on his neck becomes visible, a circular purple bruise made by a rope; Mars' lasso has caught him and nearly choked him before he was allowed loose to fight again. I daren't offer any words of sympathy; he's inexperienced and soft enough already without a girl making him look worse.

Pollo and Florus have been battling while Secundus was nursed, two men with good-sized shields, helmets and swords, quite evenly matched. The crowd still cheers, though not as loud, so I imagine their combat's not so thrilling. Their bout is shorter, and ends in the audience agreeing to a draw, for now. They both return to the courtyard, transformed from the grinning, flirting young men I saw this morning. They're swearing horribly at each other, cursing one another's families and listing ways they intend to murder each other later on. It's a very uncomfortable situation to be in the middle of, and their mood starts to rub off on the others.

Ismet the left-handed murmillo is called up against Galyn. I've hardly had the chance to notice Galyn, apart from his bad shoulder, and I hope for all I'm worth that his shoulder plays up and bars him from the rest of the contest. Ismet mustn't be injured, he's supposed to be one of my friends. He is injured, though; how could he escape it out there? He's reeling from a shield-blow to his head, and when he lies down he falls asleep at once. But Galyn's done worse. He returns clutching his right arm, the sword-arm, where the left-handed sword caught him by surprise, despite his experience in the arena. The doctor turns from Secundus, now his head's covered in cloth, to pour alcohol on Galyn's wound and bandage it up.

Ennius fights Ambrus, one of the men with a daughter. What will she make of her father's occupation, if she knows, or he lives to tell her? From the arena I hear loud curses between the clashing of swords; the two men are threatening each other, to the amusement of the crowd. It grows pretty heated, and when the referee judges they've grown too angry to hold off from killing each other he sends them both back.

There's no common sense left in either of them after that. They storm into the courtyard, both baying for blood, throwing punches at anyone they can reach, including the lanista. Ennius punches out in anger, and gives him a black eye; I can't say I'm sad about that.

"You miserable dog!" the lanista screams at him. "Guards, put them in their cells!" Soldiers grab them under their arms, drag them apart and throw them against the walls. The lanista screams on about the oath of obedience they swore to him, and how he'll have them lined up against someone tougher than themselves if they don't calm down.

Aetius meets Kiral. I almost wish I could watch the action instead of relying on the noise of the crowd. One of the youngest meets the oldest, and you don't become an older gladiator without being horribly good at it. I can imagine Aetius' brown beard bouncing as he throws out his net to snare the man watching him through only one eye. I hear the clank of his trident on the ground, and the jeers of the crowd. They raise a huge chant I can't understand.

"They're shouting 'Lance him through,'" Secundus explains, helpfully. The referees manage to prevent that, and the two return. Aetius is humiliated, and sits silent in his cell, staring at the ground, probably in dread at thought of going back for a second bout.

"They're sending you through quickly," the lanista remarks casually to Kiral, one of his favourites. "I'm not sure it was wise to ask you all to pull your blows, it's not natural." It's natural to want to kill everyone in sight, then, is it? It's starting to look that way.

Finian and Ampyx are doing battle. The doctor calls for more bandages and enlists the lanista's help, tying off wounds to stop the bleeding. Blood's dripped in streaks across the floor of the courtyard, while the fights continue in the fierce heat. The doctor calls for a pause while slaves deliver more water to the arena for the gladiators, to help them entertain for longer.

Aggression is consuming them. Finian and Ampyx return, both staggering, gasping for drink, cut all over their arms by one another's blades. Like the last pair, they have to be torn apart and locked away; the lanista seems to be amused, he likes them to be geared up for violence before they pass through the gate.

Demir's name is announced, another man with a daughter, who's unlikely to want to carry me off. That's a comfort, but we're not sure he won't happily spit me on his sword to complete the day's sacrifice to Artemis. He's against Crispus, the one who's not usually a retiarius. He seems to be getting better with his net, because he returns in triumph, waving his trident and screaming out through the courtyard; "Crispus Maximus is back! Lock up the slave-girl!" Fortunately I'm already locked up.

Crispus has the blood sponged from him, and he's hardly scarred beneath it. The three streaks on his chest vanish with ease. "That was the blood of his opponent," Secundus informs me. "Three trident wounds, and strong ones." I can only gulp, and wait to see what state Demir is in when he makes it back here.

He doesn't. Aggression got the better of Crispus before the referee could stop him. Those three streaks of blood are the last traces of gladiator Demir I will ever see.

Talos fights Oknus. Their fight is also short. It's not long before the crowd denounces Talos as a coward, I think because he stopped for a cup of water. How could they blame him? I saw them, carrying in their picnics, with coins chinking in their purses ready to buy any food or drink that takes their fancy while the entertainment rolls. He isn't free to eat, drink, rest, but they screech on, mercilessly;

"Lance him through! Lance him through!"

Oknus' instincts take over, he circles his prey. He knows the gladiator's code, to stand tall and die with honour, even if the crowd calls for your death, and Talos understands it too. The lanista can watch the action from round the corner, and I hear him groan; "No, save it!"

It's too late. Oknus returns with his mace drenched in blood. Talos never returns at all. He died to the raging cheers of his audience.

Narkis the Ethiopian has a daughter. Surely her existence will get me some consideration from him, and his African past must give him sympathy with poor Naasir. It looks as if they're ssaving my friend till last. I hope Naasir's nerve is holding out there, and I'm glad he got to live this long. Narkis is lined up to fight against the Bear- I didn't even catch his name when it was announced, because the moment he stepped into the arena the crowd began to cheer. They stamp their feet against the wooden seats and slap their sandals on the stone tiers. They're already chanting "Kill him, kill him!" before the bout has started.

The courtyard is splattered with blood, pieces of bandage and broken armour lie everywhere. The hammering of a smith's tools on the armour echoes round me, drowning out the racket from the arena, crushing every thought in my head apart from hatred. I hate the blood, I hate the death, and I detest the Roman way which has brought me here. For a while hate stems my fear, and I can breathe deeply enough to keep conscious.

Less than five minutes later the huge Bear is back in his cell, sitting in ominous silence. No-one dares suggest they lock him in. The lanista himself looks slightly sick at the way the Bear has dispatched his opponent.

"Eight pieces?" he mutters warily through the cell door. "A bit much. I asked you to hold back." The Bear raises a fist, and the lanista wanders carelessly away.

Through my tiredness I've tried to concentrate on all Naasir told me, then to make notes on who's fought and who has which injuries. I can't keep them all in order in my head, but I know that Naasir has been set against Balbus the hoplomachus. I can picture the yellow leggings, shining greaves on his calves, his leather belt and harness, his round shield and razor-sharp sword. I see it flashing in the light as he wields it, swift and deadly.

And I can picture my fellow slave in the alley beside our house after a day's work, sweating as he chops more wood for the master's fire, his shoulders bowed and his eyelids drooping. If they'd known what a gentle soul he is, the soldiers would have laughed at the suggestion he might be a troublemaker.

Some of the men in the courtyard turn towards the noise from the arena as they realise who's fighting now. He talked to them all yesterday evening, they know Naasir's beliefs, they know he's gentle, a stranger in the games, and they hush for a moment. The yells of the other cursing gladiators dim in my ears, the cheers die away. In my little space there is privacy and quiet, and I try whispering to his God to look after him. I don't feel pushed away, nor that I'm wasting my time.

But my time has come. The last bout is being fought, the gladiators who contested an hour or two ago are arming again, pulling metal over their bandages, laughing away their pain. The chief priest has come with soldiers to escort me to my place; Drusa didn't dare venture down here. The men who walked and flirted in front of me this morning jostle me, grab at me as I pass, any part of me they feel like. Their language is filthy and their threats fill me with horror.

Still, at the entrance to the stadium, the girls fluff up my hair, as if it matters. They're still full of idle chatter, touching up my lips while the soldiers pull at the ropes round my wrist. Brass horns are sounding a fanfare, my arrival is announced, though not my name; I doubt more than three people know what it is. The cheers of the crowd have dulled, maybe they know they've been cheated, and that Balbus the famous gladiator has been totally mismatched with a slave from the lower part of the city. Now they soar again, as the audience recognises a new entertainment, the arrival of a woman among the most violent men in the world.

With a blink and a gasp of breath I strain to hold my head up, and as the cart pulls me forward I enter the stadium for the first and last time of my life.

Chapter 10

The musicians parade again; there's nothing like a parade for enthusing a Roman audience. Cheers continue, and the music blares louder. From the cart, where I stand on my own now, I can look down on dancers whirling in wide skirts, jumping, girls being passed from man to man along a weaving line. The audience clap in rhythm, stirred by the music. They're still ready to be impressed by a romantic display, even after screaming and laughing as three men have died in front of them.

Jugglers are throwing batons in the air, between each other. In better circumstances I'd enjoy that; they're skilled and graceful, and their faces are joyful, whatever they're feeling inside. All that's inside me is a knot of sickness that would double me over if I wasn't tied upright.

Two priests have braved the blood-stained arena to bring in the sacrifice. They're well-used to animal blood covering the altars at their temples, I suppose. They lead me from the cart to the performers' platform on a rope, and supervise the soldiers tying me to a pole as I struggle against them. The priests want me to wave to the crowd before my hands are tied; it takes a poke in my side with a sword to make me comply. The crowd roars, and a soldier with grape-stained fingers ties my hands to the pole behind my back.

The arena is huge, I can see further than anyone can in a small town house, or in the crowded city streets. The stands tower above me, full of colourfully-dressed holiday-makers. I can only make out the faces on the front row, and the fancy stone seats built for honoured guests. There's the white mass of fabric and the purple stripe that must be the Senator. Beside him is my master; I can't tell what expression's on his face.

Now I see Narkis the Ethiopian again, one of the three men who didn't return. One glance is enough. The pieces of his body lie in a pool of blood, drying in the ridiculous sunshine; the Bear has cut one of his swords across his opponent's stomach and the other across his neck. It's the first corpse I've seen; it demonstrates just how final death is. Doesn't that scare the audience? Does the evaporating moat round the arena fool them into thinking this isn't real?

The gladiators are lined up a second time, in front of the high priest and the Senator, who claps them politely, coldly. It looks like they've brought in a new contestant, another African to replace Narkis, in their endless search for variety. That'll mess up all I've learned, because I have no chance to observe his weaknesses. I can't place his description from all I've learned; he wears as little as the others, just a loincloth, a belt and a complete joke of a breastplate that covers less than a third of his chest. He carries the retiarius' net, a dagger and an axe. Two of my possible allies are dead, is this one friend or foe?

"All right, get on with it," yawns the Senator. The Bear won't waste an opportunity to kill; he homes straight in on the new man with a growl of rage. Everyone's surprised when his swords are tangled up in a deft flick of the newcomer's net. I'm the most surprised of all; it's Naasir! Thank Someone that they gave him the tools he might be able to handle!

The Bear struggles to get his swords out of the net. It could be easy enough for Naasir to stab the brute with his dagger; never mind some god's orders for now, it's self-defence! But he doesn't even touch the dagger. He lets the swords be drawn away; we both know if he struggled his net would be cut to pieces. Shocked to be let free so easily, the Bear tries a few sword-strokes; the axe parries them all. When he realises he isn't going to be met with aggression, he storms away in search of a more worthy opponent.

The clang of iron is everywhere around me. The heat adds to the stench of excited bodies and the congealing blood on the arena floor. At first no-one comes near me, they're too busy targeting each other. There's freedom for them now to choose their own opponents if they can run fast enough across the arena and catch their target.

Oknus and Pollo are battling near to me. I try not to watch, but I can't think straight, and if I look forward I only see my master's eyes staring at me. The gladiators' leg coverings are torn and dangling, their legs beneath them covered in scars. Pollo's thigh is bleeding, but he has to fight on, there's no time for mercy any more. The little round shields provide small protection from their swords, and they swish faster than I can see. The blades are blurred until they clang; sometimes there's a pause but no clang, when a blade hits flesh.

Every wound must hurt. The thought of it throws me into a daydream of rubbing cream on Mum's wounds when my mistress has beaten her. She doesn't moan about it, she doesn't really want me to fuss, but it soothes her, I sing our lullaby to her and pretend I don't notice the tears escaping down her worn cheeks. Life's cruel wherever you turn, children die, fathers are imprisoned, ships are sunk, the crosses from Roman crucifixions litter the hillside above our town. The stink of burning animals is supposed to assuage our guilt for our faults, no laws protect slaves from brutal treatment, death or punishment in the afterlife.

Pollo's leg is twisting as he steps to avoid Oknus' sword-thrusts. He doesn't cry out, or curse his opponent, they've fought so long they're tired and dry as the sand under their feet, words are a waste of energy. The crowd hushes slightly, to watch him Pollo struggle. He's dragging his foot; Oknus takes his chance and slams down on the leg, so hard I can hear the crunch of bone.

Pollo lets out a tiny squeak as he to his knees. His only options now are to stab his opponent in the stomach or to die with pride. Oknus remains strong, although he's trying to edge Pollo away, in the direction of the water bucket at the side of the arena. He keeps his shield in just the right place to guard his stomach while he batters Pollo down. So Pollo has no choice; he faces the nearest audience and presents his neck. I look away, and when I glance down again Oknus has gone, to reap the applause from the crowd and gulp down a cup of water before seeking his next conquest. Pollo's head's twisted away from his body, his wide eyes stare into mine, then they close.

The Bear has turned towards the mighty Mars, drawn by his loud boasting; "I am Mars the Undefeated! Who dares face me?" That's the sort of thing the crowd enjoys; in unison, like the bleating of sheep, they take up the chant;

"Who dares? Who dares?" When he sees the Bear roaring back at him, he turns, for fun or from cowardice? He moves back across the arena, close to the central line of stone pillars, throwing blows at anyone who passes; the audience find that funny, but soon start yelling as the Senator does; "Get on with it!"

Striding with purpose in the other direction, the Bear has caught him, and lays in straight away. I can just see some of his sword-swings behind me. Mars continues to boast; "You'll never beat me, old man! You're tired! Go home!" It's mostly bravado; he's the one who's tired, the Bear's swings and parries seem as fast and as firm as if he'd never fought a first bout.

All over the arena the rest of the gladiators are warring, while the sun blares out, still high in the sky. Citizens are coming and going in search of drinks, waiters walk along the stands selling cool refreshments. The high priest watches the fighting in alarm. The gladiators are obviously flagging, so he orders the referees and arena stewards to take more water round and let the contestants drink.

Of course the Bear won't stop to drink; he's thrashing his opponent who had the arrogance to name himself after a god, and he's clearly enjoying it. He forces Mars back, halfway across the long arena, whacking him on each side alternately with the flats of his swords. Mars goes for his stomach, but only slits through his belt and slices the side of his hip.

That's enough to throw the Bear over the edge. People want blood, he's ready to give it to them. He pushes Mars up to the moat and begins chopping him to pieces. Roars of amazement follow every slice, and I hear the odd, very welcome scream of revulsion. Mid-slice, he glances back at me, checking out the prize. I'm next. I hate that thought. Finally he shoves his blade in one last time, and throws the body across the moat. The water reddens, and Mars collapses dead in the lap of an old citizen a few feet from the Senator.

The referee standing by with water is unimpressed by his actions. He steps in to remind the monster that there are rules to be kept, and set ways to kill. The Bear continues thrashing his blades, screaming at the audience that he will win the contest, undoubtedly, demanding to take on anyone who doubts him. He looks crazed, as if nothing will stop him. When the referee steps in, he turns, and strikes at him down his face.

The referee staggers in surprise, falls to his knees and tries to crawl back to his place for medical treatment. Stewards come to help him, but the Bear reaches him first. Seeing blood and nothing else, he doesn't hear the yells of the stewards, or the lanista running towards him in desperation. He spits the wounded referee and leaves him. He must think anything's justified in his race to claim the prize. Now he turns back towards my platform.

On my other side, Ennius and Florus are working together with brothers' instincts against Oknus. If they work together to kill the rest, and the winner is the last man standing, will they then turn on each other? Oknus is flagging; it seems that I might as well forget his name and his flaws now; with two opponents ganging up on him he doesn't stand a chance. To avoid seeing the actual moment he stops being a threat, I stare out at the crowd, asking myself how they sit there watching this. Can it really be all down to following the fashion?

Oknus is gone, but there are plenty more to watch. At the moment the priest is fairly happy, he's providing an hour of tense, varied excitement. Running in front of me, I see Secundus, still strong with the resilience of our youth on his side. He's lost his own weapons and taken up whatever he could find, a sword and a round shield. As he passes a watching soldier, he grabs his spear and runs; the audience burst into laughter, and he holds the spear above his head, waving it to make people laugh. Of course Naasir was correct, he loves to play to the crowd, and the crowd loves him.

He runs straight into Naasir's corner. How can my friend still be alive after all this? I watch closely, recalling all he's said to me about the others. The strokes of his axe are strong and straight- naturally, he chops wood at home for hours. He uses his skill to chop through the spear shaft, inches at a time, while Secundus tried to hold him off and get the sword out of his belt.

I'm delighted they gave Naasir a net, or let him choose one. Like me, he's spent time on the beach, throwing nets. He has more freedom at home than I do, buying the fish and getting to know the best fishermen. He casts the net on the floor, then, when Secundus steps contemptuously onto it, he pulls it and throws the young gladiator off his feet. At once he closes in, pressing his axe to the young man's neck. He wouldn't need massive trained strength to slice Secundus' head off, who'd blame him if he did? The public will probably scream against him if he doesn't.

Of course he doesn't. He lowers his axe and puts out his hand to help Secundus to his feet. The young man's shocked; I suppose none of them really thought Naasir was serious when he promised not to kill, or that he'd last five minutes anyway. Balbus has driven his sword into Ismet's neck before stalking away in disgust at his lack of spirit, leaving him to fall to the ground alone. Balbus advances on Naasir at once; I don't know what happened between them both in the first bout, but the real gladiator looks very discontented and eager to restart their battle.

Secundus is left alone for a moment; his face is turned my way, so I can guess the play of emotions on it. He's surprised to be alive, he actually pats his own stomach in relief that it's still in one piece. His hand runs over the blood-stained bandage round his head. He stares after Naasir in wonder, then raises his eyebrows in a split-second decision. I can't tell what that decision is yet.

There are twelve men left fighting, and six bodies littering the ground; after the Bear's attack the stewards don't dare come out here to clear up the bodies. Below me now, vaulting over a dead comrade, I recognise Ampyx the Greek, who helped me in my attempt to escape this horror. He's virtually crawling in the sand after an exhausting bout with Ambrus, the last gladiator with a daughter. She'll never see her father again.

If I were only free, I could climb down and fetch Ampyx a drink of water. My allies are dying too quickly, and too horribly, I'd quite like to help him now. I've been struggling quietly for a while against the rope round my hands; it's a tricky knot, but the soldier who ate my grapes did show the tiniest hint of compassion. At last the rope loosens; I drop it secretly and set to work on the one round my waist. That's a whole different problem; those knots are too tight, I'm completely stuck.

Ampyx pulls himself up to face Aetius and his tall iron trident. Aetius' net is dragging, so they look well-matched in exhaustion. Plenty of people are watching their bout; Ampyx' shield keeps off the worst attacks of the trident, and a twist of it pulls the trident out of Aetius' hand. He takes out his knife instead, and closes in for the final thrust.

Ampyx holds him off with his sword, twice as long as the knife. At the same time he backs towards the platform, winking at me with a leer I don't find at all reassuring. The Bear is coming for me at the same time; he could probably defeat Ampyx and Aetius both at once. Aetius' knife flashes; I scream;

79

"Watch out!" Ampyx dodges the blow and slices at the arm holding the knife until it drops.

"Cheers!" He grins at me, aiming his sword for the death-blow. I close my eyes in horror. In another moment Ampyx is on the platform. He cuts through the bonds round my waist, wrapping his arms round me instead, and asks; "What do you think of that?" He's tied Aetius up instead of killing him, and has set me free.

Chapter 11

Finally I can move my hands and feet. They're achy with the strain of standing still, watching my doom approach. Unlike the men, I haven't had to fight, so I manage to push Ampyx away before his leering face touches me again. I can hardly believe he hasn't killed his last opponent.

And there's no time to think about it. The Bear has climbed the platform a step behind Ampyx. The Bear isn't in love with me like Ampyx apparently is. I just watched him chop a man to pieces like a loaf of bread. The sight of him fills me with terror, but at least I can move now. I don't want him to touch me, to come anywhere near me; a lifetime in the sweaty arms of Ampyx seems better than facing the Bear for a moment.

So I jump off the platform, down to the ground, out of their way, and above me the battle begins. The Bear swings both his blades, Ampyx struggles beneath his blows. He sags further with each one, taking with him my hope of escaping from here alive.

Aetius' trident is right at my feet. In my hand it's as unbalanced as an amphora, but I can handle those, and this is all right, if I carry it in two hands. I have no idea what to do with it, but that doesn't seem to matter. My legs take over, my mind almost blanks in fury as the man who freed me so generously is beaten down.

Is it possible that I can free him now? I stagger back up the steps to the platform; Ampyx' blood is spattering the wood where I walk in my slippery sandals. I just keep hearing the audience' screams;

"Lance him through! Lance him through!"

Ampyx falls off the platform into the sand. He continues to fight, till the Bear jumps down on top of him and runs him through, as the crowd demands. One single stroke, and my hope of escape is dying. Even after the Bear obeys the audience, they keep shouting; "Lance him through!"

So I raise the trident and ram it down into the Bear's back. He gapes at me over his shoulder, surprised. With all my strength, anger and hatred I stab him again. He rolls onto his back and his eyebrows raise at me. Then his head falls, still, and I'm staring at a body whose spirit has left it. The crowd is stunned for a second, till, as the message is passed around at break-neck speed, they scream wildly with delight.

The most frightening man I've ever met is dead. I killed him, with a trident like a true gladiator. I am powerful!

He's motionless. I did that. He doesn't move any more, he never will. That's all due to me. I knew nothing about him, not even his name. Somewhere he has a family, a mother of his own, who will never see his face again, and may never know what became of him. I don't know what afterlife this murderer's gone to, but I sent him there.

I can't believe my own actions; I'm stooping beside his still body, too afraid to touch him, with tears creeping down my face. The Senator can see me, and the high priest, who put me in this awful position, and my master. He stands up, and raises his hands to the crowd; they respond with a sudden silence. Before I can assume that's in respect for the dead, they all begin clapping. Clapping me? If they want to see me do more of the same, they can forget it!

In the middle of the applause strong, sweating hands grab me once more. They don't paw me or aim for places I don't want to be touched, they come to rest gently on my shoulders. It's Secundus. In front of the masses, without so much as an introduction, he kisses me. And out of the side of his mouth he hisses; "Play your audience!"

"What do you mean?" I gasp, amazed.

"That's right. Surprise." He puts out his arms; is he mad? There are armed men, full of rage and adrenalin, all heading this way. I shake his hand; he holds me tight. "They like it," he tries to explain above appreciative cheers. I'm not complaining either. He hasn't killed me or attacked me, so he's a good option for now. "I think we can save your friend," he adds. Right, I've just become a Secundus fan.

Aetius has freed himself with his knife, and crept in behind Secundus. The fight resumes; Secundus is under attack, he pushes me aside and plunges in with weary thrusts and tired, floppy parries. But Aetius has left his net on the ground, and he's not expecting anything unusual from a girl dressed in silk. Yes, holding the net in my hand I recall how to spread it, over his head. The two of us pull the net round him, confiscate his knife and tie him back to a pillar supporting the stage. He's reeling in humiliation.

"End it!" he shrieks. "Finish me off, for Jupiter's sake!"

"There's gratitude," laughs Secundus, and he kisses me again. He's enjoying this too much, making me think of life and the future instead of my imminent death. There are very dangerous gladiators here, who I wish would vanish and leave us two alone; one-eyed Kiral is murdering his way to the platform, while Naasir warned me against Balbus, and now he's the one battling with the bulb-headed nightmare.

The fight is stacked against a poor slave with no training. Balbus is as armed as a gladiator can get; he has greaves on his legs, a sensible shield and a helmet on his large head. His sword reaches as far as the axe, and it's forged completely of metal. Yet the iron rings out, blow on blow, parry after parry. Naasir's arms swing the axe quickly, economically; he seems to guess where the sword will swing next. And after everything, he remains alive and fighting. That's more than the blessing of Fortuna. He wasn't always a slave in the Celerus household... What if...? Well, obviously...

Naasir keeps glancing over at me; all the time he's been keeping one eye on me, and it's costing him his concentration. If he *was* a gladiator once, he hasn't practised it for years, or known the raging urge to kill that the others are showing. I wouldn't want him to get another blow that nearly knocks his head off.

"He'll manage," Secundus hisses. I'm not so sure, but he's gone to fight off Kiral, if he can. I have to think, and quickly; Balbus is close now. All I know about him is that he's superstitious. That's no use; that means he'll only listen to the gods.

Or an image of one?

"Balbus!" I try to deepen my voice, age it, and sound wise. Tricky. As he glances at me, mid-thrust, I try to copy the fierce, uncaring gaze I saw on the statue this morning. "Balbus! Balbus!" If I keep echoing it like the priests echo everything, it might get his attention. "Leave him!"

Although I feel pretty stupid, he pauses for a second. I manage the vacant stare of my distracted mistress, through his forehead and far beyond.

"I am Artemis!" He lowers his weapon. He stares; when his enemy stops too, instead of running him through, he's convinced it's a miracle. "Balbus, Hear me, I am Artemis!" I really can't believe that the audience is following him. A chant is beginning, like the chant of the rioters yesterday.

"Artemis is great! Artemis of Ephesus!" The noise is so great, I seem to hear the roar of the lions carved on her statue.

My heart's pounding with the thrill of doing something positive- positively weird. I can raise my voice and shout clearly; "Balbus, leave this man! You will kill no more men today!" My Mum sings the song of Artemis when she wants me to be calm, even though I'm fully grown now. I climb onto the platform, with the chant ringing in my ears, and sing for the crowd;

"Run with my deer, my arrows will guard you.

Sleep without fear, no lions will harm you.

I'll keep you safe, whatever may come;

Sleep without fear, and dream." The audience is with me, many of them know the song, and they're humming along to it. Balbus is confused, but not stupid. The pause for the song has given him a chance to breathe, and decide what's best-certainly he won't tackle that Naasir again, or touch the spooky woman who murdered the toughest gladiator in the arena.

While he decides, Kiral throws a spear that lands in his back. He falls on his face in front of me. Now there are three of us and five against us. Aetius is still sitting inside a net, trying to wriggle towards anything sharp to cut himself free.

"Watch out, Ennius and Florus," I whisper to Naasir, as applause greets my song and the death of Balbus.

"Stay low," he suggests. I'm not going to step back from the danger now. The brothers are steady fighters, consistent in style, and now full of refreshing water from the stewards who wait on the side-lines, goading them on to fight. Yet Naasir believes they're easily distracted. What on earth by? There's nothing happening but their onslaught against my friend and protector, and Secundus battling Crispus the retiarius around the central pillars.

How does my mistress distract the master when he's angry? Not with music, my song scarcely worked on those two. No, she does it with a natural charm I'm sure I don't have. But if the tales are true, gladiators aren't too particular who admires them, as long as they're getting attention. "Go, Florus!" I shout, struggling to pick out which is the most handsome. He spares me a glance; I throw back a smile, and a twitch that's meant to be a wink. Ennius looks at me, waiting to hear his own name too. "Go, Florus! You can win! Leave the slave, he's not worth it!"

So he does. I suppose the excitement of battle and the sight of me tied up for him to win have driven him crazy. I put out my hand, uncertain what to do next but happy that Naasir's left with only one opponent. Ennius leaves him too; he storms up to his brother and bats away his sword.

The fight's anything but brotherly, although they're clearly not fighting to the death. "We can share her," Ennius suggests. That makes them battle faster. Naasir grabs a cup of water and a few breaths, shaking his head at me in disbelief. In a glance across the field of battle, he finds

85

Secundus has copied our trick with the nets, and hurries to help him tie Crispus to the foot of the platform.

Pleased with his victory over Galyn, Kiral returns with his victim's heavy shield, the rectangular type a legionary takes regularly into battle. It covers his whole body. Ennius comes to his senses and stops fighting his brother to face a real enemy. Florus take his chance and runs at me. He lifts me off my feet, then throws me to the ground. His blood smears the silk stola. I was too slow to gather a new weapon, so all I can do is kick.

He rolls away. I jump to my feet, with a loud rip, leaving a torn piece of silk under his knee. He chases me along the row of pillars in the centre of the arena, a bit of a comedy moment for the crowd, who are loving it all. My sandals slip, he gains on me. And quickly I do what none of the gladiators can; I slip between two pillars to the other side. It's a long run for him all the way round, time for me to find a sword, though I have to prise it from the hands of a dead man whose name already escapes me.

Florus is fast. I'm not used to hurrying, my sandals can't do me justice and I can't get them off. On top of that, while I'm running I'm trying to think of a way to defeat him without hurting him. I can't. So I run, and skip through the pillars again. At the end of the line of pillars Florus meets Secundus, angry, jealous and rested. It's over in an instant, hardly any blood, but still the tragic result the audience demands. "You killed him!" I protest.

"Yes, that's the point!"

"Not today!" He tilts his head at me, shrugs, and agrees;

"Sorry. No more."

Ennius hears his brother's cry and stares up in horror. He tries to race to his side, to see whether he can help. "Doctor!" he screams out. "Help this man! He's done good service to Rome! Hurry!" None of us have noticed that Aetius has cut himself out of the net; in a desperate quest for honour, he throws himself on Ennius, growling;

"Your soul can join your brother's!" The applause isn't as great as he expected. He wins a few laughing cheers, which swiftly die away. Nobody's watching him, their eyes are on the gladiator who refuses to kill. When he cries out in anguish; "Let my soul join the gladiators who die with *honour!*" and he glares pointedly at Naasir, the crowd deliberately ignores him. Not even throwing himself on his own sword attracts any positive attention. He dies a nobody. I'm sorry, Naasir is sorry, but we have other things on our minds.

Kiral actually snorts out a grim laugh. He's not going to go out in a blaze of humiliation, he has every intention of fighting the two men left standing, the slave *and* the dreamer. He'll take me away from the young fool who's holding my hand to play the lover for his audience, and... As he heads for the young dreamer, his laugh disappears. He laughed aloud when Naasir vowed not to kill him, but it's different now he faces a wall of three, including a woman dressed as a goddess, splattered in blood and pointing a long trident at him.

Secundus steps forward, with a dramatic shout; "You can't have... What's your name? Aysel, you can't have Aysel, I love her!" He still has the energy for a few blows, before he calls out again; "Aysel, I'm dying, save me!"

I do my best to go with the flow, stabbing the trident against the wide wooden shield as hard as I can, thudding it, and causing no harm at all.

"We'll tire him out," Secundus suggests in a whispered hiss. "Make it dramatic." He sinks to his knees, prompting Naasir to step in and carry the fight away from him.

The audience like me fighting. Now they're shouting out; "Aysel!" instead of "Artemis!" Again I hear the lion's soft roar, but that's imagination. It's a novelty, that's all. And they're sighing for Secundus' despair, watching him fall. They watch him crawl on the ground to a rope. He grabs it, staggers to his feet, and begins to whip the rope round his head.   Kiral has given up on him, fading away on his right side; he can't see the rope because of his missing eye.

He's caught, shield and all.   Naasir disarms him and Secundus helps him tether Kiral below the platform, far enough from Crispus so they can't cause any more trouble. Once they're done, Secundus returns to his individual death scene, staggering back and holding his arms out to me.   He sinks a second time when I catch him, hissing; "Shout my name, cry, or something!"

"Secundus!" I cry out, obediently; I never fancied myself as a performer.   And our audience has grown silent, at the call of the high priest.   I stare over at him, and see my master staring back, startled that they were crying my name.   I'm not sure he ever knew what my name was.

"Get on with it," growls the Senator.   Naasir turns sadly to Secundus, who's miraculously found his feet again.   He knows the rules, the winner is the last one standing, and he's praying that after all my interference they don't count *me* as a contestant.

Chapter 12

"Play along," Secundus orders, putting out his hand. What choice do I have? I place my hand in his, and he squeezes it. That should be the kind of thing that tells me to trust him, if only I'd known him for longer than a day. Naasir, the friend I've known since birth, is beside him, bleeding from wounds he's got trying to protect me; Secundus puts his sword to his neck.

"No!" I shout. Secundus winks, and kisses the hand he has tight hold of. He drives Naasir towards the Senator's seat, marked out by a bright green canopy and a mass of priests in hats and priestesses in pristine white stolas. Glancing down at mine, I wonder if Drusa will be angry that I've torn it and covered it in blood and dirt. I hope so.

Crispus stays tied up in his net without a struggle; I've heard he has some great successes behind him, so one moment of indignity in Ephesus will hardly affect his career. Kiral is grimacing with his good eye, but Naasir has plenty of experience at tying up troublesome donkeys and making nets that he sells to the fishermen.

Now I could look my master in the eye, but he's gone. The priest doesn't look unhappy, though his face looks like a storm is brewing in his mind. The Senator's amused, looking about at the crowd, cheering although there's no death. He has the power over our lives, he can order us to be killed if he doesn't like our... there's no other word for it but 'performance.' Secundus isn't scared; he's been brought up among performers. Without letting go of my hand, he steps forward to the edge of the water dividing us from the Senator and priest. The girls draw back, and the priests don't exactly lean in to protect them. A dozen soldiers' spears level at him.

Secundus addresses the crowd with a clear young voice. "Don't ask me to kill this man! Don't forget the one thing we all live for! Remember what the musicians were singing!

Remember the play!" In the drama of the fighting, many people have forgotten the romance of this morning. He wipes away a rush of sweat with his blood-stained wrist as he calls out like an actor; "They told us all about love. I have fought for…"

"Aysel."

"Aysel, because I love her, and I want to keep her for myself. But this man has loves her with a fatherly love. Who understands that?" He wins murmurs of approval, and a brief nod from the Senator. "He's even willing to die so that she can live! Will you call for that death, or will you all show love?"

He walks me along the front row, throwing his arms up to appeal to the crowd, gesturing for them to applaud, and they do. When he's sure he's winning them over, he throws me into his arms and pushes my head onto his shoulder. I rest my tangled mop of hair on blood; there's a gaping wound on his chest beneath my ear, I wonder how long he can carry on with that. He presses them on to a decision. Maybe it's the loss of blood that makes him virtually fearless, so only I can feel the tremble of his hand on my waist.

"Senator, I ask for missio. Spare his life!" He's cheeky. We don't know who would have won. Both of them are badly injured, but Naasir has experience behind him. Still, how well would he have won the crowd? It's his turn to address them now. The Senator stands, leaning forwards to look him in the eye.

"Well, tell me, you ancient gladiator! Is it possible you *are* this girl's father?"

"No, sir." Naasir is standing tall, trusting Secundus now, so I can maybe relax and trust him too.

"You're amusing. You must come to Rome," the Senator declares, with a grim chuckle. "So, if you're a gladiator, why won't you kill?" That raises a laugh. Naasir stays cool.

"The high priest forced us to fight, but my God does not allow me to kill." Ah, this is his dream! He's someone now, he has the respect and attention of tens of thousands of people, just as he hoped. And the Senator asks the exact question I know Naasir wants to hear.

"Really? Which god do you serve?"

"I serve Jesus, the Christ, Son of the unseen God." The Senator's eyebrows raise in surprise. His brow furrows. Clearly he knows much more about Jesus and His people than I do. So does the chief priest; he grips the carved arms of his campaign chair in anger, then strokes his beard in amusement. "The only God," Naasir continues; Secundus taps him on the arm; instinct tells him that's quite enough. My friend is smiling, his wounds are forgotten, the threat of death is nothing to him. I want that feeling.

A new cry begins, and I know exactly who's started it. "We make the gods!" It runs through hundreds of tradesmen round the arena, the screaming riot of yesterday is returning, Naasir's message is fading.

"See," he sighs, close to me. "Nothing stays pure, in human hands."

"The people who want to listen heard you," I promise him. Secundus has picked up a round metal shield, and hammers his sword on it like the Curetes in the parade, a clanging drum-beat that halts the racket. He screams out;

"Missio, missio!" and in their mood of chanting, the people follow as sheep follow each other on the hillside. "Missio, missio, missio!" He's going a long way to make sure we all live. It's appreciated; I stand on my toes to kiss him on the cheek, and the audience appreciate that. "Missio! Let him live!" The games are for the public pleasure, and those in charge must listen to the public.

The Senator rises, pristine in his white and purple, the long fabric of his toga perfectly draped, and holds up a hand for silence, knowing he'll be obeyed. "You can all go free, if you give us one last little show." His hand drops, a gate clangs open, and the air fills with a deep, throbbing growl.

Three times I've heard that. It wasn't imaginary. Out of the gladiators' arch wanders a lion, lithe and hungry, with a huge mane, down to its knees. Secundus hurries me back to Naasir's side, to ask him; "What are his weaknesses?" Naasir shakes his head. The lion must be starving; he wastes no time ripping into the nearest body. I can't remember who that was.

Naasir's not moving away, he's heading towards the lion, brandishing his axe. My legs won't carry me anywhere right now. If I could only get a cup of water, I might be able to think straight. But there are no stewards; they were scared of removing the bodies before, and now we're faced with a wild beast, they've all vanished. There's only one water bucket, on the side of the arena furthest from the gate.

Secundus has gone too. He cuts Crispus out of his net, while Naasir cuts the lasso from Kiral, and shakes his hand. Secundus warns them both; "Play the audience. Do you know what I mean? Do either of you fight lions?" They're fighting each other already! "Cut it out! Did you notice the lion?"

"You son of Hades! " Crispus yells, throwing himself behind Kiral's shield. He wrestles him to the ground, and they roll over in a tight bundle, throwing punches and kicking up dust. The lion glances up through his huge matted mane; he's moved on to the next corpse, closer to us. Secundus is poking a trident at the two wrestling gladiators. Crispus screams at him;

"Dumb play-actor!" He tries to stagger up and attack Secundus, but Kiral has him round his waist. The crowd are clapping a rhythm, rattling cups of water in the roasting heat. Everywhere in the corners of my eyes wooden fans are flapping. Sweat's blobbing into my eyes, either from the heat or my fear. After all those careful words Secundus used on his audience, he can't argue with a lion.

"Aysel!" Naasir's call rouses me. "Bring the bucket of water!"

"You want a drink? *Now?*" He nods; I understand, he has a plan.

"Secundus!" The young man obeys him, drawing away. Kiral gets up, grabs his shield and follows Secundus. Crispus doesn't; he lies in the dust as the lion advances. I hope Kiral ended his life properly, swiftly, before the lion can reach him. I'm at the water bucket, the furthest away from the action. If I stay where I am, I'll probably be safe, while the lion tears the others to pieces, or Kiral continues the contest.

I pick up the heavy bucket; it's nearly full, and I'm getting used to all the spectators watching me. I could do with a swig, but I ought to hurry. Step by step I heft it back towards the waiting men. Kiral has handed Naasir a shield, Naasir's moved in front of Secundus, who's rounded up three more weapons. Kiral and Naasir look at the lion, then they look at me, murmuring something, and both of them nod. What have they planned for me?

"Are you wearing a tunic?" Naasir asks, kindly. Kiral's grimacing at my silk stola, it's like a white page scribbled with a tale of murder and destruction. "Take off the stola, the blood may attract the lion."

The crowd is amused when I strip my stola off; who cares? I'm still in the softest tunic I've ever worn- and the sweatiest. I throw the stola as far away as I can. The lion takes a hint of interest in it, but hardly cares. He's padding slowly about the arena, pursued by the yells of the crowd above him. The moat of water protecting them is in danger of evaporating. I'm seeing him through a wavering heat haze.

"Why's he waiting? Why doesn't he chase us?"

"He's thirsty," Kiral hisses. Naasir agrees;

"He has the biggest mane I've seen, and this is the worst heat I've known. You need to take him the water."

"Why me?"

"We're covered in blood."

"And you're the goddess Artemis today," Kiral observes. "She can handle lions."

I don't like taking orders from a murderer; I'm holding back, naturally. But Naasir nods in encouragement. I know he's saved my life a lot in the last two hours, but I'm not happy about this. I'm shaking just as I was when they first brought me into the arena. The audience does nothing to psyche me up, they've grown almost totally silent, there's only the complaint of some heavy gamblers who bet against us all. Their day can't compare to mine.

"Go now," Kiral orders. I'm not listening to him.

"Then walk straight out, everyone," Secundus adds.

"Walk with the lion," is Naasir's idea.

"And if he attacks me?"

Kiral makes a generous offer; "I'll finish you off before the lion can."

"Thanks." So I step out, carrying the sloshing bucket, trying not to look the lion in the eye, because that always annoys my mistress' cat. He idles closer to me; the waiting is awful, I may as well close the gap with a couple more steps. The men stay close behind, and the audience stays hushed. The lion's so close I can feel his breath on my leg, and picture his teeth biting into it. His lips are slavered with bits of his recent feast on the dead men.

I lower the bucket. He drinks, noisily. He's desperately thirsty, the weight's decreasing fast. As I move the bucket away a fraction, the lion follows. It's working. When I recall the importance of playing the crowd, I dare to place my hand on the matted, steaming mane, as Artemis does on my mistress' statue- if only Lucina hadn't sent me to the agora with that statue yesterday!

The water's nearly gone, but the gate the lion came from is close by. Before my amazement settles, I'm through the gate and anxious animal trainers are chaining the lion. He's lead away, and Naasir, Kiral and Secundus are behind me, alive and laughing in relief. Secundus hugs me so hard I'm lifted off my feet. Now my clean tunic's ruined in the filth of all his battles, but I can't stop clinging to him.

"Good reception," Kiral observes. The stadium is wild with cheering, and with chants;

"Artemis is great!" Seriously, can't they let that idea rest? That was me, not Artemis, *me*! Despite the odds, Naasir and I are both alive, so is the boy he labelled as a hopeless case. The Roman Senator promised us freedom.

And a man is gone from the world today because I killed him.

Chapter 13

"LEAVE HIM!" The giant scream echoes in my ears. It wakes me from a strangely restful sleep. I wonder if I've died after all, because I'm never allowed to sleep in the daytime. But I can feel. I feel the softness of clean wool beneath my cheek; it smells like my Mum's tunic when she holds me on her shoulder if I've had a nightmare or she's had a beating from our mistress. Maybe I'll hear her sing to me, washing away my horrible dream with her voice.

"It's all right." The voice startles me; it's young, and male. I have to open my eyes now; I am alive, and still in my nightmare. In front of me is the gladiators' courtyard, and their tunnel to the main gate of the Ephesus arena. I'm in the cell where I slept last night, expecting to die in the morning; my head rests on a strong, clean shoulder.

"Secundus," I remember. And hearing my own voice, I remember it was me who screamed out and woke myself. He's had his other shoulder cleaned and bandaged, and he has a new dressing on his head. How did he manage that, between marching out of the arena following a lion and holding on to me while I slept? And why's he bothered doing that?

I'm still in the tunic those vicious temple girls forced on me. I don't know whether I want to change; the blood and dirt seem to carry the story of my life, the one that began once I left my home two days ago, a life I never dreamed of, full of lust and horror. But I can't sit here beside a clean person smelling like this, not when there's a white tunic pressed and folded right in front of me, lying unused on the table across the courtyard. "Will you keep watch for me?"

There are plenty of open cells to change in. Next to mine is Crispus'; he won't ever sit on that little camp bed again. I can look round the courtyard and recall all the names Naasir fed into me, every one of them gone for ever. The only ones left are the youngest, Secundus, and the most fierce-looking, one-eyed Kiral. I'm trying my best to ignore the end cell, furthest from mine, where the Bear sat last night in his ominous silence. Someone must have known his name. I could ask his trainer.

He's back, the gladiator's lanista. How must he feel, now seventeen of the men he bought and trained are dead? He looks less bothered than Secundus, who doesn't look as if he has a speck of guilt. He grins at my change of outfit and fluffed hair;

"That's an improvement, you don't look like a gladiatrix now!"

What in Vesta's name is a gladiatrix? And how... It's no good wondering to myself; I have to ask him seriously; "How can you smile? Seventeen men are dead!"

"Not men," he shrugs. "Opponents."

"And I murdered one of them!"

"That wasn't murder; that was self-defence. You know what he would have done to you?"

"Yes, I do!" Oh, Jupiter, I'm blushing in front of him, and the lanista. "But I..."

"That's how the world works," Secundus informs me politely. "You'll get used to it. No need to be self-righteous about it."

"I'm not! And you don't need to be patronising!" I bite my tongue, literally. Secundus saved my life, and the lanista's lounging against the table, laughing at each of us, clapping at whatever he finds amusing. His voice is still a growl, even when he's mocking;

"So you let go of her finally, Secundus? I said you didn't need to carry your act on once you left your stage! And it was just an act, I see now!"

"What's made you so merry, Corinthus?" Secundus growls back; although he looks away, I have a feeling I'm not the only one blushing.   Strange. And the lanista doesn't care. His belly bounces slightly as he explains with delight;

"You two- you three- have made me a rich man! You, boy, with your acting and your pretty love story!   And you, girl, with your interesting face, and your use of the trident!   The bookies are being torn to pieces outside. No-one bet on you and Naasir except me!" To prove his point, he throws a small leather purse at his gladiator. "Here, put this towards your theatre, you and I are going places!"

Do I get a purse of money too? No, I'm still a nobody. But he looks me over, critically, and pulls up my arm.

"You're injured here. I'll get the doctor back."   In the entrance to the gladiators' tunnel, he turns and jokes to Secundus; "Great act, I really thought you liked her!"

Secundus puts the purse back on the table, to my surprise. He's happy enough to explain; "It all belongs to Corinthus until I resign."   He says nothing about the lanista's last comment. Instead he hands me a cup of water, sitting down on a bench as if we were two friends in the agora, and asks; "What will you do now?"

"I don't know," is the truth.   "I thought you'd won me." Stupid thing to say! What am I thinking of? He chuckles, and shrugs his aching shoulders.

"I wouldn't worry about that. I'm a gladiator, we don't have any status, and we could die any time; who'd want to marry a gladiator?"

"I'm just a slave," I observe, trying to sound comforting; then I exclaim in amazement; "Marry? You were going to marry me?"

"Better than those other guys, heh?"

"It certainly is!" I laugh at my own surprise; he takes it the wrong way.

"Why? Got a better offer, have you?" I can only shake my head. It's amazing, and crazy, that anyone could ever think of marrying me, a plain little slave in a common household! He shrugs. "Still, I'm a murderer, aren't I?" I try protesting that I didn't mean it that way, but it's true enough. "And you only met me yesterday. It'd take a few more days to find out how completely awesome I am!"

Ha, I'm obviously still sleepy, I've forgotten this morning's procession, the boasting cries of the doomed gladiators and the girls flocking round them. Secundus wasn't short of admirers; no wonder he thinks he's awesome. I grimace back at him- and notice he's only joking.

"And you're not just a slave, you're a free woman, the Senator said. You can do whatever you want."

He's right, I can be whoever I want to be, if I can learn how, and if I can face the common people of Ephesus again. Just walking up the street will be awkward; nearly everyone goes to the games, it's the place to be seen and the legionaries get suspicious if freemen don't go. They'll all recognise me; they'll probably want to know if it was as much fun in the arena as it was watching. And even an uneducated slave knows they won't be interested in the truth, I'll have to make up stories for them, until the true horror becomes a legend in my mind.

"You could go anywhere." Has Secundus read my mind? He's right, what's stopping me? "Pompeii is nice, my parents live there. I go there whenever I can. Do you have any special talents, apart from the obvious?"

"Talents?"

"I mean the singing, net-throwing, trident-thrusting..." That's a talent, is it? The lanista has returned with the weary doctor; they throw up my arm again, to look at the sword-scratch under my arm-pit. The doctor takes out his cream to treat it, then, when the lanista gives him a wave, he begins on my scratched legs. I wish they'd leave me alone.

"When can I go?" I ask. The lanista smiles and says nothing except;

"I want the legs healthy, shining." The doctor nods, but doesn't look at me. Why should they care about my legs any more? Never mind; the cool soothing of cream on my skin has thrown my mind back to home, to the cosy kitchen fire and the warm terracotta colour of the pots. The sun streams in the window of our kitchen, and the smell of seething onions fills the air; here it's just stale and shadowed, with the stink of caked blood and stale urine.

"My Mum bakes lovely bread," I answer Secundus, past the interfering head of the doctor. "We could find work in a bakery. But first I'll have to earn some money and buy her freedom." The lanista snorts; I don't know why, but he's that kind of man, the sort Mum described to me often enough. I ignore the snort, and so does Secundus.

"Buy her freedom?" he echoes with approval. "Poetic." I can see his eye's on the purse the lanista gave him. He surely can't be thinking of giving it to me? That doesn't feel wise, it's death money- I'd better not carry on down that line of thought or my nightmare might return.

"Where's Naasir?" The doctor has finished with me at last, I'm covered in cream and dressings, and physically I'm going to be fine. Mentally I feel toxic, I repulse myself and I have the urge to go and make a sacrifice to someone. I wish I hadn't said that aloud, when Secundus points out;

"You *were* the sacrifice!" He hasn't lived with Naasir, he doesn't understand, and doesn't know where he's gone.

"He's out the back of the arena,' the lanista informs me. "Seeing some friends."

I have to cross the arena once more to reach him. It's empty except for two slaves with brushes and oak buckets, covering up the last traces of the day's events with a fresh layer of sand. Yet the screams of the crowd are in my head, and I wish I didn't have to blink; every time I do I glimpse Ampyx being beaten down by the Bear, and feel the weight of that iron trident in my hands.

"We *know* we do wrong, we *know* we need to sacrifice..." Someone far away, through a little back door, is crying out exactly the way I feel. They have to be talking to Naasir. I can't move a single inch closer to him, I'm physically scared of stepping on the sand. It's up to Secundus to take my hand. The warmth and his voice reassure me;

"It's all over, put it behind you. It'll get easier." Together we cross the sand; I can walk better without posh Roman sandals, and the stupid heat of the afternoon has cooled as the sun starts to go down. The sand's only sand, it was the rage of the people which filled this place with hatred, and I need never come near a circus again.

As we approach the little door, several voices grow clearer. "How can we ever be good enough for this Heaven you speak of?"

"What sacrifice could be big enough for all the sins of the whole world?"

Secundus raises his eyebrows at that idea, and leads me through the door into a garden full of trees and bushes. It's allowed to grow wilder than the clipped plants in my master's peristyle. The green of the leaves and grass cools my disappointment in finding Naasir in the centre of a small crowd when I wanted to talk to him alone. He doesn't notice our arrival, he's too busy trying to answer the questions the free crowd are throwing at him. And his face brightens as he answers, surprising Secundus and the rest even more;

"The sacrifice of God's only, perfect Son? Wouldn't that be enough?"

Some of them are giving his words a lot of thought, others are wondering what a slave could know about the human spirit. They shout out together; "The gods never gave one of themselves, just for us mortals!" and there's the inevitable question; "Which god?"

Naasir throws up his hands, exasperated. "There is only one God, don't complicate matters! Didn't you listen to Paul, who spoke in the agoras? And the lecture hall?"

"Tell us again," a white-haired old woman suggests, laying a wrinkled hand on his bandaged arm. "We forget so easily." He nods at her; it looks like her calm understanding of human nature's all he needs to restore his patience.

"It's already done," he continues, while the crowd shift closer and some sit down to listen more easily. "The Romans crucified a man named Jesus, twenty-four years ago. He was God's Son. The miracles he did are proof that He was; I mean, that He is."

"That's too easy!" someone shouts. Exactly what I said this morning. Now he gives us all an answer.

"We're hard-hearted and slow to believe, sir. It has to be simple. Paul came here to teach us all about Him, and Paul did miracles." The old lady nods in agreement, and, as Naasir points out the long wound which should have taken his head off, she creaks to her feet and raises her stick to invite the crowd's attention.

"This is the truth. My son was struck blind and he could work no longer. His children were hungry, his wife had to work his trade for him, and I was left with no-one to care for me in my old age. I tried all the gods, all of them. I was desperate when I turned to Paul from Tarsus, but he prayed one prayer in the name of Jesus, the Christ, and when he put his hand on my son, he could see again. Down with the old gods!"

She waves to encourage a chant, people seem so willing to chant along. Naasir has noticed me above the people who are sitting now; he sends me one of those long-suffering glances I've seen a thousand times. He does it whenever our master carries on at us, even though we've completed his tasks as well as possible. Naasir bears all that in calm silence, but now I find he can raise his voice enough to shout easily over the old woman's head.

"Thank you for telling us. But Paul didn't come hating anyone, whatever they believe, and neither do I. I won't kill, I only want to show you the way to life, to life that lasts for ever." I shoot him a smile; he seems to be doing well. He smiles back, and goes on, promising as clearly as the Roman Senator promised our freedom; "You only need to believe, and turn away from all that's wrong." He raises his hands and places the palms together; that's how he prays, but other people aren't ready to pray. They have so many questions, we all do. No-one takes any notice of his slave's collar now they've seen his actions inside the stadium.

"You don't kill? You mean you never did?"

"I didn't say that..."

"Can you do miracles? My daughter..." And Secundus yells out;

"How do we know what you call wrong?"

Naasir turns to the young gladiator with a weary sigh. He's been marching and fighting all day, fighting the instinct to kill which he's hidden for thirteen years. This morning he felt unequal to the task of spreading his message. Now he's doing his best, and the people who looked for him particularly after the circus are corrupting his words when they're only just out of his mouth.

On top of all that, there's a disturbance at the back of the little crowd. Secundus raises his sword; that must be his natural reaction to trouble. Three men are battling their way through to where Naasir sits on a tall stone. Two of them wear heavy togas despite the heat, and one has a cloud of white hair round his open face, and striped robes that remind me of the priest in the Jewish synagogue; they're certainly not soldiers. As they reach him, Naasir's shoulders straighten and his pained expression melts away. The three men greet him by shaking his hand, and he stands with them like an equal, not a slave. I like them for that!

"Here are some wise men who have taught me, and know more about the one God than I can tell you. Stay and listen, they can explain much better than I can." He sidles away from the crowd, through the standing stones in the grass and heads for me and Secundus, who's hissing in my ear;

"He is actually crazy!" To his face he adds; "Naasir, you should never turn your back on your audience." It's true, now the novelty of a peaceful gladiator has left them, the crowd's leaving too. There are only seven people left, settling down at the feet of Naasir's friends to hear more. He's not at all surprised.

"Go and listen," he suggests to Secundus. The young man takes the hint that he wants some peace, but he doesn't want to sit, he wants to celebrate his victory.

"Tell me later," he offers. "Corinthus has ordered us a meal, and I'm starving."

Chapter 14

The townspeople head out of the garden in the pink of setting sun, worn out with the fun and excitement of watching the games in the glamour of the Ephesian stadium. If they're heading straight home to share their stories with their families, they'll have to dodge the people who've changed out of their sweaty day-clothes and headed back into town to the taverns. There, I suppose, there'll be gossiping about us, and cursing of us, and drinking away the pain of lost bets until the sun's ready to rise again.

It'll rise on a free woman, not a slave any more. I'd like the chance to walk and plan the future I want, but first I need to talk to Naasir. It doesn't make sense to take my freedom and start my life again if I'm just going to live it like anyone else, and die carrying my guilt. He's offering me the gift of a longer, more interesting life than that. Still, we're both as hungry as Secundus is, and we only have a few spare moments to whisper as we head back to the gladiators' courtyard to eat.

"Sorry about that woman, Naasir, interrupting you."

"That doesn't matter, she wanted to tell her story." Now I've reached him, and we can walk together, alive, I want to throw my arms round him again, and hug him like I hug my Mum when she's in pain. But I know he's broken and bandaged all over, and he'd be uncomfortable with hugs anyway. Instead, he smiles down at me, and I do my best to smile back.

"She had a good story," I agree, glad that he's not tired of me, despite his exhaustion. "You said nothing stays pure. Are you all right?"

He nods, uncertainly, I think. He's standing in front of one of those stones in the grass, beside a small hawthorn bush; now I see what all these stones are, they're gravestones.

105

"What does it say?" For some reason I don't doubt he can read as well as he fights.

"It says 'Dacmus, won six times, drew three times, lost once.'"

"Was he a gladiator?" I stoop to brush the parched grass away from the stone.

"Yes, they live outside society so they're buried outside the city graveyards."

I'm trying to be quiet and respectful, but I can't help gasping; "What? That's unfair! Society forces them to fight in the first place, for society entertainment!"

His response is quick; he's had years to ponder it; "Society itself is unfair. We slaves know that, don't we?" Yes, we do, too well! Doubtless, this gladiator who now lies beneath the ground knew it too.

"Was he a friend of yours?" Naasir kneels beside me, resting his hand on the inscription, and murmurs;

"Yes, he was a good friend. We spent some good times together. He was a skilled musician. I went to his wedding."

"Who killed...?" An instant too late, I sense I shouldn't have started to ask that question. I know the answer before he gives it.

"I killed him. With a trident." I want to ask so much more; I daren't open my mouth, he's kneeling in silence, eyes shut, while a tear escapes them. I've never known a man to cry, and I'm relieved that he can weep for these men, when no-one else seems to be bothered. My heart's aching for them, and cursing that Senator; he's the symbol of our oppression in my mind. There's someone I wouldn't weep for.

"Naasir?" He doesn't answer, so I hope he's heard me. "Does trusting in the one God take your guilt away?" I have to wait for an answer; it's no problem, I'm growing used to that. Having spent so many years in quiet, he wants to use the right words.

106

"Yes, He can take away your guilt. You can be clean again, inside." His hand's still resting on the tombstone as he adds; "But I can never forget what I did."

"Will He want me as a worshipper?" I prayed to Him this morning, and we're both still alive, against the odds. I want Naasir to say yes, to touch me and work some heavenly magic; I want the power he has to face the future, and death, without being afraid. His acceptance doesn't come as willingly as I expected.

"Aysel, I said it was simple, but do you know what you're asking? In this world we are misunderstood, and persecuted more than slaves are. It's not too bad in Ephesus right now, but in Rome... in Rome we have to worship God in secret, or people are likely to stone us."

I don't see why I should worry about what goes on in Rome, nor why I should be robbed of the peace and certainty that's Naasir's. "That doesn't matter to me," I tell him.

"They've taken innocent followers and fed them to the lions in the circus," he warns.

"The circus? Wow!" I might joke about our survival, yet the memory of that lion sends a shiver right through me. All right, so I'm foolish to mock him, and probably deserve his next observation;

"You're so young. But if you die...." I'm not going to die for many years now, facing death once at fourteen was enough! "And then... I need the wisdom of the elders." His friends back in the graveyard? He'd better hurry, the lanista's beckoning from the courtyard, food's ready, and this time I'm sure I can eat. Naasir preached to all those people he didn't know, so what makes me such a difficult case? Just in time, he spits it out; "Secundus worships the Roman gods, when he believes in them at all."

"And? What's that got to do with me?"

"You're very fond of him."

"I am not!" I protest, offended as our mistress when her friend asks if she's dyed her hair; she always dyes it, and

107

hopes no-one notices. Naasir puts a comforting hand on my shoulder.

"He's really charmed you, hasn't he? He's a typical gladiator." Is he, I wonder? Maybe it's the smell of warm pastry and onions that's making me dizzy, but I'm sure Mum didn't warn me against men who let you rest on their shoulder to sleep. She said nothing about men who talk politely, hold you gently, and even kill for you. Hmm, he killed for me. "I'll talk to God about him," Naasir offers. What's the point? Secundus kills people for a living.

He's at the entrance to the courtyard, beaming and offering us both a slice of the pastry. I smell cheese, I see cheese, and I'm actually allowed to eat it! I've tasted plenty of crumbs before, the ones that are left when Aunt Yildiz makes cheese pastries for a party, and the scrapings of cheese sauce are always worth the wait. But to have it spread thick on rich baked dough seems like more than I deserve. Well, it's gladiator food, and I'm going to eat till I'm stuffed.

I'm relieved to see that there's no need for table manners, because I really haven't got any, particularly tonight. I cram in the cheesy bread as fast as I dare on such an empty stomach, hardly tasting the olives and onions the baker has dressed it with. After all, once I walk out of the stadium as a free woman I won't be able to rely on meals paid for by the Celeruses. Not that I'd want to, I'd rather starve.

None of us will starve tonight. There are pies with real meat in, expensive meat I've never been allowed before. It tastes better than it smells, and leaves me completely speechless. I can't manage a word anyway, with my mouth so full. Kiral's quiet, too. He comes out of his cell to fill his wooden plate and his large pot mug, then retreats without a word. He may be the toughest and worthiest survivor of the day, but I'm sure he's still smarting with humiliation.

"Want a drink?" Secundus is asking. I take a thirsty swig from his tankard- it's wine, I'm not falling for that again! So I take a leaf out of Naasir's book, and fill another cup from the bucket of water; it's not as clean as weak ale, but it's hugely refreshing. The gladiators feel a duty to finish off leftovers, and work their way doggedly through the whole amphora of wine.

The drinking has its effect on the lanista pretty fast. He claps me on the back, laughing in his usual angry growl;

"Eat, drink! Fatten yourself up, girlie, have anything you like! We are going to be so rich! Did I tell you the bookies were being torn to pieces- I mean metaphorically, you understand...?"

Yes, he told us. And he can tell us again, if he just leaves me to eat in peace. He's going to be rich? Lucky him, but I want nothing more to do with him.

Secundus is growing merry, too. He throws me a berry pie and a huge, careless grin, and chuckles. "Will you make these in your bakery? Have you thought any more about where you'll go? I'm going to buy my dad a theatre, not in Pompeii, in Rome! In Rome, why not? The Senator said we ought to go there. Why don't you bake in Rome?"

"We might," I shrug.

"Great. I'll bring Primus to taste for you, he knows his pies! And we can get to know each other. Who knows?" His chuckle's infectious, and every time he smiles I forget some of the horrors I've witnessed. I suppose that's all just gladiator charm.

"Drink," Kiral hisses at me. With his bulk leaning over me, I obey, wondering why he's bothering to be kind when he doesn't have any natural gladiator charm. Ah, he's put more wine in my water cup. The lanista's laughing with him.

"Eat more," he suggests. "Food will help absorb the wine!" I need to absorb it, it's making me dizzy. Most of the food's meat and pastry, ideal for filling up beefy warriors. Fortunately there are also nuts and grapes. Drusa wouldn't let me eat the temple nuts, so I'll choke down as many of these as I can, and hope she never darkens my path again.

The grapes are impossibly sweet for someone raised on a plain diet of bread and broth.   I'm very sleepy, and my troubles are dulling a bit.   I don't know where newly-freed girls go to sleep, but they might let me rest here for a few hours.   Seeing me yawn, Secundus wraps a firm arm round me.   It's the cosiest feeling I can ever recall.

I shrug him off.   Now our stomachs are full, I need to talk to Naasir.   Or to sleep all night.   Secundus has started on the slave before I can.   "Come on, then, Naasir.   How do we know what's right and wrong?"

Naasir pauses in the middle of a bite of meat pie.   Then he carries on eating, until Secundus drives him to answer.   "I'll tell you, but you won't remember any of this in the morning." He sweeps his glance over me, too, knowing I'm sober, and listening.   "God has given us commands to live by.   You must honour Him and not serve the... the invented gods."

"Fine," Secundus agrees, with a cheerful nod and another swig from his mug.   "Makes sense.   If I were a god I'd have that rule."

"You must not swear by any god, or lie, or steal, or be jealous."

"No problem, my friend, I never did any of those.   Heh, I'm sounding pretty good!"   Pretty unbelievable, too, I can't help thinking.   If we're all supposed to keep those rules to gain a good afterlife, no wonder no-one's ever good enough.

"And you're pretty drunk," Kiral chips in.   Is he taking all this in?   I thought he'd gone to sleep.   "Sounds like a boring way to live life!"   He's finished his tankard, now he drains the amphora; when he lifts it and tips it, not a single muscle quivers.   He could probably lift me up in one arm and not even notice my weight.   I hope they lock him in tonight. "Any more fabulous commands?"

"You must not kill," Naasir replies calmly, though he knows that's a dangerous thing to mention.   Kiral growls, leaps up and advances, ready to kill the slave at once; the lanista puts one hand on his chest, and whispers;

110

"You'll get your chance." He pushes the gladiator into his cell, and fumbles for his key.

"Naasir, stop winding him up." Why does he think the gladiator will have his chance? By morning they'll be hammering off Naasir's iron collar and setting him free, like the Senator promised us! "You've all upset Kiral enough for one day!" the lanista rails. Secundus rouses himself from a moment of muddled reflection to observe;

"You two are like old friends." He stops to stuff in another sausage; they're all still eating! "You are, aren't you? Did you work for him?" Naasir shakes his head, unwilling to talk about his past. The lanista's happy enough to discuss it.

"We worked together for a while, when I was a young gladiator. I was a bestiarius, so we didn't fight each other." He leans down to breathe an alcoholic blast on me as he explains helpfully; "Bestiarii fight animals, lions and bears and things like that. Naasir reckons we mortals are more beastly than beasts, don't you, mate?" Naasir nods; I have to agree; animals don't build arenas, nor volunteer to fight in them.

Suddenly the courtyard's ringing with song, Kiral's begun a morbid chant;

"Hold your head high, never look down,
When you feel the knife, wave to the crowd,
If you're going to lose, however you tried,
At least you can choose to die with pride,
Gladiators die with pride!"

Secundus shouts at Naasir over the dismal song; "Were you any good, in your gladiator days?" Again Naasir shakes his head, and looks away, so the lanista fills in his own details.

"He's just reaching his peak, aren't you, mate? He's the oldest gladiator I know, I suppose that makes him the best!" Kiral's grumbling that only cowards die old; that doesn't dull the lanista's grin. He's almost rubbing his hands in glee as he declares; "He's going to make me a fortune!"

Naasir's finally given up eating, in time to let out a pitiful sigh. "It's always been about your money, Corinthus." He's jeered down at once by a yowl from Kiral;

"What's wrong with money? What else is there?" Yes, what else? Naasir was right, they've already forgotten the unworldly things he talked of moments ago. Kiral's off again, with his chanting dig at us;

"If you're going to lose, however you tried,

At least you can choose to die with pride..." Secundus hasn't forgotten all of Naasir's words; he's staring into his mug, eyes wild, smile strangely wonky, brow furrowed in confused thought. When the lanista jangles his purse of money and pushes it back into the young man's hands, he looks up and lets loose a drunken laugh;

"Naasir's life's all about one God. There is one goddess, Fortuna, and she's smiling on me!"

"Push off back to your theatre, you stupid little actor," Kiral growls from his dark cell, twitching his good eye. The lanista pats him on the back, burbling;

"Just another fight or two, and you'll have enough to buy that the... thea... thea... thing!"

"Brilliant!" Secundus declares with a squint. His mug's empty, and he's disappointed. "But I'm not leaving my little... little... what's your name again?" He lurches forward for me to catch, and I have to shuffle back to his bed with the weight of all those muscles leaning heavily on me. Imagine a lifetime of that! He's tapping his cheek with a wobbly finger. "Kiss goodnight, before you walk free?"

I'm already well out of his way. There's a spare piece of cold cheese pastry, I'm sure I can squeeze it in, once I've twisted it shyly in my trembling fingers for a while.

"GLADIATORS DIE WITH PRIDE!" Kiral bellows, deliberately out of tune. I won't be able to sleep quietly here with that going on.

"When *are* we free to go?" I ask the lanista, though I'm too tired to stand for long. He just laughs in my face, a long, burping, drunken laugh. "Where should we go first?" Only the sight of Naasir rising in front of him, taller, scarred and angry, shuts his grim laughter up.

"Stop it!" the slave insists, and the trainer obeys him. "Stop teasing them both, it's not right. Tell them the truth!" The lanista can hardly get his words out, and stutters so long I march up to him as well, to demand;

"What's the truth? Tell us!"

"The Senator said you must go to Rome!" he answers me, with a hint of surprise that I don't follow his meaning at once. "Did you think it was only a suggestion? That was an order."

"Rome?" I squeak, horrified. The lanista nods carelessly, and rattles his purse with glee.

"Rome! I have to present you all at the Circus Maximus in two weeks."

Chapter 15

It's a grim truth. We're not free, the Roman Senator has broken his promise, and it's caught me by surprise. I don't know why; I'm learning how the world works now. That's how Kiral will have his chance to kill Naasir, and I'm sure he'll pull no punches. That's why they want my legs healed and shining. I should have seen this coming. Secundus has sobered up slightly since he understood the news; he grimaces at me and groans;

"We gave too much of a performance. My fault, I'm sorry."

"It's certainly not your fault!" I want to tell him he did a lot of good out there, it was a life-saving performance; the fault lies with the organisers of this horrible entertainment. Then again, I don't want to encourage his attention any more, and he looks ready to doze off to sleep.

Suddenly I wake to find I've dozed as well. The cells are almost silent, and dark as Hades. If I let my mind wander I can hear the ghostly voices of yesterday's contestants filling the courtyard. When I try to wipe my eyes my hand's pulled back; I'm chained up.

Naasir wakes with a huge gasp. He's been sleeping on a straw mattress beside me, and we're chained together.

"Sorry to wake you," I whisper. He shakes his dark, spiked hair, and stares, motionless. "Bad dream?" I would imagine so; I don't know how I managed to sleep myself with the nightmares that clog my head. He nods, that's all.

Then, for once, he chooses to share the dream without being pushed.

"I was in the circus in Rome, I think. The Circus Maximus. I was telling them all that life's more entertaining than death. I told them about God's love, about the love of Jesus, and they were all listening. The Vestal Virgins were there in their red braids, with their thumbs up. Caesar was there, listening!" He stops for a wry laugh. That's not likely to come true,

114

though his face is glowing with the idea. It gives me the chance to ask;

"Was I there in your dream? Er... alive?"

"Yes," he says, to my relief. "And then the referee killed me, for cowardice, because I refused to kill." What in Vesta... I mean, what in the world? "And then it wasn't me. It was Jesus dying; I saw His cross, and His friends crying. There was a thief crucified beside him; at the last minute he asked Jesus to save him, to take him to his beautiful kingdom after death."

It sounds so vivid, I half expect a bright light to fill the grim cell we're locked in. I picture the scene, just as he says, two crosses made of wood, the sort I've seen before, usually in a crowd of others, dying bodies hanging there to remind us all who's in charge, and keep us always afraid.

"Too late, was it?" I prompt him. I suppose a thief would have a lot of bad to turn away from, and no time to prove himself.

"No, it's never too late, not even for a retired gladiator. I was dying with him, and I think I saw the gate of Heaven, and Jesus standing there..." The dream is fading, taking his glow with it. He covers his face with his hands, dragging my chained hand with them. "There's so much I don't know. If only Paul were here, or the elders, or..."

He stares up through the little stone window, to the moon; he doesn't seem so old now, or as broken as he did at home. Inside is a man as full of life and hope as any freeman, and I'm the only one privileged to witness it. "It's silly, but do you know what I wish?"

"What do you wish?" I ask in a whisper. I wish for so many things that my mind crowds up the moment I start to think of them. He only has one, for now.

"I wish I had met Jesus in person, here in the world, in the flesh. Many people did, Paul knows some of them. What stories would they tell? How full of His love for mankind would they be?" His face droop again. "Silly. I was fortunate to meet with the followers in Ephesus; Paul spent weeks persuading them to accept slaves as real people. Gladiators rank lower than slaves, they're even less respectable. Sorry, I shouldn't have said anything at all."

He tries to lie down again, to sleep, and let me sleep too, but he can't, if I don't move my chained hand. I don't want to move, I'm content to stare up at that moon outside the window, and smile at his dream. It seems that the gleam of heavenly gates is hanging round us both.

"Naasir, I want to meet death like you do."

"Really?" In the darkness I can see his bright eyes, wide in amazement as he asks; "How? You mean with terror, fear, sick to your stomach?" Is that how he felt? He hid it well!

"No." I soften my whisper, no-one else needs to hear me. "I mean, with the knowledge that I'm going to a better place, through those heavenly gates you dreamed about. Don't put me off, I'm determined, and you're not going to lie down until you talk to your God about me."

He puts on his silent, don't-want-to-talk-to-anyone face, as usual, yet there's a tiny hint of a smile on his cheeks. I raise my eyebrows enquiringly, hoping he'll see that in the dark; I daren't break whatever train of thought he has. He nods; finally.

"I can't do it properly, not like Paul does..." He must say that a lot! "But you hardly need words."

His hands are shaking as he puts them round mine, pressing my palms together as he likes to when he prays. My heart's beating faster, and the blood makes my head ache more. Being promised freedom was a wonderful feeling, but this should mean so much more, if it works, and lasts longer than my freedom did.

When he prays, Naasir's voice alters, it's shy, uncertain and worshipful. "Dear God, my friend Aysel wants to know your love, and to come into your kingdom. Please show yourself to her. Please accept her, make her one of your children."

Is that how he talks to his God? Like a friend? He reminds me of little Mir talking to his Mum, Aunt Yildiz. How does he dare? He's not even armed with an expensive sacrifice! Drusa doesn't like people to bother Artemis with unnecessary troubles or chat, but Naasir's happy to say plenty to his God, without wreathing his words in mystery.

"I'm asking because of the sacrifice that was made by your Son, Jesus. He gave up his life for Aysel, although she didn't know Him. Please make Him known to her now. Forgive her for killing, you know all about that. Thank you. And Amen."

"Amen," I echo, vacantly. I don't know what that's for. Then I sit up, away from Naasir, and lean my head on the cold stone wall to wait for my transformation. I don't turn into a beautiful angel, or grow gladiator muscles which would be useful in the dreaded Circus Maximus. There's no flash of light, not so much as the miraculous wafting stink of sacrificial smoke to distinguish the moment. I'm still just me, little Aysel the slave, weak, worried and plain.

I am loved. I have never felt so loved before, not even in my Mum's arms when I was little and scraped my knees. The air doesn't feel empty as it did a minute ago, the darkness doesn't frighten me and fill my thoughts with evil. Instead it feels like a thick fur, wrapping me warmly, safely.

I am clean, inside as well as out, innocent like a baby. Yes, I'm still worried, but not deeply afraid. My heart may tremble, but my spirit's calm, the vision of the heavenly gates Naasir spoke of is in my mind too. I dare to look, I understand that I'll be welcome when I get there.

At the same time I feel more alive than ever. There's so much to live for; I want to fight my way back to my Mum and tell her there's hope, and a world beyond the miserable world of slavery. It doesn't matter much that she's told me nothing about my father, because I feel as if I have a new, everlasting one, and an African older brother. I should thank him, if I could speak right now. I want thank everyone who's shown kindness to me, even to thank my new God in my own hesitant words for whatever's filling my spirit with love.

Naasir's watching the smile grow on my face; in the darkness he squeezes my hand, seeing his prayer has worked.

A sharp ching in the dawn-lit courtyard is followed by a clank of metal on the sandy floor. They've cut Naasir's collar away. He no longer needs a sign round his neck saying he belongs to the Celerus household, because he now belongs to Corinthus the lanista, and he's the businessman's favourite gladiator, even though he refuses to kill. Now his neck's free, the scar right down it stands out even more than before. He's rubbing the callous-marks the collar left round his neck over fifteen years, while he stands at the table in the courtyard which is becoming far too familiar.

He's been writing. He's educated, much more than I am, I can't read a word! I'm not surprised, I've just about decided not to be surprised by anything any more. He writes one final word on a piece of deer-skin. Maybe Naasir learned letters from our master; that'd be a miserable job, I'd much prefer spinning in our kitchen to working with angry Panaius Celerus.

Naasir passes the quill and the vellum to the lanista. Corinthus takes it away, looking like he actually intends to send it to whoever Naasir's addressed it to. By then breakfast is served. Breakfast! I feel like a real lady, eating soft rolls and butter first thing in the morning, made by a baker in town and brought directly to me- if only I could imagine away the dirt and smells, replace them with the musky scent of incense and walls painted brightly to look like marble.

"How are you?" Naasir asks.

"Fine." I feel the same, like I'm walking in a cloud. My heart's warm, life doesn't seem as bleak as before; all right, the next two weeks may be awful, but life stretches on lovingly a lot further than that.

"Can you swim?"

"No."

"That's a pity."

There's no time to say anything else; Corinthus the lanista is wandering behind my back straight into my cell with a blood-red bundle. He jabs his thumb at me to go in. When I throw open the bundle a pair of sandals falls to the floor. The red thing is a stola made of fine linen, so wide it'll drape down over my arms to hide my bandage and a dozen scratches. It also reaches to my ankles, so the wide skirts will hide my injured legs. It's too beautiful, and the more I stare at it, the more it feels like a symbol of the blood shed yesterday.

"Get a move on!" yells Corinthus- do I now have to call him my master?

I throw the stola on over my tunic. It comes with a thick woven belt of green and yellow, and a comb to sort my hair out. At least I can dress myself in private, without those temple girls fussing round me. Mind you, if I told them who I was talking to last night, and who's now going to run my life, I'd be interested to hear what they'd say!

Corinthus shouts and waves a knife about, until Naasir agrees to strap a full leather suit of body armour over his tunic. While he's struggling with that, he can't help me with my sandals. Kiral's in the courtyard, sparring dangerously with Secundus; he takes one look at my dress, then shakes his head and deliberately moves the fight so his back's turned on me. Then Secundus sees me struggling, and leaves the fight willingly enough. He stoops to buckle on my sandals. I have to have help with them, I just wish it didn't have to come from him. I'm heading on a different road to him now, and I don't want him to think I've fallen for his charm.

The thing is, now I know what it's like to be filled with love, I know that I do love him. Although we only met two days ago, it feels as if we've shared a lifetime. And we probably have less than two weeks together, before he has to kill his way to glory again.

He stands up again, and claps his hands to his head. His eyes squeeze shut, and he laughs at himself. "Heh, Naasir, does your God have a rule about not drinking?" My friend looks up from his buckles, and shrugs;

"I'm not aware of one."

"Well, he should think about it. Drinking turns me into an idiot!" Kiral claps him on the back with a roar.

"Better an idiot than an actor!"

I'm startled by hands appearing from behind me; Corinthus my new master is strapping a wide leather belt round my hips, complete with a dangling scabbard. "This is not yours to keep," he warns me, as he slides a legionary's sword into the scabbard. He ties it in with a thin cord. Not mine to keep? As if I'd want to keep a weapon like that! He grabs my hand to strap on a cuff, the sort that archers wear in contests, and finishes off by handing me the silver circlet I wore to make me look like Artemis. It has two fresh solder marks, how much longer will it last? He stares at me fiercely until I put it on my head, then he grunts and leads us all away.

We have left Ephesus stadium behind us, to set out on our journey to the next one. Less than a hundred yards along the street we hear shouts. If they're from those men I met outside the gymnasium, let them come, and see me now! It's easy and natural to rest my hand on the smooth iron pommel of the sword.

"Aysel Artemisia!" I hear. It starts with a few voices, and others join in; "Aysel Artemisia!" Corinthus' ches swells when he hears it, although within moments it's joined by curses from men who bet against us. Again and again people scream out, gathering in a crowd to watch us. "Aysel Artemisia!" Now they know my name, it's weirdly flattering. I concentrate on not feeling the honour, or being pleased with myself. And they keep on and on; it's a bit of a tongue-twister, but they persist, until a new voice yells over them;

"Secundus the lover!" Quick as a wink, the gathering crowd takes up that chant instead. He smiles, he lifts his hands to acknowledge his fans, he waves at them, and they shout louder. We're going to struggle to get through the crush developing on the quayside, if we want to reach the ships. Girls are throwing him flowers, stretching out to touch him just the way gladiators like it.

He gives a sweeping glance to pull all the admiring eyes to him, then takes my hand and kisses it gently as if I were a rich Patrician lady. It raises a cheer; I understand; we must play to our audience. He's very convincing, walking with his hand in mine, pushing away the finely-jewelled and painted hands that reach out to him. The way he wraps his arms round me to protect me from the crush near the water, you'd think I was really the only girl he cared about.

Not surprisingly, Naasir is at my back, close at hand, preventing people from crowding us into the sea, seeing I can't swim. But surprisingly, another chant begins, quietly, rising to a painful crescendo; "The Beast! Beast! Beast!" Who... I don't need to wonder. I glance back at him with a questioning face. He whispers in a downcast sigh;

"I never thought I'd hear that again."

"Naasir the Beast!" they yell. In all the world I can't think of a man less beastlike. But they're certain, and he's just acknowledged that was what they named him long ago. Was he a beast? Will his beliefs- our beliefs- change me as much as they've changed him? His head's low, while Secundus is waving my hand merrily in front of everyone. I have to shake my hand away; I can at least walk with Naasir and take away some of his shame in his old life. With my hand on his ageing shoulder, I'm hoping he can feel that encompassing love that won't let me go, and remember he's not alone.

There's a tower on the quay. I see three men standing there, two in neat white togas, one in a Jewish type of robe. Naasir's elders have come to see him on his way. They obviously don't fancy getting trapped in an over-excited crowd, but they clearly know how to influence one. Slowly the edges of the crowd are changing their accusation of

Naasir, still hoping for him to look up and wave at them all. I can't make out the new words until they penetrate to the centre, where we stand waiting for a plank to be lowered onto a ship. But the moment he hears it, his whole face brightens in a smile.

"Naasir Christianos! Naasir Christianos!"

"A follower of the Chosen One," he interprets for me. I like it. I hope the elders can tell I'm waving at the three of them. Now Naasir lifts his head proudly, and puts up his hands to acknowledge the shouts. He blinks at me, then takes my arm and holds it up beside him, demonstrating that I'm a follower too, although he's the only one who knows it.

Finally one of the grasping hands reaches me; I pull my arm back, and find myself dragging a Roman lady into the middle of the chaos. It's our mistress.

Chapter 16

Naasir, Secundus and I form a triangle of protection for Lucina to stand in. She's crying enough to wash the chalk from her cheeks with streaks of eye paint. "I... I'm sorry," she stammers, wringing her hands in her wrinkled stola. She's thrown an unwashed palla over head and shoulders to disguise herself on the quay. She's not too good at disguising herself, coming into the middle of the chaos like this. "I'm sorry, Naasir! If only I'd known! It's my fault!" He doesn't bow, he doesn't look worried that she may take her anger out on him as she used to at home. He squeezes her hand and talks to her as an equal; "If it's anyone's fault, it's mine. You sheltered me, I shouldn't have gone out so often." "I don't want you to die because of me!" "If I do, you know where I'll be," he reassures her. Does she? Our mistress, who beats us regularly... or used to, till a few weeks ago...? "Did you deliver my message?" Lucina's soft white hands cover her face, her shoulders are heaving as she starts crying again, and splutters; "I didn't dare! He's so angry! He... he bet against you!" Naasir can see the sailors coming to hurry us on board the ship. He grabs her hand and insists;

"You *must* speak to him, it might not be too late, if he can follow us. Think of Aysel." She looks at me through her tears; she obviously hasn't thought of me particularly. She looks me over; my outfit's richer than hers now, she's never been able to afford dyed linen. She really is afraid. "I failed. Er... Aysel, I'm sorry." I'm not, I don't much care for this conversation, I'd actually prefer to get straight on that boat and never see her again.

"Tell my Mum I'm well," I demand, shocked by my own daring. Well, she's no longer my mistress, and she seriously could have thought of bringing Mum here with her, if only for moral support! She nods, with a sniffle, and tries to wriggle away, but Naasir isn't done yet.

"You can still save Aysel, if you get him to come to Rome. If it's a question of money, sell that shrine!"

"He has to finish organising the Volturnalia festival, in two weeks!" Lucina's struggling to pull herself together, while the sailors and Corinthus are pulling us away. Naasir has to draw Secundus' sword from behind his back; a quick swish, and the sailors squirm out of the way; they don't want to mess with such an old gladiator.

"Mistress, it's up to you. If ever Aysel needed her father, she needs him now!"

Lucina nods once more wiping away a tear on her palla.

"God be with you," Naasir adds.

"God be with you," she echoes. He hands the sword back to Secundus, and lets himself be manhandled onto the ship. A soldier with a long spear pokes Kiral to follow. I'm not keen on walking up a narrow board in slippery sandals and ankle-length skirts. That's no problem; Secundus scoops me up in a second, and carries me across the water. He keeps one arm round me as the ropes are loosed, waving to his fans with the other hand. He's the only one of us smiling; boy, he loves showing off!

As they push me down the ladder to below the deck, my head starts to buzz. Shaking it doesn't help, yet I keep shaking it; I thought back there that Naasir was talking to Lucina about Panaius, until he said that about my father. He's alive, is he? Why did nobody ever tell me? Maybe it's a metaphor the followers use, he's dead and I'll soon be with him.

"Naasir, is my father dead?"

"No."

"So where... why..."

"It's not my place to say." All discussion is closed. That's vastly unfair. I don't want the discussion closed, and I don't want to keep quiet and mind my own business as I always have.

"We're not in any place, and we don't live with Lucina any more, so tell me anyway."

"Not now." Not ever, he means, I'm getting used to his way of talking. We're down in the hold of the ship; it's dark and makes my eyes fuzz after the sunshine on land. All I can smell is damp wood and old wine. There are hammocks strung from wooden beams, close together, and I'm not shown to a private space as I was in the stadium. At either end of the hold masses of amphorae are stored, tall and wobbly. They chink together slightly as the waves rock the boat; one's already cracking. That explains the wine smell.

Naasir's planned ahead, and scoots me to the end hammock, making me tie my woven belt to it to mark it out. He takes the next one.

"Thanks," is all I need to say; he understood before I spoke, Secundus and Kiral are close behind us, but to reach me they'll have to get past him. It's a good few days' journey to Rome, I'm glad he's with me.

Back on deck, we watch the sailors casting off. For fourteen years I've lived close to the ships. I've seen the gulls veer in the sky, welcoming the ships to shore, eager for scraps to snaffle. I've heard the cries of the sailors as they loose their sails ready for a voyage, and occasionally I've watched the wind filling those sails and blowing a crew and cargo away to distant shores. I've always thought it a beautiful sight, and the creak of any wood has filled me with hopeful dreams of escape and adventure. Where do all those ships go?

This one's taking me to meet my doom. The waves that once called romantically to me now hit the sides of the ship like slaps to my stupid face. However hard I try to stand firm and not to be afraid, I can't forget the dying men around me, nor the roar of the lion. Next time, in Rome, the centre of the world, I'll know what to expect, and that will feel even worse.

Naasir stands beside me, legs comfortably apart to absorb the rocking motion of the ship. He looks far out, between the other ships coming and going, to the empty sea, in his own world. Until a large wave throws me off my feet; he steadies me with a strong hand.

I remember how brave I felt while he was praying. "Can you pray again?" I wonder.

"If you like. But you can pray yourself, it's not hard." How could a young girl slave dare to do that?

-I dare you!- I hear a voice, soft and kind, but there was no sound. It's inside me. -Pray to me. I'll always listen, Aysel.-

I'm done for! I've held myself together pretty well, put up with horrible indignities, but this sudden, huge well of love inside me has shaken me up so a tear's rolling down my cheek, the one next to Naasir, typical! It's too big, too much for me to take in, I can't answer the voice, I can only think a tiny -thanks.- But I'll find the words; trapped on a little ship for days, Naasir can't escape me and my questions.

Question number one! "Where's my father?" Number two. 'Why can't you tell me about him?" Three, four, five. "Where is he? Does he love me? Why's he never come to see me?" I see a flicker of hesitation in his face when I ask that one. "He does come to see me? When? Why haven't I ever heard about this? It's not fair!"

"Fathers aren't always fair, or good," is all Naasir will tell me about it. Seeing Secundus coming across the deck, he moves to my other side so he's accidentally between us both. The young gladiator's sniffed out a story, and he asks innocently;

"Was your father no good?" Naasir's probably sensing my desperation for some answers, so he gives in, and chooses to answer this one.

"I don't want to speak ill of my father, he saw that I was decently educated, he taught me to love our country, he was kind to my mother. He had one flaw, he drank too much. He was drunk the night a lion came into our village. My mother had to take his sword and run out to defend us, her children. She lost the fight."

At the same moment I put my hand on his shoulder, Secundus murmurs to him; "I'm sorry."

"It was a long time ago," Naasir assures us; that hardly matters, clearly he feels the pain as if it happened only yesterday. "My uncle had some experience with lions; he took a bucket full of soup and lured it away from the village." Ah, so that's how he got that crazy idea from yesterday!

"Good trick," I have to admit.

"He never came back," Naasir adds. "The lion turned on him. My father missed him and my mother badly, and started drinking all the time. His trade failed, he fell into debt, and he was forced to sell one of us into slavery. As the oldest male, that was me. My mother called me Naasir, 'defender,' and that was the only defence I could offer to my family."

I was curious, and now I know. Did the loss of his Mum and his freedom give him the fire to fight as a gladiator and survive? I can't ask that. So it's over to the actor to fill the silence.

"Wow!" he says. "Bad luck, man! My dad... Well, my dad's awesome. He writes the best plays in Pompeii. Sometimes he let me and my brother act out plots to test them; I always had to be the girl! He used some of our ideas, too, and he took us to the theatre to watch them on stage. I'll take you both to meet him one day, if... you know, if we survive."

"You will," I tell him. I won't say any more, or look straight at him. He ought to ignore me, forget me, and move on to someone rich or well-known. It may hurt, but we're on different paths, which will be too obvious in eleven days or so.

"We're all in this together now!" he laughs at once. "We did a good show, that's what they want to see in Rome. Can we give them that? The romance?"

"Just for one day," I agree. Heh, I sound sulky, that's not how I want to be! I just feel strangely green and dizzy. The deck's so new and clean, where's the edge of the ship?

"Seasick?" asks Secundus. That would be a good explanation. He's an annoyingly good help to me, leading me to the edge, stopping me from falling over the rail and holding my hair and scabbard out of the way. In the space of a minute I'm well enough to stand up and regret having had so much breakfast. Embarrassing. That must surely have put him off me!

On the rare occasion I've been sick at home, I get a cloth to wipe myself and a glug of water. Then it's back to work as usual. Corinthus the lanista is more careful of his investments than Panaius the clerk was; he orders me to scramble back down the ladder to the hold for a rest, while the ship's cook works on a milky soup. I'm allowed milk? It would be so easy to think this was all a luxurious dream!

By the time I'm better and the scent of spilled wine is getting on my nerves, Secundus and Naasir are sparring on the deck. Feet scuffling on wood are a lot louder than on sand. Naasir's showing the younger gladiator how to correct his weak stabbing action. Their trainer's clearly happy about the extra lesson; he's come prepared, with wooden practice swords and one of those huge sacks stuffed tight with straw. That's taking a hammering now, as the two men take up their iron swords again to stab it over and over.

Next Naasir starts to show Secundus some ways of disabling his opponent without causing much injury, let alone killing. Corinthus isn't the least bit impressed by that.

"This isn't the theatre!" he bellows in his habitual growl. So the two men turn up the speed, twisting across the deck, huffing with the effort. And still neither of them come out of it with a scratch.

The lanista climbs off a bollard to break up the play-fight, asking; "Aren't you leaving someone out?" His knife is jabbing in my direction. But I'm a peaceful slave-girl! I don't want to learn to fight! Seriously, though, it's going to come in useful. To show willing, I pick up one of the wooden swords; it's not that much different to a rolling pin.

Naasir takes it away again. His trainer protests; "Don't you think it's dangerous to leave her?"

"I think it could be dangerous to teach her," Naasir replies, and to me he adds; "I mean for your eternal soul. I don't want to give you the skills to kill again. We'll be there with you." Corinthus scoffs at his confidence.

"Naasir, your conscience is going to drive me crazy! It's just a game! Come on, stop pretending you were happy as a slave hidden away in that poor household! You're glad I found you and brought you back into the public eye, you love the attention!" I yell back at him before Naasir can muster a calm word to retort.

"Naasir's not crazy, you are! He has the conscience to remember murdering is bad, and watching people being killed is *not* entertainment!" The lanista like my fire; he pats me warmly on my arm, the one with the scratch underneath it which still aches. I pick up the other wooden sword. "And my conscience is awake as well. You can teach me some moves, and let me decide what to do with it when... when the time comes."

It's a tough lesson, the ship itself seems to join in, tossing us everywhere on the waves, so it's hard enough to stay upright. Naasir wants more power from my arms, Corinthus wants me to use my hips, a trick the male gladiators don't fully understand. Kiral looks over from his sparring with Secundus, and can't help laughing.

I have to take off the fine linen dress to move freely in the tunic, the costume I'm used to. That amuses the sailors; their whistling distracts me from parrying a lot of Corinthus' gentle sword-strokes. "Concentrate!" he screams. "This is not a game!" I wish he'd make up his mind about whether it's a game or not.

To strengthen my arms, the trainer shoves me in among the sailors reefing in the sails, so I have to help them pull on the salt-covered ropes. My hands are soon sore from that, but he keeps shoving me over every time the wind changes, and each time there's a man less, so I have to pull harder.

It reminds me of the circus; each time I opened my eyes there was one less man left alive. Kiral's sparring with Secundus; the young man's muscles are big enough, in my uneducated opinion, but the one-eyed monster's more powerful, faster, and has time for evil laughs between parries. Secundus' only hope seems to be in befriending the older man and hoping they don't meet in the arena.

Kiral sticks out a foot, tripping his opponent, then hammers down fake blows on him with grim delight. On second thoughts, Secundus' hope lies in Naasir's prayers; if he dies with us, at least he could come with us both through those heavenly gates my friend described.

After a small meal of plain bread and luxurious ham, I'm allowed back down into the twilit hold to rest my aching arms and legs. I'm relieved the lanista didn't offer me the leg massage he's now giving Kiral. I'm glad to be as far from that gruesome face and fierce sword as I can get.

Down in the hold I have a new struggle. I have to sleep in a hammock, and I've never seen one before. It's nothing more than a long net strung between two wooden pillars; as soon as I try to sit on it I end up on my back on the floor. I try again, and fall on my behind. Now I can truly say every part of me aches.

I wish I could be at home in the kitchen, rolling under an old sheet with the comforting scent of a straw mattress beneath me. No, I do not! There's no time for self-pity any more. I am going to climb into that hammock and pray for the people I've got to know since I left home, and then learn all the fighting skills I can!

If I crawl in at an angle and stay low, I can stay in the net. And actually it's pretty comfortable. I suppose I just needed to keep an open mind. Now, how do I reach the blanket that I left down on the floor?

The men will be heading down here soon, now the sun's nearly gone. I need to do what I came for.

"Hello," I whisper to the empty air. One moment of silence and concentration is all I need to recall the strong, invisible arms that now hold on to me. I wonder if God has a proper form of address, but I've had it with the high ceremony and fancy words I witnessed in Artemis' temple, and the cringe-worthy impersonation of a goddess that Drusa forced on me. So I talk as Naasir did, as if to a friend.

"Thanks for giving your Son up for me. I didn't deserve that. And thank you that if I die in the Roman circus it'll be quick, not like being crucified, I can't imagine how much suffering that must have meant. Sorry I killed a man, you know all about that. And you know my friend Naasir, he's been very kind, protecting me and everything. So, when we get to Rome, if you don't mind, he'd love to meet someone who met you in person. Would that be all right?"

Drusa doesn't like worshippers to fuss over trivial things, but nothing's trivial about my brief life right now. I have loads of things on my mind, and it's all pretty urgent. "Please, Jesus, can you look after my Mum and stop the mistress hitting her? I hope she won't any more, if she's one of your followers. And maybe you could help her find my father, although, honestly, I can't see what good that would do. You're listening, you obviously care, Naasir says you're our heavenly Father, so I don't need another father who's never around.

"And I'm really sorry to bother you, but Secundus the gladiator... It's a big one, the other gods wouldn't even care about him, but..." The first of the sailors are heading down the ladder. I'd better pretend I'm asleep; fortunately I can pray to this God in my head. "Please show Secundus who you are, and help him to stop killing… But don't let him die because I said that… Please protect us all. Er, thanks. Good night." I think it will be a good night, the ship's motion is rocking me like a baby, I can snuggle down into the hammock. I get a little rest, but I'm more at ease when Naasir hands me a blanket and climbs into his hammock. He'll sleep, and probably pray, between me and all the aggressive gladiators and sailors.

A soft rustle is all it takes to shake me out of tonight's nightmare. Something's moving among the amphorae of wine near my hammock. Rats? I hear they like to live on ships. No problem, I can just kick my blanket back over my feet. Rats are really not going to worry me right now.

The something is under my hammock, and much bigger than a rat. I listen hard; close by, Naasir's snoring has stopped. A calloused hand claps over my mouth, its rough fingers are shoving a salty old cloth into my mouth so I can't scream. The other hand drags away my blanket.

All my Mum warned me about men flashes through my mind. I can just make out the looming head of one of the sailors. Then the head lurches back, his hair's being yanked by a stronger man. Judging by what I can hear, he crawls away up the hold as fast as he can. He must be running from a gladiator. Large hands, pale in a slight ray of moonlight, spread my blanket on top of me and tuck in my feet.

That's all. Soon Naasir's snoring resumes. It's quiet, and I feel strangely safe. I prayed for protection, but I never expected it from Kiral.

Chapter 17

Days more training have passed, on our way to Rome. When we stopped on the island of Sicily, Corinthus went happily about his dirty business, buying new slaves to train; the rest of us weren't allowed off the ship. At least the pace of my training didn't slacken, I'm slightly enjoying the exercise and having something to keep busy, it beats being locked in a cell and ignored. Only now the ship's full of new gladiators Corinthus has bought to replace the last ones, and another trainer to take the pressure off him now he's doing so well. He offered the job to Naasir, and got offended when he refused. He grumbled all day, and kept muttering;

"Just what I always said, he's a rotten businessman!" He reckons that's the only reason Naasir failed in the gladiator business. He was also burbling all through the trip, something about giving time for news to circulate.

So we've reached Ostia, the port we need to stop in to get to Rome. Ships are almost stacked up here, there are so many, and a mass of traders and merchants fill in the spaces between the ships. Masts and brown linen sails tower everywhere I look. If I wasn't chained, and could run away from this gang of thugs I'm in, I'd be totally lost, and probably knifed by some thief wanting my sword.

"Look, news travels fast!" Secundus grins. Posted on the wall of a wooden shed is a paper with a long list of words. "I'm here! I've never featured on a poster!" He grabs my hand and drags me over to see it.

"I can't read."

"Oh! Really? I'll read it, then. 'Volturnalia festival, Circus Maximus, seventy gladiators, featuring...' A lot of people I don't know, and then at the bottom, look! 'Naasir Bestia, Won six times, drew twice,' and... and! 'Ephesian newcomer Secundus Amator!' I'm not from Ephesus, but who cares? They always play with the truth." He's grinning from ear to ear. However, I reckon the Romans have done him an injustice.

"You're not an amateur, you act as if you were born to it... I suppose you were." Behind us the new gladiators who speak Latin are laughing at me, and Secundus looks too embarrassed to translate- but only for an instant.

"Amator means 'lover'."

"Right. I see." He holds out his arms for a hug. I don't move. You could cut straight through the tension. Kiral watches Secundus' expression turn to embarrassment, and almost laughs. I'm actually glad that Corinthus springs back at that moment, beaming;

"I've found a blacksmith! Ah, a poster, a nice one, too! With my gladiatrix, top of the bill, more or less." He points at some words high up on the paper, and looks to see whether I'm impressed. I don't understand.

"There!" he cries, stabbing his knife at what I guess are the relevant words. "'Aysel Pulchra, gladiatrix, killed Ugur Magnus, who was unbeaten in fifty-seven fights!' Come on, we need to fit your breastplate."

I have to follow him, past a line of women and girls gutting fish; the pace of their work's amazing, they slice down the spine with knives that run close to the palms of their hands. The knives flash even faster than Aunt Yildiz slicing carrots. Fish guts slap into buckets, and fish into tall baskets, while more, freshly-caught, slap down on the tables. That's the work of some free women!

The lanista bounces along to a stone workshop full of clangs and the hiss of bellows. Fire rages in a huge brick hearth, smoke rises from the workshop chimney and hangs over our heads like a storm cloud. The heat inside is tremendous, and the noise of a clanging hammer on iron rings shrill in my ears. I'm relieved the gladiators don't follow us into the busy space, particularly when my master and the blacksmith start measuring me and discussing my best features- I didn't know I had any.

"She needs more... shape," the blacksmith insists, miming curves with his rough soot-blackened hands, and Corinthus agrees too easily.

"I'll feed her more meat, and cakes," he suggests, charitably. Why, to fatten up the lamb for the slaughter? The blacksmith measures my waist again, shaking his head. "She'll be all straps and no design!"

"So? I need her to last a while, my little gladiatrix." It sounds like I'll at least be wearing some protection this time, that's something. So I let them plan over my head, and indulge in my own thoughts.

Gladiatrix? A female gladiator? How far is he going to take this farce? I'm nearly 'top-of-the-bill' for killing Ugur Magnus; at last I have a real name for him. And he was unbeaten? He must have been a well-trained murderer. It doesn't sooth me; that's what Corinthus wants me to become.

"The sword."

"What?"

"Give me the sword," Corinthus orders. Quickly I untie the knotted cord and hand over the weapon I never wanted anyway. He passes it to the blacksmith, insisting; "Go ahead, it's pretty old." While I watch in curiosity, the blacksmith puts the sword into his raging fire until the blade is glowing. Then a few quick strikes on his anvil snap it in two. By the time they've negotiated a price for all the work, the sword's quite cool. "Here, you won't cause any harm with that, so you needn't tie it in any more."

My face must be stunned, because he sighs deeply, and slaps my scabbard. I slide the broken blade into it; there's only just enough length left to hold it in, though the pommel still looks impressive. This circus is becoming more of a farce every minute!

A cart draws up outside the blacksmith's, on a road as wide as Curetes Street and twice as busy. A crowd has gathered; I'm getting used to that. I wouldn't put it past Corinthus to have paid some of them to throng us, just to make us look

135

popular. He pushes me and Secundus onto the cart, leaving the others to walk; that'll get them on our side, won't it! I've heard it's a very long walk from here to the city of Rome.

Of course Secundus is delighted to be raised up on the cart, it's so like a stage. He milks the applause and the shouts of; "Amator, Amator!" And of course I'm growing very sick of the attention given me by people who just want to watch me die. But he's taken my hint and isn't playing the lover now. I find his new, calm and gracious stance beside me helps me relax enough to ask;

"What do they mean, Aysel Pulchra?"

"Pulchra means 'beautiful'," he answers evenly, waving a hand to the crowd. But his cheeks are red again, as if he's actually shy. He's a very good actor! As we creep in our little procession along the road towards Rome, he says very little to me, although I can tell he's not angry at all.

Corinthus has a woman walking in front of his ten gladiators, waving a scarf, clearing a way when people crowd the road, shouting out to everyone who we are. That keeps Secundus occupied, waving to passers-by who are screaming to see him. People love these men; the title of Gladiator alone seems to make them stars. Girls seem to emerge from the countryside wherever they go, to follow them and sigh in delight, as if they're mystical dryads who've melted out of the trees beside the road.

Sometimes Secundus takes my hand as we wave to the crowd; he always puts it back where I'd rested it. Still, I wish he wouldn't, I've got enough to worry about, without having to bury the thrill of his touch before it gets to my heart. As we near the great city, he wonders; "What's the game plan this time? Has Naasir spotted any weaknesses?"

"He hasn't mentioned it yet. But there are seventy gladiators, that'd be a big plan. I don't know." He squeezes my hand, and I allow myself to leave it, it's comforting; let the older men make fun of us youngsters, they don't understand a thing about us.

When my mistress sent me to shop in Ephesus, I stared and stared at the tall pillars, at the rich houses on the hill and the towering arches of the aqueducts. I thought no city could be bigger; I was so wrong. Rome sprawls for miles. On the edges are absolutely hundreds of wooden houses, single-roomed dwellings thrown together with bits of canvas and rope. More little children play in the streets there than I have met in my whole life in Ephesus. After the relative calm of the sea voyage it's pretty noisy, people shouting their wares, doing business over the racket of hammering trades.

We pass a tanner's, where they're treating animal skins, scraping off hairs and cleaning them with noxious mixtures to make soft leather for selling in the city. Then there's a fuller's, where women in old grey tunics are washing hundreds of yards of wool. The smell is unspeakable, but this is why they work so far out of the city. Some of the stretches of wool on the washing lines must be as long as our peristyle garden was. We had one of those long wool robes in the Celerus house. "Togas," I remark to Secundus.

"Senatorial togas," he adds when we spot some on separate lines, each one with a purple stripe sewn all down its length. Senators are a rare sight at home, but hundreds of them live in Rome.

"Aren't Senators elected by the people?" I wonder. He nods, then his mouth twists into a puzzled wiggle. We haven't got round to discussing politics yet, in the middle of our training sessions.

"What's your point? Are you wondering why we elect people who think killing is fun?"

"You'd think old men who represented everyone would be wise," I respond, surprised that he's read my mind.

"We can't all be Naasirs." He's not joking. I think the size of this place has shocked him as much as me. We're into the stone city now; I notice the people here are no richer than those by the sea in Ephesus, and there are many, many slaves with collars, never mind those without. I can spot many of them by their resigned trudge and their plain clothes. They stare back at me up on the cart in my red linen stola as if I'm a noble woman. "Why don't you give them a wave, make their day? They love you. Who could blame them?"

"They love my dress," I have to point out, realistically. "Secundus, how many slaves are there in the empire?"

"I have no idea," he admits readily. "A lot, possibly more than there are freemen."

"So, if they decided it was unfair, and got together... I'm talking rubbish, aren't I?"

"No, you're not. A lot of people feel that way. What's it like, being a slave?"

"I don't know. What's it like being free?"

Actually, Secundus has tried it both ways, he's been free and given himself to the lanista with a vow of obedience, so now he belongs to Corinthus just as I do. He's become a slave just to win fame, and some money for his father. With that he's given up all his status and become a total outcast. He must really love his father.

We have to leave the cart and walk through the city. It looks like nobody's allowed to bring carts here, the only people not walking are rich Patricians being carried in seats with poles. If Lucina could have afforded one of those, I bet Naasir's arms would have been as muscular as the rest of the gladiators.

We're into a district of the city where the houses are very like ours, stone at the bottom and wood above. Some of these are four storeys high, and washing hangs from every window. Downstairs are plenty of shops, for bread, meat, pots, betting, anything you want. On the corners of some terraces are taverns, with no lack of customers, even in the morning. On the side of one of the betting shops hangs a set of posters. One has a quick picture of a chariot and four horses, with a list of names beneath it; another has a scribble of two brawling men, and another list. Secundus laughs, and point out; "There we are again.   'Aysel Gladiatrix and Secundus Amator, as seen in Ephesus!'"

"Playing second fiddle to the charioteers," Kiral puts in, jabbing a finger at the other poster.   Secundus doesn't care; he's famous now, apparently, and smiling with all his gladiator charm.

The woman leading us is getting hoarse with shouting, but there's hardly the need to any more.   Gossip has travelled faster than we've walked, and by the time we reach the richer part of the city early in the evening, people already know who's coming.   Up here on one of the seven hills of Rome there are shops selling furniture and wall hangings, and others with fine linen hung on display outside.

Secundus points out a fine wine store his father loves, where he apparently bought the drinks for his wedding to Secundus' mother.   Corinthus stops there for a minute, untying his heavy purse from his belt, and returns empty-handed but delighted. As we continue our march to cheers and amorous cries, he keeps muttering; "Bargain, absolute bargain!"

Jewellery shops dazzle with shimmering gold, bright amber and colourful precious gems. Corinthus dives into one while we all stand, helpless to move in the crush of stolas and feminine sighs. Secundus is in danger of being knocked down by crowding girls, but one of the newcomers is actually thrown to the ground by their grasping hands.   I can see the appeal, Achlus is a stunner, and I think he knows it.   At least he takes ages playing with his hair every morning.   When the lanista returns his men are struggling to scrape Achlus off the pavement.   Finely-dressed citizens look down their noses as they stare at the accident, and everywhere we're met with screams.

"Come up at the front," Corinthus commands me.   "We're in Rome, here's the Forum, let them see my best attraction." His new gladiators agree that I'm the best-looking of the bunch, not that it's much of a contest.   Two of them volunteer to hoist me onto their shoulders for our parade up the hill.

"You're not touching her legs!" he spits at them both. "That goes for you all!"

Kiral growls at him from the back of the huddle; "Getting soft, are you?" The others laugh with him, swiping at each other and jabbing their elbows about; they daren't tease their new trainer, when they've just sworn the oath to be 'burned, bound, beaten, and killed by the sword.' So Kiral appeals to me to continue the argument.

"Kid, tell them what you think of them!"

I'm dumbstruck. We head to a wide area below the hill, paved and full of people, and we're surrounded by white temples and palaces, looming so high they block out half the blue sky. The temple pillars must be a dozen times my height; as a slave I can't help thinking of the labour which must have gone into building everything on this hill. Away behind the Celerus house, thousands of slaves are worked to death in the huge stone quarry. Is that where my father works, and why he can't communicate with me?

"Wave!" Corinthus orders. He has to prod me with his sword to encourage me; here in the heart of Rome, I feel lost, tiny, close to my end, surrounded by blackness. "Draw their attention, let them see we're only up here to make a sacrifice."

He forces me on through the mass of people, and the world feels even blacker, as if to smother me with a dark cloud of something I can't explain. "The temple of Julius Caesar," Secundus reads for me.

"Not that one," Corinthus snaps, pushing us to the right. "We'll go to the big one!"

"The temple of Castor and Pollux," Sceundus reads again. I'm not surprised size is all that counts for the lanista, and this temple's huge. I see white pillars tall as old trees, richly carved golden wreaths topping them, and masses of flames and smoke. It's making me dizzy, the fear I felt for my life when I stood on the steps of the Artemision is flooding back, overwhelming me. I can hardly see where I am.

Corinthus has bought a whole sheep, just for the altar, to pray for the success of the coming games. I suppose he picked this temple because it stands alone, a good place for a public show. Someone else thinks it is, too. A man in torn robes approaches us all as we stand waiting for attention from the priests in their rich embroidered capes. Locals sidle away or clear a space for the stranger to pass. Either they're afraid of him or he smells bad- it turns out to be both. He carries a tall stick, which he wafts at our little band menacingly.

Kiral square up to him in challenge; the smelly man isn't afraid of any of the gladiators.

"Warriors!" he cries, taking in all the people at the bottom of the temple steps who've followed us here hoping for a show. They seem to be getting one. "Praying for success in battle? Who wishes to know his true fate?" People line up as soon as he says that; this could give them some great betting tips.

Hitching up a broken rag of a hem, the little man walks up and down, staring at us. Suddenly he halts in front of the handsome Sicilian gladiator with a face full of lipstick. "Achlus, is that your name?" He nods, surprised and uncomfortable. The soothsayer rattles a cup under his nose; the gladiator has no money of his own, so Corinthus throws in a large coin, and looks away; his grimace is heavily sceptical. Pleased with his audience, the smelly man raises a finger, and intones; "Achlus, beware of tridents! Avoid those with tridents, and you will fight again!"

Achlus is impressed. The little man looks over us all again, before he proclaims; "Takis! You are Takis?" The gladiator nods, uncomfortably. Again the cup rattles, and Takis has no money. Corinthus glares at the soothsayer, and growls;

"I paid you plenty. Do them all." He's taken some wind out of the performer's sails, but he soon gulps it back, and moves on to Takis' fate. "Takis, you are a born winner, but you should never have married. I fear for you."

"How can I avoid death, like him?" Takis pleads. Soothsayers should surely offer comfort to people who pay him. This one doesn't answer at once; he thinks about the question until quite a crowd is gazing curiously at him. Then he shakes his head slowly, and proclaims with his hands lifted; "The gods tell me if you go into battle you will die."

Takis is horribly moved. So am I. How does the stranger know all this? The gods have told him? There's a terrible sense of power here, a grim power I've never experienced. "Secundus, the one they call Amator! Come forward."

The dreamer's unwilling to take centre-stage with this man, who's waving his hands and his stick and moaning in concentration. He sways on his feet in front of the young gladiator, while Secundus's foot starts to tap in impatience to learn his fate. Behind him the rest are discussing the soothsayer's authenticity; they decide he's genuine, and some of them actually sound afraid. "Secundus Amator, choose carefully who you follow, that will decide your fate. You are called the Lover, but your love is misplaced!"

Corinthus doesn't like the sound of that; he wasn't convinced by the man at first, but now his sacrifice is being slaughtered above us in the temple he's more ready to listen and believe. Still, he doesn't want anyone spoiling Secundus' performance. I don't like the sound of it either. How can the Soothsayer know so much? What if he's right, and all Naasir told me is wrong?

"Gladiatrix, come forward!" I'm properly worried now; he's going to tell all the people what I've done, how I've left the old, fierce gods for one who's all about love. He'll laugh at the love for a gladiator, love that I've now got to hide for ever; I'm sure he already knows about it. What does he mean, it's misplaced?

He can't get up the stairs to me. Kiral and Secundus have both moved in front of me, and Naasir's stepped up in front of them. I can't see his face, but his shoulders are squared and the little man's bravado's slipping. He turns his eyes down for a moment, before continuing; "Naasir Bestia, long retired."

"You read that from the posters," Naasir observes. "Tell me what they called me last in Ephesus." There's a challenge, the new gladiators don't know the answer, hardly anyone does. Again the soothsayer looks down, and frowns. Then he declares in a voice of triumph;

"Naasir Christianos! Christianos?" He isn't happy with the name. "Christianos?" He's almost spitting the word. His eyes widen like a madman as he stares. The crowd's enjoying his discomfort, they listen for his verdict on the African. He just stares.

"Jesus the Christ knows my fate, I don't want to hear what demons tell you." There's no retort. The poor little man looks about ready to fall over in panic. "Stop scaring my friends and go away."

And he does; he slinks back against his will, shoving a way for himself with bowed shoulders. Just before he disappears into the Roman Forum, he dares at last to shout back; "You can't win *and* lose!"

Chapter 18

It's only a short, silent walk from that temple to the palace
of the Roman Emperor. The walls are tall and inpenetrable,
poshly-dressed soldiers are all round it; they sneer at the
gladiators for their dirty occupation, while Corinthus' new
gladiators keep teasing Naasir, telling him to 'go away.' But
no-one raises a hand against him. They don't know how to
treat a woman in a fine gown with a silver circlet, fortunately.

Directly below the palace in a long, lush green valley, a
race track is cut and covered in sand. Surrounding it seats for
hundreds of thousands of people tower upwards, and through
its centre runs a stone barrier topped by statues and shrines.
It's full of animals now, roped off, probably waiting to be sold
in the market next door, or to be carted up to the temples
above us. It looks peaceful and sort of distant now, but I'm
not fooled. We've reached the enormous Circus Maximus,
and next week it will be us penned up waiting for slaughter.

Beneath the steeply rising stands there are wide, shaded
spaces for market stalls. Next week traces will be there
selling snacks and souvenirs of the Volturnalia games. The
stalls are divided by neat wooden walls, and some are fitted
with shelves and strings to display the merchants' wares. At
one end of the huge stadium is a built-up stone area with
tunnels and courtyards and acres of large cells.

Our team walks under more arches, only built of brick,
seeing we're no-one special until the show. I can hear
arguments coming from the cells long before we're there.

"I don't care about that scabby barbarian!"

"No, he lost his stupid village!"

"Not a village, a kingdom!"

"I'll talk to the sacred birds!"

"Dumb birds, get me a real bird!"

"Yeah, I haven't seen a woman in a week!"

"You insult the gods!"

"Shut it, he's an augur! Be afraid!"

The place is teeming with men, mostly young ones, some cursing at each other, some clanging weapons together lazily. They're so noisy, Panaius Celerus would probably shout them down and read them the riot act if he were here. I don't suppose any of them care much for Roman law, it's not exactly protecting their interests.

"Damnatii," says Corinthus, pointing at a group of thugs lounging in one cell. "Condemned to the arena instead of being killed straight off." How generous of the government, to give the men they've damned a chance to wait longer for death! "And barbarians, who don't even speak Greek; give them a wide berth, my girl, or you'll never make it into the arena." Wow, that's not much of an incentive. I never wanted to see the arena in the first place.

Corinthus has booked one cell for everyone, eleven of us. The new men muscle in quickly, nabbing the best beds or spaces on the floor.

"Where will Aysel go?" Naasir inquires; the trainer simply shoves me through the door. "You can't put a girl in here."

'Woman,' my mind retorts; fortunately I don't say it out loud. Secundus spreads himself out to save a corner near the door, beckoning to me. Is that the closest I can come to safety any more?

"There's an empty cell next door," Naasir points out.

"That's for the noxii, when they come in. There are always some screamers. She won't sleep a wink!"

"She may, tonight. Show some compassion! Takis, would you mind?" Naasir unwinds Takis' orange scarf in a flash, and throws it over my head like a veil. What's he doing? "Look at this, Corinthus, will this make you see reason?" The trainer does pause for a second, I don't know why, or what point Naasir's trying to make, but it does no good.

"Nice try," the trainer jeers, before he shakes his head, frowning, and locks the door.

Kiral is on one side of me, Naasir on the other, Secundus at my head. I should have a grain of safety, stuffed between them. Still, it only takes a moment for trouble to brew. Takis wants his scarf back, so he reaches for my head, pulls it to him and kisses my forehead. Someone else elbows him away and grabs my arm, laughing;

"Out of the way, I've been waiting for days!" Secundus punches him in the stomach, Kiral decides to join in the fight. Stuck in the middle of it, I find I can pack a decent punch. Two or three of those catch the men by surprise, before I'm thrown to the floor and have to curl into a ball to protect myself. Secundus is growling in unusual anger, Naasir stands over me, throwing men back; even he's kicking at stomachs. Corinthus returns, opens the door, and drags me away.

So I'm in a cell completely alone, and I still won't sleep. I pray for Naasir; that helps. And for my Mum, and Secundus. God listens, despite my doubts today; I'm not as alone as I thought. I move on to prayers for the other gladiators, surprising myself. And I pray that I can fulfil Naasir's wish, even though I don't know when I'll be free to go anywhere. That throws up a problem I can't ignore.

Naasir has no game plan. I may as well cut my own throat now, except that I must not kill. Secundus is depressed; he'd counted on Naasir for a plan, and no amount of whispering between the two of them will encourage him to find one. Seventy men are too many to study properly, too much death, too great a horror to contemplate.

And no-one wants to train alone with Naasir, they find him spooky; and I can't blame them, he rattles me too. How can he win *and* lose? While the rest are piling into one edge of the arena for morning drill, he offers me a brief idea.

"Paul says Jesus is the reason for him to live, and to die will be a gain."

"So this time you really will..."

"We all die eventually."

True, that could be in a practice session. Secundus explains the damnatii are barbarian soldiers, captured by Rome. They have to fight as punishment for being taken alive; if they fight nobly they can gain forgiveness from the gods, and, more importantly, from Caesar. They have the experience of fighting for the lives of their wives and children, not only themselves, and, to judge by the little I've picked up, they're totally wild.

Last time, Naasir warned me to beware of the quiet one, and it looks like that's true again. There is one of the damnatii who has pale hair so long he wears it plaited like a girl. His eyebrows are so pale they make his pink face look ghostly. He's as broad as he is tall, the motions of his weapon are as clean as Naasir has ever seen, with any weapon he chooses. He never needs to raise his voice among the others in the evening, they always listen with reverence.

He has a group of followers among the blond and ginger bearded warriors in their hot baggy trousers. They bring his food, pick up his weapons, they even bow to him. "I think he's one of their leaders," Naasir guesses. "I haven't found anyone to translate so I can talk to them."

And there's another one who scares me just looking at him. Kiral says he's an augur, a holy man who reads people's fortunes by the motion of the birds in the sky. He looks the same as any Roman gladiator, the same dark hair, olive skin, terrifying muscles, a sharp frown. And he also exudes something, an unworldly power similar to Naasir's. But augurs have always been respected in Rome, so the others listen easily to him, and do his bidding in fear of their lives.

"A holy man, who fights?" I ask Naasir. "Should we bow to him too?"

"I'm not bowing to any Lord but my own," he answers, "but I'll leave it to your conscience."

He says that a lot now. I think he's a bit touchy that I dared answer him back on the ship and asked to be trained. He's teaching me to slash and to thrust, saying; "You can aim for the legs if you need, that'll surprise them; they'll be expecting you to go straight for the neck. You can aim for the neck if you want, I'll leave it to your conscience." He shows me how to swing a trident to protect myself. "You can use the blunt end, or the fork, you know how that works. But I'll leave..."

"Leave it to my conscience! I get the message!" Of course he's about as worried about the coming games as I am, but he's worried about me, not himself. And I can't even parry a blow from Secundus, nearly the weakest man in the arena, when he's only sparring.

Sometimes I can't manage so much as flinging out a net, like the fishermen's boys on the shore at home. Just remembering that is enough to bring a tear to my eye, knowing I'm never likely to go back there; if by some miracle I do, it'll never be the same, because of the way I've been forced to change.

So I flick the net out, and only catch Naasir's wooden sword. It's so tangled the weapon's wrenched out of his hand, and we have to start the bout again, while he lectures me about concentration. I wish he could teach me about God and my spirit instead, but whenever it's quiet he's locked in with the gladiators and I'm in solitary confinement. He's probably teaching one of them instead of me. I need to get out, and find someone who can help Naasir know more.

Who are the noxii Corinthus spoke of, the ones who ought to be in my cell? Why aren't they here yet, imprisoned like the rest of the entertainment? Can they be more dangerous than all the gladiators I've seen?

"You're not going to do that, Corinthus? We were friends once!" Naasir's voice wakes me up at dawn, and the rattling of my door follows. I scramble off the tiny pile of rushes they gave me grudgingly. There's little point in folding my blanket or worrying about my hair or my stinky tunic, I'm probably just off to another sandy knock-about with the grumpy trainer.

"It's just a bit of advertising," he shouts back at his men's cell.

"If you do this, Corinthus, I have nothing more to say to you!"

"That'll be a relief, you talk a load of rubbish!" As I trap on my useless ornamental sword outside Naasir's door, he whispers quickly;

"If you get any chance, escape."

"Isn't that sin?"

"What he's doing to us is sin. God be with you."

I have no idea what's going on, the lanista tells me to shut up and walk. But at last, after days of battle and argument in the dark, stinking tunnels, I'm out of the circus. I'm tied up to Kiral's hairy hand, since his trainer knows he won't run away without the money he's owed, or without his chance of proper glory in the arena. I can't look at him; I'm on his right side, so he couldn't see me anyway.

But he talks, and surprises me. 'You don't need to be scared, not of me. I don't want to hurt you."

"Huh?" We humiliated him in Ephesus, and he's always been mad about it. Then again, on the ship he kept me safe...

"I owe you and Naasir my life. If I'd died in Ephesus, I wouldn't have had the chance to fight in Rome, that's a great honour." Yes, to him, maybe. "Naasir talks about forgiveness and repentance, turning, all that stuff. So, how about you forgive me, and I turn away from hurting you?"

I can't believe I'm hearing this, but a great deal of unbelievable things have happened in the last week. I may as well believe what he says. "All right, that'd be good." So we walk quietly through the streets, wherever Corinthus is leading us, staring at the way the rich people live, and I try to relax in the company of a proper gladiator. That's going to take a lot of practice.

We stop outside an enormous bath house. I should be all right here, these places are built for Roman citizens, and I don't think slaves are allowed in. But I've been wrong many times before. "In the slaves' entrance," Corinthus orders us. There he hands me over to two strangers, while his new deputy gives a heavy bundle to a bath house slave; odd, I haven't thought about my missing collar for a few days until I saw that one on the slave.

The trainer and deputy take Kiral away, promising him a soak in a bath for the trouble of escorting me, and they leave me at the mercy of the jealous slaves. "Where do we start?" the woman asks, unwilling to touch me. Fair enough, I'm caked in sand and dust, my hair still has straw sticking out of it, and I didn't realise until I stepped into this clean, decorated place how badly I smell. The man gives her a stern warning eye;

"You heard him. We have to make her fit for a wedding."

A wedding? What wedding? I don't want to know, I certainly don't want anyone marrying me! At least a woman has to give her consent to a wedding, and I'd rather die right now than do that. As I'm marched away from the fresh air and wide streets, I'm stretching my neck up tall, as a gladiator would so his stronger opponent can cut his throat.

We're in a huge hall full of echoing noise. The floor is covered with tiles; mosaic pictures entwine on it, pictures of water creatures, legendary sea monsters, tales of the water gods, anything and everything watery. Behind tall colonnades the walls are of bright red, green and grey marble; I don't know whether it's real or painted marble like in the public spaces of the Celerus house. Gaggles of women, all ages and sizes, chat round the cool pillars in their pretty stolas and jewels, having their hair dressed and nails painted.

In the centre of the room is a giant bath, wide stone steps lead down into it, and hundreds of women are coming and going into it, none of them wearing a thing. I am not doing that! Nobody's seen me naked since I was a toddler, except that Drusa and her girls, and the water looks murky...

I've got away with that. The two slaves scurry me past the smart, clean women, into a side room where they've already had a copper bath drawn. The woman brandishes a pumice stone, the man picks up a sponge.

"Give those to me," I tell them; "I know the drill." To my relief, and theirs, they hand me the stuff, sneak willingly off and pull the door shut.

I'd better make a good job of it, or they'll come back and do it for me. So I scrub as hard and fast as I can in the cold tub, even my back, although I'm stiff from sleeping on a virtually bare floor and I struggle to reach far enough at first. Then I polish with the sponge and a ridiculous amount of rosemary scented oil- it's at Corinthus' expense, not mine. When I've shaken myself dry and unwrapped the bundle to find clean underwear and my other tunic, I have no choice but to call the slaves back.

Lucina makes us do this to her just about every day! Surely it'd be more fun to do things for herself. I wonder whether she talked to Panaius about my father. Probably not, she usually gets bored very easily; still, if she is a follower like us, and she valued Naasir enough to come and talk to him... It's all pretty pointless. Citizens don't care about their slaves that way. If the father who's been absent all my life suddenly wanted to come to Rome and say his farewells, he could never afford it. A slave would have no influence to help me, and they'd probably throw him into the arena with us, all for their perverted pleasure. He's out of my mind.

The two slaves spend every day doing this sort of thing for rich citizens, but they're not confusing me with one. They'd probably talk politely to a rich client, this morning they just talk to each other over my head. Well, I know how to fix that, how to get a bit of respect out of them, the men do it all the time. "You're wasting your time," I tell them. "I'll be filthy again by the time I fight in the Volturnalia festival."

"Fight?" the woman echoes, pausing with her instrument of torture in her hand, the dreaded hair comb.

"Yes, with the gladiators, at the Circus Maximus." Her eyes nearly pop out when I say that; suddenly she wants to her all about the glamorous lives of those adorable gladiators, and I feel horribly like one of them.   Still, she combs my hair more carefully now.   The man's still rubbing oil into my legs as roughly as he can manage, so I can't resist pointing out the evidence to convince him.

"Can you pass my body armour?" I ask.   He shakes out the bundle, and finds a stiff padded tunic and the shining breastplate Corinthus has had made for me.   There are no doubts now, he virtually bows as he hands me the padding, and gestures for the woman to help me lace it on because he hardly dares.   When it comes to the stupidly tight straps round my waist, he has to help, and his eyes are carefully cast down.

They've given up on the idea of painting my nails; instead they're braiding my hair tightly to keep it neat in a fight, and strapping vambraces on my wrists.

"It's not right," the woman keeps muttering.   "Not right for a wedding."   That's true; obviously I'm not going to be the bride.   Not with a sword-belt round my waist and a sword which looks vicious as far as the scabbard.   They needn't know it's snapped off below the hilt, need they?

It's the boots which finally make them gape without stopping.   They're so new they creak, they're smarter than Panaius' winter boots and stretch up to my knees, just as well, considering my tunic scarcely reaches my shins.   The outfit's complete; I don't need a mirror, the awe in the two slaves' faces is enough.   The woman's so worried about the sword, her collar's beaded with sweat.

I'm a slave too, nothing more, a slave with no intention of killing.   "Thanks for your help," I tell her.

"Enjoy the wedding," she shivers back; I've accidentally clenched my fist and put it to my heart to salute her, I'm turning into a warrior.

Chapter 19

"I don't like the shoulders," our trainer announces, not to me, to his deputy. Of course he has to agree with his boss. "Get rid of them altogether."

"Her shoulders won't be protected."

"That really doesn't matter, does it? Get something done with the tunic, while you're at it. It's too long." Too long? It barely clears my knees.

"Yes, sir. Shall we take the shoulders out of the tunic?" Corinthus likes the sound of that. Kiral's been taking in the silly breastplate, with cups as big as Lucina's, and the breathlessly tiny waist. Now he taps on my back, and asks;

"What are these two channels for?"

"Wings. They've got a Victory complex here." Victory? I've seen her statue on the temple of Caesar, the goddess who carries a torch and a laurel wreath, and has a huge pair of wings.

"How will I fight in wings?" I wonder. "Naasir said..."

Corinthus snaps instantly; "Don't speak his name! He's like a one-man plague! How long before you catch it?" I have no chance to ask him what plague he means, although I know already, before he whinges on; "And you, remember your place today. You're an advert, that's all. Keep your mouth shut."

"She never talks much anyway," Kiral points out. He's been cleaned up, too; he looks almost human, apart from his eye. And he's more inappropriately dressed than me, with only his harness, and a bare, awe-inspiring torso. Corinthus is white and resplendent in a real toga. It doesn't mend his mood; he obviously struggles with its drapes and folds. But picking up a rich cake from a baker's cheers him up enough to growl at us;

"Listen, you two, this is my daughter's day, it's her wedding, and I don't want anyone messing it up."

"You have a daughter?" I squeak in surprise. He throws me an icy stare. How in the world can he live with himself? Naasir told me in Ephesus that we were likely to have sympathy from the gladiators with daughters, and that seemed to be true, they summoned up a drop of compassion for me. It was Corinthus who bought me and shoved me in with the men, without a trace of pity, and all the time he was looking forward to his own daughter's wedding. It makes him almost as terrifying as the other lanistae here in Rome, and nearly as ruthless.

We stop outside a blue door a lot like the Celerus'. Garlands of leaves decorate it, I can hear music playing, and I can't hold back a well of excitement; I'm going to my first wedding. The house is the same shape as ours, with the same stone ground floor and wooden upstairs, and the door is opening for me, the front door!

A stern woman stands in the doorway. She frowns, gasps; "Corinthus, brother, it's been too long!" Then she looks at me and Kiral- all right, just at me.

"Advertising," Corinthus returns, with a grin that's suddenly a bit sheepish.

"You're not bringing that… person in here, to a wedding!" she tells him firmly. Again she's looking at me.

"See reason, sister," he pleads. "I'm known in Rome now, because of these idiots. And look what I can afford now!" He digs into his purse, and takes out the ring he bought when we arrived. "A proper engagement ring. And did you get the wine I had sent? It's some of the best. And here's money for the musicians, and honey cake!" It appears the old lady sees his reason, and lets us in, but she still stares at me like I'm the lowest form of life, and orders me to hide in a corner.

The whole atrium's full of garlands, neatly clipped plants are decorated with flowers, their rainwater pool in the centre has flowers floating in it. No tragic mistress sits here, dipping her hand miserably in the water. Under the tiled roof round the edge of the atrium are musicians, one on a shawm, one on a harp, another on a lyre, and there's even a drummer. Their music is bright, slightly raucous, and guaranteed to cheer.

Guests fill the atrium, spilling over into the triclinium where the food's set out, and into a study like Panaius'. I'm naturally heading out the back way towards the kitchen when Corinthus drags me back. "Keep your place," he growls at me, yet the moment he meets an important guest he introduces me with delight, carrying on about my- non-existent- skills in the arena.

"You look very stern," his mother tells me softly. She dares to pat my hand, the hand of a social outcast, to show her son she's more of a worldly woman than he thought. "I suppose it comes with the job." I'm staring carelessly at the stone pillars painted like marble, still amazed to be in such a bright, happy place and to be talked to by the host's mother. Then I catch the lanista's mother's tone of panic. "Corinthus, we're running late, and no thanks to you. Now Glaucia's messed up the knot of her belt, the girls will have to cut it off!"

"So?" Corinthus shrugs. "She can marry without a belt on. I'll buy her a new one."

"No, she can't! No Knot of Hercules? What's the groom going to untie when he takes her home tonight? That was my belt! It was woven by my mother! What's the point of your fancy wine, if the biggest tradition is broken?"

Yes, yes, I'm good at untying knots. I'm not going to tell her, and risk rescuing some unknown girl's wedding!

-I would, if I were you.

If I were Jesus, the Chosen One, after all I've been told by Naasir, I wouldn't be so selfish. Didn't he once bring a Roman centurion's servant back to life, from a distance? So while the household slaves bustle about feeding the guests, I venture on my own up the stairs. It's easy to pick out the bride's bedroom by sounds of panic. I remember the compassion Naasir keeps showing me, and open the door, whispering quietly; "Mistress?"

The room explodes into screaming. The bride in her white stola cowers against the far wall, her brides-maids race to her; one of them collapses in a faint on the floor. "What's wrong?" I ask, stupidly. They're staring at my armour, and my sword.

"Heh, I'm not scary! This sword won't harm anyone." As I draw it the usual *swish* of a blade is nothing but a *sw*... I stow the useless hilt next to a shrine in a plastered alcove, and hold out my hands in peace. "I'm not a gladiator or anything..." The very use of that frightening word's driven one bridesmaid into a tearful panic. "I'm just a slave who's good with knots. Do you want me to try and unknot your belt?"

The bride must be desperate; she pushes past her one remaining guard, and stands in front of me, with quivering hands. It's no special knot, it's just twisted and knotted over and over, the sort I've been unpicking from home-made clothes for years.

"How... how can you do this?" whimpers the bride. I've never spoken so much to a lady of the house, but I've never been in an upstairs room or to a wedding either, so I tell her straight;

"My mistress beats my mother. Then she ties her up in the peristyle. I have to climb out of the window at night to untie her. I'm sure nothing like that goes on around here. Nearly done." Their silence is predictable; of course the same must go on in Rome, but I think she gets my point, and if it happens less here I'll be glad I spoke up.

The bride is smiling. She looks quite like Corinthus, except a lot prettier, and softer. The other girls are draping her with an orange, flame-like veil as I take back my sword and leave them to it. I'm glad I helped; in my bleak world these past few days I've started to forget what simple kindnesses are.

The music stops, news passes round that the bride is ready. Guests gulp down any nibbles they were whiling away the

156

time with, chosen witnesses step forward. Corinthus gives Kiral and me a final stern warning before joining his daughter, who's absolutely gliding down the stairs.

Through the decorated front door, followed by some of his family and friends, comes her groom, in a red toga with bands of bright embroidery. Judging by the richness of his robes, and the simplicity of this house, Corinthus' daughter has done pretty well for herself. And the young groom's no older than she is, unlike Panaius and Lucina, who have more than thirty years between them. I wonder if that's a good foundation for a marriage.

No, I'm not thinking of Secundus, I mustn't, I daren't. While the bride's parading with her perfectly decked maids round the pool, I remember him leaning drunk on my shoulder- he hasn't touched a drop of drink since. And I remember him stabbing Florus in front of me. That's a lovely image to have in the middle of a wedding.

The bride takes her groom's hand, symbolising her agreement to the match. Anyone can tell she's happy, even the lanista who buys and sells men to be killed. He actually smiles at his daughter, who smiles back, waving her new ring I helped pay for. Although the priest is waiting, the couple stop by the pool for a kiss. Their s chorus a whisper of appreciative sighs. They're guided to the household shrine, which is decorated with flowers and more garlands to match the wreath the bride wears on top of her veil.

Two of the gods they've picked to guard their house are Mars, god of war, and Victory, the one with the wings who we call Nike in Ephesus. They fit in well with Corinthus' line of work, although they're about as incongruous at a romantic occasion as Kiral and I are.

The priest's praying to the statues. Funny, I used to accept that without a hint of question in my head. After that, the couple turn together and look into each other's eyes. I can see they're happy, and excited at the thought of being together.

Do they know how fortunate they are to have found happiness, and to be allowed to live it?

"Ubi tu Gaius, ego Gaia," the bride chants, in a shy little voice. At an elbow from me, Kiral tries a translation; "When you're Gaius, a holy man of some sort, I'm Gaia, his other half." She's promising to be part of him, to live her life in step with his, in peace together.

They truly are the happy couple. When offered stools to sit on in front of the household altar, she shoves them closer together so he can sit without taking his arm away from her waist. Now Corinthus' cake takes pride of place, as the priest offers it sincerely to Jupiter, perched on the top shelf of the shrine. Slaves take the cake away to be shared among the guests later, and it's time to eat.

It's also time for more entertainmment. Apparently that's us. Kiral only needs a nod from his boss to throw down his cloak and draw his sword; in a few careful strokes he's cleared a space between the front door and the fountain. Corinthus' mother scuttles across the atrium, between a dozen guests, ordering him fearlessly; "No, no, no! Not in here! Not now!"

"Mother! Advertising!" The lanista hands me his own sword, and commands us;

"Fight! Take it easy, Kiral, like the paegniarii."

"What are paegni… things?" I wonder.

"Play fighters," Kiral grimbles. Ah, I should have known that, I've heard Corinthus threaten often enough to make Secundus one of those. So I'm a paegniarius or something now, am I? The lanista's Mum has managed to force us out of the house to do a demonstration in the street, but she might have known that most of the wedding guests would follow us in fascination. Corinthus stands on the side-line, cursing that she's stolen his book and he can't gather bets for the great event next week.

Play-fighting, at a wedding! The man's totally mad. Even Kiral thinks it's weird; still, I missed the morning's practice, and this is about as useful. The gladiator's been studying my technique behind my back. Instead of using his knowledge against me he aims gently at the angles I find difficult to parry, so I start to improve. It makes us look pretty good to our impromptu audience, to judge by the cheers, gasps and whistles.

They're easily pleased. Any man who's ever fought could see how useless I am. My breastplate is heavy and chafing on my shoulders, and at the back the channels stop my arms from wheeling properly. My wrists are still weak, and my beautiful boots are slippy. If Kiral really went at me he'd run me through by accident. That would be a novel event at a wedding, for all those novelty-seekers gathering round us.

The bride has followed the rest of the wedding party into the street. There are cheers for her arrival, not as many as there are for my short tunic, but she's on the warpath to her father. She pulls him by the arm and nags him about how unsuitable this is, watching me at the same time with an obvious awe. Finally Corinthus sees that he'll be the one spoiling her day if he doesn't obey; he calls off the battle. Kiral winks at me, glad to stop and head to the buffet table. The bride takes my arm and leads me back into the house.

In the triclinium two long tables are groaning with food, two slaves enter from their kitchen to refill any gaps. I know plenty of the dishes by sight, we prepare them for the Celerus parties; there's a whole roast piglet, with half its ribs cracked away and eaten, and sausages filling its inside. There are oysters, supposedly the food of love, though they don't work when Lucina tries them on Panaius. I see stuffed olives and dates, lobster, fresh figs, and I can't touch any of it.

The bride has me tightly by the hand, but it still it takes her a moment to gulp up the courage to speak to me, and tell me what's on her mind. "Thank you, for earlier. I want to give you a gift." I think I can see one right now, an open window. I could force her to let me free, run away from here and leave Rome behind, Naasir too.

Again I find myself speaking to a mistress like an equal. "There's no need to thank me, and there's only one thing I'd really like," I tell her humbly. "It's for a friend of mine. I want to find someone in Rome who knew Jesus."

"That's all? Is he a Jew? That's a common Jewish name, I'll ask the girls."

The bridesmaids return the moment she calls. One of them opens her eyes wide in surprise, the other gasps. "I suppose you mean the Nazarene. You live dangerously, don't you?"

"Do I?" I ask, trying not to look down suspiciously at me.

"Yes!" she lowers her voice to a whisper. "They've been taking his followers away, putting them in prison. But there's still one man who talks about him in the Forum most days. You know Abram, girls?" They nod like a dramatic chorus. It sounds like I've found my clue; I'd like to meet this man who's so determined.

"Can you take me to him?" The bridesmaid's unwilling, the others are afraid, yet the bride's convinced she has to thank me still. So in the end she agrees to take me, after we've eaten. "I'm not allowed to eat." The bride won't have that; she pushes a plate into my hand and insists on filling it herself. I daren't disobey her command on her joyful day, and I feel so relieved to have some good news that I'm more than happy to sit in a corner and eat like a free woman.

I won't touch the figs; I still have a superstitious aversion to them. I dither over the grapes, unsure how many I can politely take, and whether I can eat them without spilling juice on my tunic, that wouldn't look too tough. And I'm filled with a sense of déja vu; I'm being watched, just like I was in the agora back home.

A smart, middle-aged man in an anonymously white toga is looking at my costume. He's been watching my fighting display and eavesdropping on my brief conversation with the bride. In battle I won't be able to hesitate, so I won't now. I look him in the eye to demand; "What do you want?"

"You admire the Nazarene? So do I. He talked of justice for all, of equality." I'm surprised to hear such talk from a citizen in a toga. "I hear you used to be a slave."

"I still am; I'm Corinthus' slave."

"I see," he replies, with a twist of his head. "I can't imagine what the life of a slave must be like, but I believe it's wrong, just as you do. Many of us believe the same." He talks freely, not quietly, he doesn't mind who hears.

"Won't you get in trouble with other citizens for talking that way?"

"I don't care. The Roman world is unjust, it's ready for change; we need equality, morality, freedom and moderation. That's what you think, isn't it?"

I have to agree. "From what I've seen, Rome's a bad place; people are amused by death, the system is unjust, even your bath water's murky!"

"That's true," he laughs. "I like the way you talk. My master agrees with you." He follows my gaze for a moment, to a woman picking up a feather from the table and looking around. Then he jabs a thumb to show her the way she should go. "A case in point; slaves are built like you, small, probably starving, while citizens use vomitaria so they can carry on stuffing themselves at parties." What's are vomitaria, what's the feather for? I don't want to know, not when there are much more pressing questions.

"Who's your master?"

"Seneca!" he exclaims with pride. It sound as if I'm meant to be impressed. But I don't know how I can be.

"Who's Seneca?" His face reddens as he stares at me in disbelief.

"Why, the great philosopher! The tutor to Caesar's nephew Nero! Do you mean to say you really haven't heard of Seneca?'

"No," I shrug. "I'm a slave."

"I see. That's strange. He's heard of you."

Chapter 20

At last I'm being talked to like an adult, an equal. Flavius talks with such a lively way, so full of enthusiasm for the world, it's exciting just to listen. He's lived a long time in Rome, and he fills his talk with tales of his family and friends. Many of them long for a world where everyone's respected for their deeds, not their birth, even high-born men like the Emperor's nephew believe it. He and his friends have been watching the decline of Rome under Claudius Caesar with sadness, and gradually their beliefs have forced them to admit he's not up to the job.

Not all men love the games. In every corner of the Empire there are men campaigning about the treatment of gladiators and prisoners, protesting at the constant killing for entertainment. Flavius says the circus is dragging people's morals into the gutter. If only Nero were in power, in place of his uncle, he would pass new laws and clean up the whole empire.

In his educated words Flavius paints me a picture of a bright future world, without murderous games, without slaves, with freedom to learn, work, travel however you wish. "Are you sure this man Nero would do all that?" I wonder. Flavius is quick to reply;

"He's tutored and guided by Seneca, who leads us all in our aims."

"But how long will we have to wait for Nero to be in charge?"

"I see it's hard for you to understand. That's my fault," he apologises. "Just picture a world where everyone is free to worship whichever gods he chooses, with no exclusion or punishment!" I struggle to imagine that, yet I want to. Can it really be possible to make the world a better place so quickly? If it were, Naasir, or men like him, could worship the true God without fear. I can hardly wait to get back and tell him.

The meal has finished, the food's being cleared away, the sky's a little darker, and still we sit talking. Kiral raises an eyebrow at me; I 'm sure we'll have to leave soon. I must talk faster. "Why have you told me all this?"

"Because we need your help, of course!" My help? I've never heard that before, from anyone except my Mum, who's painfully far away. "Aysel, you're in the public eye, you talk well, you're a true slave. People, especially slaves, will listen to you. I hear they listened to everything you said in Ephesus, your singing, too."

News does travel fast. And I can scarcely believe it, I'm wanted, I could be useful to someone just as I am. I could help change the world. Except that I won't be alive to do anything useful.

"I'm fighting in four days, I'm going to die."

Flavius sighs. "I'd forgotten that. It's not a big problem." Oh, really? Doesn't he think so? "Come to the Forum tomorrow morning; I'll wait there for you. If you want to help us, Seneca will see that we buy you from your trainer, he won't dare to argue with a man who works for Caesar. Just come and meet him and you'll see."

He'll buy me, just like that, a woman he's never met before? I wouldn't complain. The panic that always lies in the pit of my stomach is starting to dull already. Naasir told me to find some escape, and here it is. I can take him too. So there are decent, wise people in Rome after all.

The sun's going down, we've talked so long. "Time to take her back," Corinthus growls drunkenly at Kiral. The gladiator grabs my arm, taking out the lanista's chains, but the bride has my other arm.

"She's coming in the parade," she tells her father. "No-one I know has had a gladiator in their wedding parade!"

"Gladiatrix!" he mutters, and gives in.

I see why he wanted to leave. His sister has emerged from her place close to the food table, and she's suddenly very discontented. She grabs her niece by her woven belt,

163

complete with its complicated knot, and shouts out that she's not letting her be taken away to a strange man's house. Is she crazy? Hasn't she seen their smiles, their touching, the glow on the bride's face?

She's upset the bride; she's wailing too; the groom's friends think it's ridiculous, they're actually trying to pull her away from her aunt, the whole scene's a farce. What will the neighbours make of it? And neighbours are gathering, carrying torches of burning oil. They're chattering loudly, gossiping, and laughing!

"Should we do something?' I ask Kiral, putting my hand on my sword-hilt... Yes, that'd scare the men, wouldn't it, a broken sword? He shakes his head and holds his ground. The bride could teach Lucina a thing or two about throwing a temper; she looks desperate enough, yet she hasn't dropped a tear, her make-up's perfectly intact. The men have pulled her away, and she's laughing almost as much as they are. It was all an act, a part of the wedding traditions.

I march among the bridesmaids, who've drunk enough of Corinthus' fine wine to dull their fear. They shuffle in their long skirts, I hold my head high, just as I intend to when I go with Seneca and Flavius and all the Stoics in Rome to demand Claudius' abdication.

I can see it now, in my mind as the sun sets over the chaotic city. Everywhere collars are clanging to the ground, slaves are raising their hands in joy, citizens are panicking that they'll starve, their clothes are growing dirty, uncared-for, and they're racing round in search of food. I'll be kind, I'll spare them some compassion. They can have the vast amounts of food stored in Caesar's palace, to keep them from starving till they find their feet.

The slaves can be put to work taking down the circuses; one flaming torch would be all we'd need in Ephesus, to set fire to all the wooden stands, but the Circus Maximus would have to be removed stone by stone, and what better symbol of our coming freedom? Soon I'll be back with Naasir, and if he's not locked away I can tell him the incredible news that he can help us save this world, that we needn't wait for the next world to have justice.

People are flocking to join us right now, as if the rebellion has already begun, except that they know nothing about it. They carry torches to light the bride to the home of her new husband, where he'll untie that Knot of Hercules and wrap her in his arms as he did before. She needn't fear him as my Mum fears men, I can tell by the glow in his eyes, and the way he holds her hand; it's the same way Secundus held mine on our ride into Rome.

The crowd of public stops at the groom's garlanded front door; they're not invited any further. Corinthus bought a silly amount of nuts the other day, now I see they were for people to throw over the couple at the door. They're left, trampled, for animals to find. In fact, Aunt Yildiz comes home with nuts for us slaves sometimes; she must have known where there was a wedding.

Genuine wedding guests, with Flavius among them, push through to the front to watch the final pieces of the wedding ceremony. The bride has carried a torch all the way from her Aunt's fire, now she gives it to her groom, a symbol that she's going to keep his house warm and his food cooked for him from now on. His friends carry her over the threshold so she doesn't fall, that's always considered a sign of bad fortune.

That's enough for Corinthus. He beckons to Kiral to tie me up again, and marches us at a fierce pace back to the valley where the Circus nestles. "Extra training tomorrow," he warns us, with no thanks for our performance earlier; it's just as well I never expected any. I never expected to feel this rotten, either. I thought Secundus and I had got into a brother-sister kind of friendship; so does he. But I can't get the image out of my head, of the bride and groom looking into each other's eyes, except with the faces changed... It's the worst kind of injustice I've ever felt. Seneca must help me end it.

We're back in good time; the gladiators have trained solidly all day until sundown, and they're lounging about in the courtyards, eating. It's our usual vegetable diet, bread and stew, I'm glad I've already eaten better than that. Naasir's in a corner with Secundus; I gasp in a deep breath and swallow it down, pushing the young gladiator out of my mind. Then I pull Naasir away and hurry him into my cell to share my news.

"I talked to a man at the wedding today, and I think I've fixed up our escape!"

"All of us?" he gapes. I'm pleased to see his dark face brighten, he hasn't smiled for ages.

"Yes, both of us! All we have to do is go to the Forum tomorrow morning. I've asked Kiral, and he said he'll escort us."

"Why should we go there?"

I don't like his suspicious look. I need to try and convey the excitement in Flavius' voice when he spoke of his great mission. "Because we're going to save the world, that's all! The real world, right here! I talked to someone called Flavius at the wedding today. He's a wise man. He told me there are men all over the Empire who believe that slavery is wrong and the world's just twisted up."

"Very wise." I don't know why he isn't drawn in yet. Maybe he's had a bad day of training and he's worn out.

"Flavius told me all I have to do is meet him at the Forum and his leader, Seneca, will buy me from Corinthus."

"Why you?" Naasir inquires, with a lift of his eyebrow that I take for jealousy.

"Because I'm the only gladiatrix in Rome. He says I can speak for the women. But you're the gladiator who doesn't kill, he'll need you too! I mean it, you should have heard how he talked, and you will. They want to clear up the world, get rid of greed and murder."

"How can they get rid of murder?" He is truly tired. Maybe I'd be best discussing this in the morning. But I can't shake the excitement.

"They're going to get the slaves to rise up in the city and force Claudius Caesar to retire!" I bet he didn't see that coming. "I bet when the soldiers picked us up at home you didn't think we'd be at the front of everything when the world changes for the better!"

Still he doesn't see the vision. Seriously, I saw his gates of Heaven clearly enough when he described it! All he can do is sigh, and try to walk away. I catch him with arms that are much stronger than last week. "What's wrong? Why aren't you happy?" He shakes his head, and sighs again.

"No, I didn't think it would be this way. First Lucina, then Corinthus, now someone else, a total stranger. Instead of taking care of a child, they all want to use you."

"They're not using me!"

Finally he throws up his hands and shouts in anger at me. "Caesar won't retire! They'll have to kill him, and who could do that better than a gladiatrix? Then they'll blame you, and kill you! So they'll start a new order with killing!"

"It'd only be one life, for the freedom of..."

"It's been done before. Slaves rose up, the government killed them. Rome was a republic, ruled by men elected by the people, headed by Julius Caesar. Jealous men killed him, and made this Empire. Now they worship him like a god! And how do you think Claudius came to power? It's all twisted, every good intention's corrupted!"

"Naasir, you're wrong!" My voice is echoing through the courtyard. I don't care, he can't burst my bubble, when I was so happy. "These men are different, it'll be right this time!"

"Nero will be no better than his uncle," he predicts.

"You don't understand anything! We can't all be angels like you, we can only try to do our best!" That's enough for him, he wrenches his arm away and leaves to return to his own crowded cell. He just has one more thing to add;

"Go, if you want. I'll leave it to your conscience."

"LEAVE HIM!"

"Shut up, kid!" one of the damnatii screams back. I'm in a cold sweat, my nails bite into my palms, trying to grasp an invisible trident. The world is dark- no, I haven't opened my eyes yet, and when I do I'm just staring into the corner of my stone cell. My head's fuzzy, and full of panic. In three days my fate will be decided.

In three days I'm likely to die, and last night I didn't pray. Mum always made me pray before I went to sleep, on the off chance that it would do some good. And now I have a real God, who I know listens to me, what have I done? I've ignored Him and screamed at the friend who showed Him to me. It confirms what I've always thought; I'm an idiot.

I'm not happy to wake up realising Naasir's right yet again, but I've got to face the facts. That Flavius may have talked of banishing greed, but he looked fat enough and ate enough to need a feather for his throat by the end of the wedding. He denounced entertainment by the gladiators, but he was happy to watch us fight, and to want to use me, one of the dregs of society. He and those other men, all wealthy citizens, will certainly murder Caesar to put his nephew in his place. I'm sure Nero could be as sweet and well-meaning as Flavius says, and values the pure and selfless aims of Seneca and his crew. But I heard the audience in Ephesus when Naasir told them about the true God- nothing stays pure in human hands.

Kiral's at my door already; he's keen to take me out again, to the Forum. He's decided to meet this Seneca in person so he can make a better life for himself. He won't care how the power in Rome is changed, as long as he can harness some of that power for himself. But they won't harness me; no-one's going to make me kill a man again.

As we cross the sand, Naasir looks up from his morning bread. "Going to the Forum?" Naturally he has a disappointed face, though I think he's trying to smile.

168

"Yes," I reply, "but it's not how you think. I'm going to see..."

"I don't want to be any part of it, but God bless you."

"You too. See you later." Ha, that surprised him; if I were going where he thinks, I wouldn't see him again at all. That's not as good a surprise as a visit from another follower would be, though.

I walk quietly beside Kiral as we head back up the hill. I might not be on my knees, but I'm learning God is everywhere and I can talk to Him. It's almost enough to make me smile. I've thought of Him as a presence as big as the starry night, but walking under the wide sunlit sky inspires me with thoughts of Him as my Father who cares for me.

I can't ignore Kiral for ever, and I'm curious, as always. "Kiral, how did you get Corinthus to let us out?"

"I told him we were commanded by Seneca, and he's coming to get us if he doesn't let us go." Not a bad plan. I still have trouble taking in how pleasant he's become since Ephesus. Of course we've all changed, I've probably changed the most, and he's been in a room with Naasir, something's clearly rubbed off on him.

We're back in front of the temple of Julius Caesar; it seems stranger to see it there, so tall and white and spangled with gold, now I know he was just a man like anyone. Close by is the Roman Forum; it's a lot bigger than the agora I visited in Ephesus, which is no surprise. The cries of the stallholders gathering to sell everything under the sun confuses me less than it did. That must be due to the chaos at the Circus, with seventy men training at once. There must be a hundred stalls, and a thousand people crowding in, all confident of where they're going and what they want to buy. I'm getting used to the colourful rush of it now.

Round the sides of the rectangle are shaded cloisters, their pillars marked with dirt from dyes, skins and food. One has a poster stuck on it, and I can recognise the letters of my name. I notice green and yellow colours are very common, one stall's selling little cloth flags; at the back are a few red and blue ones, but the whole table's full of a sea of yellow and green. "What are the flags for?" I wonder. Kiral's amazed I haven't heard, he's travelled so much he reckons he knows just about everything.

"They're for the race teams. The Circus Maximus was built for racing chariots. They're the big entertainment, not us. We're like the starter and they're the main course." I see; except they won't have to run the risk of being eaten.

"Is that why we're just fighting on both the mornings?" That sounds a dumb question the moment it's out of my mouth. As if I'm going to last more than one morning!

"Yes. And you're lucky, you're only listed for Day Two." Ah! If I could read, I might have known that. So I have a day of grace; I'd better use my time wisely. "There they are." Kiral points with a roughly scarred hand at a group of men debating under the shelter of the cloister. After yesterday's wedding I didn't think I'd ever see finer clothes; I was wrong again. These men wear deep-dyed tunics with beautifully-woven bands down them, and togas which seem to be embroidered all over. I can't help staring; some of the embroidery's actually gold. The message is clear, they are the richest of the rich, and proud of it. There's Flavius the philosopher; he must have dressed down for the wedding!

"Coming? Aysel?"

From one corner of the Forum I can hear a call; it's not a loud, clear one like Paul's, but it's enough to be heard through the crowd. I see a man in long robes, woven stripes, and a thick beard.

"No, thanks, Kiral. I'm not staying. Say 'hello' to Flavius for me. I'll be over there with Abram." Kiral unties me with a shrug, gritting his teeth, probably to stop himself remarking on how stupid I am. It all depends on your point of view, really.

Abram's not an old man, though you might think so when you look at his beard. His nose is the same shape as Paul's, and his eyes have the same twinkle, but he's less comfortable talking in public. His hands stay mostly by his side and his voice goes up and down so some of his words are lost. He's not the kind of orator you'd expect in the Forum, and that's making people turn their heads. I see, he's doing what he thinks he should, sharing the love of his Lord with everyone, even though he's afraid to do it. He doesn't accuse, or scream out, or threaten, or kill, and yet with his help the world *is* changing.

And, just like I did in the Ephesian agora, he has a soldier watching him.

Chapter 21

I'm glad I've had the sense to come plainly dressed today, that gladiator get-up would have scared the poor preacher stiff. Unfortunately they keep shortening my tunic, and now it's above my knees, I must look a state. The kind old man in the Ephesian synagogue wouldn't even look at my ankles, so I hope I don't make this gentleman too uncomfortable. I suppose he's uncomfortable already, standing in front of such a crowd.

All around us people bustle about their business, in soft browns and greens and plain wool, selling, bargaining. Here and there are men in brighter coloured clothes, richer than the rest, and ladies in pairs, too fine to be seen in the street alone. On one side I can see a woman with scarlet lips, blushing cheeks and tight curls, all overdone, exchanging money with a droopy type in a toga. On the other side is a bunch of skinny people like me, with wooden signs round their necks- slaves for sale.

I stand between the preacher and the soldier, listening carefully as he shouts his wares; eternal life. Other people are listening, yet nobody else wants to bother too much with him, not with that soldier glowering a few feet away. It looks like the preacher's had enough, either of talking or being stared at. He prays a quick blessing; "Dear God, please bless these people with your love. Help them learn more about you. Amen." Then he moves aside to shelter in the shade. That's where I join him.

"Are you Abram? Can I ask you something?" He's startled, confused, then he points out;

"I would like to talk, but there's a soldier behind you, watching me. I don't want to put you in danger." I shock myself with an unimpressed grin.

"What, that foot-soldier? I could disarm him in a second."

"You? You're a little... a young lady," he gasps.

"I'm Aysel the gladiatrix. I need to talk to you about Jesus. Where can we talk?"

He purses his lips in disbelief and starts to walk away. I have to hurry to keep up, pleading as I walk.

"All right, that's not the whole truth. I'm a household slave who was forced into the arena. I have to fight for my life in three days, and I'm hopeless." Man, he walks fast! How can he go at such a pace in those ankle-length robes? "I'm going to die and I want make sure I go to the right place afterwards!" I'm sure he can hear me, but that soldier must really have shaken him up.

Ah, he's trying to hurry away from the soldier, who's right behind us as I race after him. It's time to prove I'm no liar. The soldier doesn't expect the feminine manoeuvre Corinthus taught me; a quick high kick, and his gladius is in my hand instead of his.

"Get lost!" I tell him, brandishing the sword. As I throw it back to him and he slinks away, Abram chooses to believe my story. He veers round at once, taking an alley-way, then another, down far from the Capitoline Hill, into an area full of tall brick apartments. I hope I can remember the way back to the stadium- huh, I'm going back, am I?

He leads me round behind a potter's shop, up an outside staircase, and pauses at a plain wooden door. I didn't expect the comforting scent of rotting fish in the heart of the city. It reminds me sharply of my home by the sea and my Mum's firm hand on my shoulder.

"Excuse the smell," Abram whispers. "My neighbour makes garum sauce." There are amphorae of wine stored on the stairs, so the garum business is obviously a good one that pays well enough.

"That's all right, I like garum, and I live by the sea anyway." I give him a smile as he dithers uncertainly at the door. I hope it's an open and honest smile, but I can't be sure. I never had to worry about the faces I pulled as a slave. And the gladiators wouldn't care what I look like, being female is

173

enough of a charm for them. Anyway, the smile works, and he opens the door.

There's a large room inside, cool and smelling of lavender, maybe to mask the fishy smell. It has one door to another room, and a small fire in the middle of it. There's no pretentious wall painting, although the wooden floor's well-scrubbed and neat. The three chairs are plain but smart, with cheerful cushions embroidered with Jewish-style patterns like the neck of Abram's robes.

A young man, younger and skinnier than Secundus, sits on the floor by the fire, mixing egg and soot. Without looking up, he mutters; "Morning, Dad," and takes his home-made ink to a desk in the corner of the room. He's serious and careful, and his tongue pokes out as he concentrates. He's using his ink to write with a rough quill on a well-scraped piece of hide. I wish I could have learned to write too, before I die. I could have written to Mum. Well, there are more important things for me to learn in the next few days, and Abram could be the key. It's hard to believe I've found him, I'd better ask him all I need as quickly as I can.

The old man's in no hurry to spill the beans. He wanders over and places a hand on the young man's shoulder, telling me; "This is Nathan, our youngest son. He translates, and he writes music." He's so proud of his son he can't keep it hidden. "How's the psalm coming on?"

"Nearly translated," the boy replies, as he stops writing to dip his quill in his ink. "It'll be ready when Gaius gets back."

"Why don't you read it now?" his father suggests. "A genuine piece of scripture for our guest?"

The writer looks up politely, and freezes. He takes in my legs and tunic with one eyebrow raised, then the other eyebrow follows as he studies my face, shocked. Half my mouth smiles at him, which seems to put him more at ease, until his father feels he has to add; "This is Aysel; Aysel Pulchra."

174

"The gladiatrix?" Nathan gasps. He's already out of his seat and halfway to the door. "What... what have you brought her here for?" He can't escape; the door's opened, and in it stands a Roman woman, hair braided like Lucina's, in a spotless green stola.

"What indeed?" she asks. "A gladiatrix? Abram?"

"This is my wife, Persis," the old man proclaims without a hint of shyness now. "I can imagine what you're thinking, we don't look like a couple who have anything in common. It's been observed before. She's Roman, I'm Jewish, she's beautiful, I'm plain- and old, now!"

She pinches his cheek with a grin.

"Darling, the gladiatrix asked me to tell her about our Lord, so how could I refuse?" She's not happy at all, she's grimacing like Corinthus' Mum did when I appeared on her doorstep. She's trying to keep calm by spinning, but her hand trembles as she drops the spindle, and when she picks it up again the thread winds back into a tight knot. Obviously she was rich enough once to avoid learning to spin. In a moment I've taken it from her without noticing I did it, and I'm burbling;

"I'm not a warrior, I'm a household slave who was forced to fight. See?" The thread's straight now, the wool teases through my fingers, I don't need to look to wind it on. It's so relaxing, I can almost forget the stress of the circus, the rigorous training, the cursing and pinching I've been getting from the nameless gladiators. And my skill gives Persis the proof that she needs.

"Will you stay for lunch?" she offers. I can't see anything to eat but yesterday's loaf of bread, and the moment I think of staying I'm filled with an uncertain feeling.

"I don't think I should. I have friends who'll get in trouble if I stay away too long."

"Friends? Gladiators?" Abram gaped in surprise. He's not taking me seriously enough.

"Yes! So hurry up and talk."

175

"Fine. I'll tell you the story of how I met Persis..."

"Tell me about Jesus! NOW!" I have the spindle poking his chubby stomach. His eyes are wide, his wife gasps and his son wavers, wondering whether he dares come to his father's rescue. "Sorry. I didn't mean it. But I really don't have much time. There's so much I don't know." I've seen the students near our home sitting at the feet of their Greek tutors, so I sit on the floor in front of the preacher, with the spindle resting in my lap. His wife hands him a stool, and he pats my head.

"Now, then, I'll talk quickly. Persis' father was stationed in Judea, in my home city of Jerusalem. Even then she was the most beautiful woman I'd ever seen." She grins slightly, and waves him on. "But whatever I did, I couldn't persuade her to follow our Jewish God. Our rabbis- our holy men- taught us to be afraid of God, and to hate strangers, particularly the Roman invaders. And then there's the law of circumcision..."

"Abram!" his wife hisses, frowning at her own spinning attempt. "She won't want to hear that!"

"True. So we were trapped. We were very much in love, but that was all we had in common. I don't suppose you understand..." He stops for a second. He's noticed me nodding. His eyebrows rise again- I'm just one big surprise to him. "Do you? Well, God always has a plan. He had a good plan for us. Persis had gone out to the mountain with her friends one day, and I followed her at a distance; you see there was no point in me troubling her any more. And on the hill was a preacher. Yes, it was Jesus.

"We'd heard plenty about him. At first the gossips talked about a preacher who was turning our understanding of the scriptures upside-down, then they started to tell about him doing miracles, healing the sick, making lame men walk, even raising the dead back to life."

"What did he look like?" I inquire as he pauses for breath. I can imagine someone like the mighty statues I saw on

Curetes Street, far away at home, someone powerful and noble-faced- in those stripy Jewish robes, of course.

"Well, he looked like the rest of us do, he had longer hair than the Romans, and a bit of a beard, I think. His appearance was nothing particular, it was the way he talked that I remember. What we heard on the mountain amazed us. This is what I try to teach in the Forum now; he said 'Blessed are the poor in spirit, the kingdom of Heaven is theirs. Blessed are the meek, they will inherit the Earth. Blessed are the peacemakers. They'll be called the sons of God...'"

His son's stopped his work, he's turned round and listens closely, taking in words that I find confusing and hard to believe. Meek people like slaves, inheriting the Earth? How can this boy understand it, when Secundus still follows the pretend gods? Abram's smiling down on both of us.

"You see? He turned the world on its head. Persis became a follower of Jesus at once. She heard how He spoke with authority. She felt his words were straight from the God she'd never met. My heart was harder. I still wanted what the rabbis had promised, a warlike Messiah who would defeat the Romans and establish a Jewish empire here on Earth. Persis hated my anger, and correct me if I'm wrong, dear, but you couldn't see why I didn't think he was the Messiah, the one we Jews had been waiting for."

Persis nods quietly. When I put my hand out, she puts her spindle in it so I can sort out the new knot she's spun. "Finish the story, dear; Gaius will soon be back."

Abram doesn't want to go on, that's clear by his sorrowful face. "Yes, I should. I kept God waiting a long time- but he's patient. I tried to block out all the stories I heard about Jesus. I saw him all over Jerusalem, and in my business in the countryside. I was there at the Feast of the Passover; that's an important Jewish celebration. Some of our leaders accused him of breaking our laws, because he healed someone on the Sabbath- our holy day... Rules, traditions! So they... well, I was in the crowd, shouting out for his death, and they..."

"They killed him by crucifixion," I conclude for the old man across my spinning. "My friend told me. My friend the gladiator." I can see Nathan bursting to ask what a gladiator knows about this man of peace, but he daren't interrupt his father.

"Yes, indeed. When he died, I finally realised something very special had gone out of the world, but that's not the end."

"He came back?" He nods. "I know, he's alive, in here." Man, I've done it again, slammed my fist on my heart. He doesn't mind the soldier's salute, he's smiling in even more surprise. He'd better watch out, an old man probably doesn't need that much shock. "So what happened to you and your wife?"

He throws her the warmest grin, that she returns with such love I'm jealous, and keen to get back and see Secundus. I might only look from a distance, but we only have a couple more days. "Once we both became followers, there was nothing to stop us being together."

"Except my father…"

"And mine! We ran away and came eventually to Rome. Other followers were starting a group here. We left our wealth behind, but we have our treasure in Heaven. God blessed us with three children, and told me to preach in the Forum. I haven't been arrested for it so far, maybe because I'm not very good at it. I don't seem to have that persuasive turn of phrase that our friend Gaius…" He pauses, allowing us to hear the slap of leather on the stone steps outside. "That'll be Gaius now."

He bursts in, a man in his thirties, not noticeably rich or poor, brown-haired with a prominent forehead like the Greeks. He claps Nathan on the arm, and laughs; "Is it finished? Read it to us! Abram, I did it! I stood at the gate to the Circus Maximus and denounced their depravity! As if murdering for entertainment isn't depraved enough, setting women up as gladiators is the final straw! If you'd heard me, calling down fire on the head of that... that gladiatrix! Er, hello."

No-one says a thing. I spin, drop and tease out another stretch of thread. Then another one. I am *so* relieved I didn't wear any armour this morning. The newcomer struggles to see what's embarrassing them into silence. At last he observes; "You have a visitor." Still the silence goes on, until Nathan looks over his writing and catches my eye. His mouth twitches, and he replies;

"Yes. This is Aysel. Aysel Pulchra." Gaius' head twists, then shakes. He steps back in disbelief, and I remember where I've seen him before.

"You were one of the men in Ephesus, in the theatre, you caused a riot. I was there, the gladiators were training." I'm a bit worried he's going to fall over in shock. Can't he see I'm just an ordinary slave in a simple tunic, spinning like any woman in the empire? "I was supposed to be a sacrifice, but my friend Naasir saved my life, and they made me into a..."

"Naasir?" Gaius exclaims. "He didn't meet with us two weeks ago, I wondered why. They put him back in the arena? After so long?" He's talking as if Naasir's a friend of his, too, not just a slave. He practises what he preaches, that everyone is equal. "Couldn't Lucina stop them?"

"She didn't know until it was too late. Listen, Gaius, Abram, he's in the circus now. He only wanted to talk to someone who'd met Jesus. He probably wants to make sure he believes what's right. And we'd welcome someone who can teach us more. Will you come and talk to him? I know it won't be easy."

How can they turn down my request? Both men agree, they'll come if they can. Gaius has been orating at the gate, so he may be able to get into the cells. "Take care you don't get locked in," Nathan smiles, not a very funny joke, but it raises a grim laugh. "Before you go, do you want to hear my translation? It's from the Jewish scriptures, I've put it into Greek."

He has the manuscript on his clean hand; it's only a page, it can't take long. I take another tube of wool, spinning out peace and calm in my worrying heart; it may only be a page from hundreds of years ago, but it turns out it's all about me and my life.

"I love the Lord, for he heard my voice,

He heard my cry for mercy." Nathan's voice is soft and musical as he reads his own angular writing.

"…the cords of death entangled me,

The anguish of the grave came upon me;

I was overcome by trouble and sorrow.

Then I called upon the name of the Lord." I've never heard of a holy book, let alone hearing something read from it. I know so little.

"The Lord protects the simple-hearted;

When I was in great need, He saved me." Very true; dare I hope he'll do it again?

"…For You, O Lord, have delivered my soul from death,

My eyes from tears, my feet from stumbling,

That I may walk before the Lord

In the land of the living." Does he mean in Heaven, where I'll never have to die again? The way Nathan talks, I can almost see that Heaven.

"I believed, even when I said; 'I am greatly afflicted,'

And in my dismay I said; 'All men are liars.'

How can I repay the Lord for all his goodness to me?"

Nathan reads with such conviction. Of course he gets to talk to other followers a lot, when I've only talked to Naasir, until they locked me away from him.

"Precious in the sight of the Lord is the death of His saints.

Oh, Lord, truly I am your servant." I want to hear the young man sing, holy words like this, that must be even more like Heaven than his reading in his melodic voice.

"You have freed me from my chains…

I will fulfil my vows to the Lord

In the presence of all His people,

180

In the courts of the house of the Lord-

In your midst, Oh, Jerusalem..." That bit must be for Naasir, he kept God's law not to kill, and told everyone in the Ephesian stadium about him. There's so much I need to learn, and so little time. Nathan's finished, the lullaby of his voice stops. His father claps briefly, Gaius puts a hand on his shoulder, Persis smiles at him. I put down the spindle and leave them smiling. Behind me they're praying that God will protect me, and hugging each other.

I head back to the only home I have. My head can hardly believe what my feet are doing. I'm walking back to my death of my own free will, and it doesn't matter where I go after death, the dying bit's still a terrifying idea. The thought that I might survive almost makes me laugh aloud. But I'm not running away, I'm not letting Naasir think I've gone off with Flavius' crowd like Kiral.

I stand at the gate to the arena. The stone arches tower above me, the sandy race track stretches out before me, divided by a central row of idols and temples. Inside, seventy men spar with wooden practice weapons, stabbing and cursing, rolling in the dirt, throwing punches. Right in front of me one of them is led out by two soldiers, one of them carrying a tall whip. I've arrived just in time.

"Jupiter, Juno and Mars!" Corinthus my trainer stops, staring through the gate. "Never! What in the name of all the gods...!" I have to look twice; they're not punishing the man I imagined.

"Leave Kiral, and I'll come in," I shout. The lanista's hopping from one foot to the other. I was his poster girl, and he thought I was gone. "What are you doing with him?"

"Ah, nothing. Let him go, the girl's come back. Open the gates." The soldier with the whip drops it to let me in, and Kiral leads me back to Corinthus' little group of half-baked warriors.

"Flavius didn't buy you?" I inquire.

"No. Absolute liar! Where've you been?"

181

"Hunting the truth," I reply. Poor man, so lonely and friendless he had to come back here! In our little band we find Naasir, who's as shocked as the rest are to see me. My friend's unscathed, and keen to hear where I've been. "I found a man who met Jesus- his wife did, too. He's coming here, if he can. And I found Gaius, who knew you in Ephesus. They read me some holy stuff. Scripts?"

"Scriptures?" Yes, that was it. Naasir's more pleased and excited than I ever would have guessed. As they drag him back into the training session, he shakes my hand like a man, and whispers; "That was my last wish."

Chapter 22

An hour yesterday, in the company of honest, clean people, felt like a day, or more. The vision of Heaven is still in my head, bright as the sun and bigger than the sky. This place is the total opposite; nothing's clean, not even the drinking cup we share when the sun beats relentlessly during our training. The cells are black as ash, cool but damp; superstitious snakes are drawn on the walls, to give the gladiators luck in battle but misery in sleep. At least my cell's empty, until the noxii come in tonight. I have no idea who they'll be, but Secundus has already stolen a knife for me to keep under my pillow. Prisoners of war, enemies of the state, untrainable, undisciplined- I'm glad I got some sleep last night, despite the oppression of the darkness, because I don't think I will tonight.

Since I shocked them all by coming back, Corinthus has decided I really want to be a part of his little troop. Yesterday he mounted a sudden campaign to teach me survival skills.

"Try this," he was yelling, "and you might survive. I'll teach you more before the next time."

"Next time?"

"Yes. You needn't fight more than once a year, if we advertise you well enough. Think of the future, freedom, wine, clothes, a villa!" I haven't mentioned that I want none of those things, not if it means killing another person. I'm happy to learn the survival skills, although it's left me aching in every part of my body.

Yesterday was all about the hips, the weapon he says the men don't use and don't know how to fight. He taught me to swing a shield, duck under it, to throw a man over it, onto the ground behind me. It was almost fun; he picked Secundus to spar with me, and I threw him onto the sand time and again. The first few times he jumped up, grinning, then it got tiring, but he wouldn't let me stop learning. So he started doing dramatic falls, even a death scene that was so over-the-top it actually made me smile. Corinthus responded as he always does; "Dumb paegniarius! Don't think I'm betting on you!"

We couldn't talk much while we were training, and there's not much I could have said. To ask him, "Hold me like you did in Ephesus," would be a bit misleading, particularly after he pointed out that we were fighting the way he and his brother always used to. So we sparred as friends; he could be a very good friend, if we had more than the next two or three days.

After Secundus, Takis was sent over to help me out. I remember he's the one who just got married; he wears her wedding veil as a scarf, it's getting tattered already. When we were at the temple he was really rattled by that soothsayer saying he should keep out of battle. According to Naasir's rules he could be my friend, a comrade-in-arms.

It was Takis' job to be thrown over my back. Corinthus taught me how to duck in five different ways, and I had to try them all on the unlucky groom. He took it with surprisingly good humour, considering he'd been on edge since the moment I met him. He gave more aggression when the lanista demanded it, but never enough to harm me.

"Lay it on harder!" Corinthus was screaming in the end. "Where's Takis the Vulture?" The gladiator got up, stretched his aching arms until he reached his full, impressive size. He thought for a moment, with his head on one side. Then he answered softly;

"I'm changing my name. I won't be the Vulture any more."

"Right! What are you now?" The way he stared into Takis' eyes, I had a feeling he knew what was coming, though I couldn't guess.

"Takis Christianus."

Corinthus face-palmed. He cursed as he had when I came back here, and shook his fist in Naasir's direction, muttering;

"Wretched one-man plague!   Takis, you'll fight to kill, or you'll be whipped into it!"

"I know, sir, I'm not stupid."

"Are you sure about that?"   He stormed away for a few minutes, giving us a brief rest. Takis hissed at me not to congratulate him on his transformation, he knew it'll likely end in his death, and he didn't want me to get into trouble. I drank some muggy water, amazed at Naasir and his powerful words, still more amazed that these sort of things could happen in this horrible kind of place. I might have known what my friend was doing, all those nights I've been locked away from him in another cell.

"So you *are* a friend?" I asked him, simply.   He nodded. And he was taken away, to be replaced with someone who'd fight me more fiercely.

Achlus has changed his fighting style; he's taken to fighting as a retiarius, that way he's the one with the trident, so he can avoid being attacked by one, as the soothsayer advised him. That aggravating little man has rattled a lot of the gladiators, one or two found ways to visit him again and find out what Naasir had prevented them from hearing.   They weren't too happy when they were brought back.

Achlus; I keep wanting to call him Oknus. He's awkward with me, as Naasir said Oknus was, though he's the only other member of Corinthus' group that I know at all.   When he looks at me with an uncertain face, I see Oknus' black beard poking upwards, the way he lay when he breathed his last. But he's Achlus, alive and tough; I've watched him fighting other men, hacking recklessly, like he has nothing to lose. Even when the trainer yelled yesterday, he couldn't hack into me like that.   Maybe he has a child of his own who Naasir hasn't been able to mention to me.

Achlus and I beat up the stuffed dummy till the sun started to sink.   Now that I have arm muscles and the strength to thrust a weapon, stabbing into the straw felt good. Achlus praised me for it, so I stabbed over and over, faster each time.

185

I see what Naasir meant when he said it might be dangerous for me to train.   Still, who actually *wants* to die?   And training is my best chance of avoiding it.

So I woke up this morning, aching all over, stretched away the strain, and knelt below my stone window to pray, with a grain of hope, in spite of the vast number of unknown gladiators outside.   I strapped on my armour, ready for one last day of rigorous training.

Instead, they've taken me away from the drill ground, through a tall iron gate and down to a new place, where the smell's even worse than above.   There are more cells, with more strong gates.   The first has a face leaning over it, a long, hairy animal face, high above my head.   It scares me stiff for a while.

"That's a giraffe," says my guide.   He reaches up his hand, and the animal's head leans down on a gigantic neck to lick him with a long, black tongue.   Through the bars I can see its legs are enormously long, too, and its skin's the colour of egg yolk, mottled with brown.

The giraffe lifts its neck up again, to some leaves tied on a hook by the door.   The word 'majestic' comes into my head; I don't know where I've learned that from.   This creature ought to be out in the wilderness, maybe somewhere beyond the walls of Ephesus, eating from tall trees and galloping-how fast could it gallop, with those legs?   Not fast enough to outrun the might of Rome, obviously.

"What's it here for?"

"The same as everything else.   It's here to be hunted and killed.   We have three."   The other two are next door, one's small and looks like a young one; I'm certain of that when I see it bend to drink from its mother.   I feel a connection with these poor creatures, we're all here to die, but at least I'm an adult, unlike the little giraffe.

"Are they fierce?"

"No! Look, they eat leaves!"   My guide leads me on, past two stalls which are covered with cloth.   From behind one I hear a low growl I recognise; lions, not just one, but three at least. The hope I woke with starts to fade. Opposite them is a line of horses, quietly munching from troughs of hay. They look as innocent as any work-horse down at the docks, but a groom's brushing one until its coat shines, and another man's testing out some headgear, a huge, showy plume surrounded by metal spikes.

A blast like a trumpet throws me against the wall. My guide laughs at my wide eyes, and announces; "Elephants. Come and see them." I've seen pictures, but they don't give you a true sense of elephants; they're so big they fill their stalls with scarcely space to move. Their tough grey hide is in keeping with this dark, stone place, but their fan-like ears and small black eyes make them look sweet and sorrowful.

The elephant in front of me reaches out- with its trunk. I must admit to being scared, slightly, until my guide reaches out his hand to stroke it. It beats having a sharp trident pointed at me, anyway. The elephant uses its long trunk to sniff me; that can't be a pleasant smell. I force myself to stand tall, like a gladiator waiting for the death blow in his throat, while the trunk plays with my plaits; it's probably best not to show fear.

"This is Chica," the man tells me, scratching the trunk. "She's a parade elephant. You two are going to lead the parade." What? He explains as well as he can manage; "They say that Julius Caesar had a parade to the Senate with elephants and torches, so Nero wants one. You'd think he was Caesar already, the things he demands. Chica can carry a torch in her trunk, and they want the goddess Victory to ride on her back."

"That's me?" I joke.

"Yes. They've got you wings and everything."

"So I've heard. I can't wait." So I've got this new trick to learn, and as usual there's no way out. He's opening the gate, leading her out on a rope, whispering in her ear. She's enormous, one wrong step and she could smash me against

187

the wall. He throws a heavy saddle up across her back, and she doesn't flinch. Then he gestures for me to climb up.

It takes so long for me to pluck up the courage, and then the balance, that by the time I'm on her back any sign of breakfast's been cleared away ages ago. That hardly matters; it's so worthwhile when I'm led into the arena. Now the men's heads turn, now they stop laughing at me, now I'm the one looking down on everyone.

And I look pretty stupid when I fall off. And I'm admired again when Chica reaches down her trunk and scoops me back onto her neck. I whisper thanks in her giant ear, I hope she understands. At least she walks gently with me, while I try to scramble to my feet. It can't be much harder than fighting on the deck of a ship in high winds.

It drives me mad, to see those men practising below me, when I can't practise any more. I concentrate on what Naasir told me; "Whatever your hand finds to do, do it with all your might." So I'm determined to make the gentle elephant my friend. I stroke her and sing in her ear until she seems quite at ease with me. My guide and trainer's pleased with my progress, and lets me ride her all around the race track.

"She's a good kid, she'll do as she's told," he promises his boss. Is that what he thinks? While I ride I'm looking for any clues in the arena to help us in the next two dreadful days. The building could be part of our game plan, if I ever get to exchange more than two words with Naasir.

I spend the rest of the day with the elephant, since they're obviously not going to train me any more. I take my bread and cheese down to eat with her; it's good to be with another female at last. And just for good measure, I dare to befriend the elephants either side of her. If we're going to parade through Rome together in the morning, we might as well get along. Being in their uncomplicated company helps me forget the lust and greed I'm surrounded by. I even find myself talking to Chica, telling her where I came from, wondering aloud if my mysterious father's been told where

I've gone, and if he'll miss me. She curls her trunk over my shoulder, and snaffles a chunk of bread. She can have it, thinking of home I've lost my appetite.

The sun's setting over the stone oval of the arena, the day before the games. Outside, in the mighty city they call the centre of the world, free men and women will be picking out fresh clothes to wear on their holiday to watch the games, careless of the fact that men's lives are going to be put to a complete stop just for their entertainment. I'm glad the elephants won't be made to fight, they're too calm and gentle to deserve that, gentler than I've become in the last few days.

So I snuggle close to the locked door of her stall, and whisper. "Chica, I feel so angry with the men who put me here. I feel like I've only got one kind thought left in me. I love someone I just can't be with. He's probably going to die tomorrow." She rustles my hair again, although she knows I've got no food.

Quick footsteps on the stairs stir me from my daydream. Secundus is here, looking for me. He's dressed in a clean blue tunic without a trace of armour, and his hair actually looks clean. If I could just run a hand over it- no, that's just part of the gladiator charm.

"Time for the party," he grins, and holds out his hand to me. I can't take it, and I'm certainly not in the mood for a party; but I still have some curiosity left, so I follow him out of the menagerie, out through the cells and training ground to the arena.

The sand is being raked, ready for morning, and in the royal box close to the track edge slaves are hanging purple curtains. Surrounded by these grim reminders of the coming games, Secundus lets out an angry snort. I wonder what he could possibly find funny right now.

"The Emperor's nephew's coming with all his posh hangers-on, to watch a show that's totally unrehearsed! He could go to the theatre and get something a lot funnier, and more professional!"

189

"So could you," I point out, "instead of working here."

"I could, and I'm going to, if I live." He faces the box where they're now draping garlands round the stone pillars, holds up his hand in salute and sneers; "Moritori te salutant!"

"What's that?"

"It's what we say before we fight. 'Those about to die salute you.' Everything's better with some rehearsal. Still, tonight it's more like 'those about to stuff their faces salute you...' Are you ready to eat?"

I can't help pointing out that the gladiators seem to eat a very large amount. Secundus agrees readily.

"That's our last defence; if your stomach's full it's harder for your enemy to injure your vital organs."

"I see. So that's why you're all a bit paunchy?"

"I am not paunchy!" he replied indignantly. Then, before I can apologise, he laughs; "Not yet, anyway. Wait till after the party!" Despite everything, he makes me laugh aloud. It still surprises me how all these men can cast off any thought of dying tomorrow and laugh and party as if they'll live for ever.

We pass the little temple built on the dividing wall in the centre of the track. Metal brackets hold huge torches; they flicker weakly against the sun at twilight, though they'll be all that lights us back to the cells later. Secundus stares up at the temple; he has a comment on most things tonight, including that.

"All hail Jupiter, boss of gods! He never proved much use to me or my family. They can burn those torches, but he won't listen. There he stands, stony-faced. Get it, stony-faced?"

I laugh with him, before I remember my new life. "I shouldn't insult the gods, really..."

"No, I suppose not. I can imagine what Naasir would say. But they are useless, it's good to have found a new way." Yes, it is, I was fortunate to land here with Naasir... Hang on, it didn't sound like he was talking about me... Secundus has stopped short, with sudden alarm on his face.

190

On some of the arena walls posters are hung, some with chariot pictures and lists of names, a few with pictures of gladiators. Secundus stares at one, and raises an eyebrow. He must still love this game, if he stops every time he sees his name published. But when he walks away his usual grin has gone.

"Does it say something bad about you?" I wonder.

"Yes."

"What?"

"You'll find out soon enough." His voice is strangely quiet. I want to press him to tell me, but he snaps back into a fake cheery mood, waves a hand at the door in the arena wall, and announces; "Here we are!"

Chapter 23

We walk near the front gate of the Circus Maximus, where the chariots will enter tomorrow afternoon. Close by is a door which leads beneath the raked wooden seating. In the space below, facing out into the city, shops are being set up in the twilight. Tomorrow they'll selling bread and meat, pastries, baskets, souvenirs in yellows and greens for people to remember their racing teams.

There's a large room beneath the seating, low and cosy at one side, tall and echoing at the other. The room's completely built of wood, yet there are candles in every corner and on the long tables in the centre. Before I enter I can hear the music of a trio of shawms, loud and harsh, with drums beating breathlessly. The beat fills the air with noise and excitement that feels forced and fairly desperate. The musicians' message is clear; you *are* having fun, you *must* enjoy this evening, we'll drown out any sane thoughts you dare to think.

Cluttering round the door as we squeeze in, there's a crowd of women as unlike me as you could get. They're cleaned, polished and pampered, stinking strongly of perfume, with curled wigs and thin stolas draped to show their shape to the best advantage. They're all coated in chalk and painted as thickly as I was when Drusa and her girls sent me into the arena in Ephesus.

The moment we arrive they surround Secundus with no sign of shyness. He has hands stroking through his hair, more tapping his shoulders for attention, and more stroking his chest while the girls drool over the muscles beneath his neat tunic. I saw them do the same in Ephesus, drawn by the gladiators' charm and fame. He handled it calmly, smiling at all of them, waving, whispering in their ears. Then he sent them off graciously like some young king. He was well-named Amator, looking at these girls now, thinking they're madly in love.

This time he's frozen. For the first time I witness him uncomfortable in an audience. He tries to push their hands away, tells them sharply that he's not interested in what they're selling. They don't believe him, they only think he's playing hard-to-get. In fact I'm sure he's looking at me to help him. Weird.

One glance at my dirty legs, sandy short tunic and macho breastplate shows me how unattractive I am compared to these women. So what, if he needs help? I grab the closest woman by the shoulder and spin her round. Feeling the firm hand of a gladiator, she cuddles straight up to my breastplate. Then she senses the ridiculous shape of it and steps back with a screech.

Her colleagues stop pawing at their handsome young man for a second, to stare at me.

"Heh, it's the girl! She's one for the boss, call him over!"

"Nice breastplate!"

"Think you're tough, do you, girly?"

I square up to them, ready to show them how tough I am. But I've been working on my self-control, and I recognise now that it'd be better to diffuse the argument before it begins.

"No, I'm not tough, not really," I tell the women. That takes some wind out of their sails. "But I'm not interested, and he's not interested, that's all." One of them gives us both a knowing glance, whatever she thinks she knows, trying to think up a witty comment; I know that look, I often use it myself, and I can never come up with the witty thing. Fortunately the women see someone else coming, a darker-skinned, older man with a forbidding face and fearsome scar; they step quickly away from us, and him, and move on to another gladiator. "Naasir, finally we can talk!"

I'm pleased he's missed me too. He folds me in a hug at once, just a quick, polite one. At the same time I spot a new expression on Secundus' face that I can hardly believe; it's the jealous glance I was using a moment ago when those women were all over him. The pressure of tomorrow's battle must be driving us all mad.

A stranger in a toga steps up and takes Secundus' arm. "This is my lawyer," he explains. "Excuse me." And he's gone again, leaving us two in peace to talk. It's just as well I don't expect Naasir to sit down with me for a quiet chat, or I'd be disappointed.

"Come and eat," he orders. When I insist I don't feel like much, he shoves a bowl into my hand and tells me firmly; "Look as if you are. Then we can circulate. You wanted a plan of campaign?"

"Yes!" At last, we can talk plainly, and he has ideas. His plan worked last time, so maybe there's hope again. I grasp the bowl and look over the long tables that groan with food. There's some sort of porridgy stuff I think I should be able to manage; I slop a gloopy ladle full of it into my bowl. Before it comes near my mouth, I can smell honey and cheese. In porridge? Maybe I can disguise the strange smell with a dash of garum, the spicy taste of the sea. Or maybe not. I have to eat it; it's actually a taste which isn't too hard to get used to.

Naasir's drawing me further along the table; I've missed the chance of grabbing grapes and broad beans and nuts, the sort of food that's more than fancy enough for the taste buds of a slave. Now I recognise patina, the same Aunt Yildiz cooks for Master Panaius whenever jellyfish is available. The egg in it's too rich for me, and the jellyfish is undercooked. Not as undercooked as the next plate, though. "What are those?"

"Bits of a bull," Naasir sniffs, turning away. They're round and squishy, and floating in a suspiciously red sauce.

"Which bits?"

"Don't ask. They're meant to give you courage in battle, but these'll only give you a bad stomach, they're still oozing blood." All right, I turn away from them too. I have to warn Secundus, though, he's just put three in his bowl. "Sh, don't talk to him. You don't want the others to think we're a team."

"Are we?"

"Of course. But look over there." I peer over the light of the candles into a gloomy corner. There sits the man with the blond plaits, in a cluster of other pale-haired men; he's bigger than any of them. "That's the chief. No-one else speaks his language, but he's from the North. See how his men serve him? They'll stick with him in battle."

"So should we try and split them up?"

"That wouldn't work. We're better off befriending him. When I pass him, I give him a little bow, as I would to our master. You should try that, it won't do any harm." I've downed the sticky porridge while I watched the pale-haired men pouring drinks for their lord and checking his plate's full. In the middle of the table is something I'm convinced is goat. I've never tried it, so I may as well, if I can reach that far.

"And look behind us now," Naasir orders.

The goat will have to wait. I turn, to see the tall, dark Roman I've been trying to study in training.

"He's the augur," I know. Like the northern chief, he has his followers, all in awe of his skill in telling the future in a time-honoured way. Basically, he's a bird-watcher, in his spare time away from the arena.

"Good. I've talked to him a lot. He thinks I'm a joke; I hope I get the chance to prove him wrong. But he loves the old traditions, like valuing women. He hates Corinthus for putting you in the arena, so I don't think you'll have much trouble from him. Remember to give him a little bow, too. Look closely at the men around him; they're unlikely to harm you, either."

"What about you?"

"They know I'm only trying to protect you. With their help, I might stand a chance of keeping you alive." That's comforting to hear, but has he realised that, when I came back for him, I didn't intend to leave this place without him? I'm distracted by some finger-sized things, plain, brown and shrivelled. They look pathetic, and yet they're displayed on a plate with leaves as if they're something special. "Duck's tongues. Not bad."

I decide to risk one. It's chewy. Still, it looks better than the next dish; "That's gross. It looks like… hm…"

"Brains; in eggs, of course."

"Naasir, seriously?" It must be another symbol of making the gladiators strong for the fight. Across the table, Secundus is really going for the paunchy look; I'm sure he's taken another three of those disgusting bull's bits. I have a sudden vision of a wife struggling in his kitchen to undercook those for him. It's swiftly followed by a vision of his tombstone. I have to shake that out of my head.

"Heh, I noticed the men with spears like to side with the augur."

"They do, you're right. If you can get behind them, he may get them to shield you." I agree, though I'm not at all happy with how he focuses everything on me. Hasn't he given any thought to his own escape?

"Now, you remember Takis?" Of course I do.

"He wears his wife's wedding veil as a scarf." Naasir nods, and begins to explain;

"I've been talking…" At the same time I add;

"He's calling himself Takis Christianus."

"Ah, you've heard! I didn't know he was going to tell anyone." Quickly I whisper what was said in our training yesterday, openly, to our lanista. Naasir's impressed; he confesses he didn't know if Takis had meant it when he promised to follow our God. "Keep eating, or we'll look suspicious. I should leave you, really."

"Don't." Pumpkin with rose petals is the last thing I think I can manage; I help myself slowly as I look around. "You haven't mentioned the animals." He looks blank. "A man showed me round the menagerie. There are giraffes."

"Giraffes?" he grimaces. "Oh, that's cruel!" I reassure him they're amazingly tall, but not meant to be aggressive. "True.

I mean it's cruel to the giraffes; to hunt them, for sport. What else?"

"There are two stalls full of lions. I couldn't see them, but I'm sure there are more than three."

"Lions, or lionesses?" he demands. I don't know; does it make any difference? "Lions, like the one you met, are more passive; the lionesses do the hunting, in the wild. They'd be worse. I don't know enough about fighting animals. Maybe we won't have to; maybe they're for the bestiarii. Corinthus used to be a bestiarius. That's what they'll be for."

He nods clearly at me, trying to make me think that'll be the truth. It's no use, we've met the seventy gladiators, and none of them specialise in fighting animals. "I'll try to find out what sort they are," I offer.

"I'll do that. Now we should split up," he sighs in response. "We'll talk more later."

At once he merges into the crowd of gladiators, lawyers, families and random women. Once he's a couple of feet away, he wouldn't hear me at all, the musicians are blasting out such a loud tune. Looking about me at the colours lit by the flickering candles, at a sea of faces talking, hugging, dancing, I could imagine this is just a party... except that slaves never go to parties... so it could be a celebration of my freedom, not a last meal for most of the men in the room.

I daren't stop to think again. I must try what Naasir suggested, and pass by that chief so I can give him a little bow. He looks regal enough, holding his head high as if he wore a rich fur collar and a gold necklace. I'm sure he must have been stripped of all his wealth when the Romans took him captive, but they didn't get his nobility. He's perched on a stool as if it's a throne, and he casts his eye across the room like a monarch studying his courtiers. I pick up a tankard to take to the weak ale near his seat; as I go, I nod deeply in his direction, then raise my head to go on.

He gazes straight at me, directly into my eyes. He has a stern, solemn face, and I've hardly ever seen a blond-haired man before, so I stare back. A step later, I'm bowing more deeply, while his followers watch me with interest. He puts out his hand, and says something soft that I don't understand. Whatever he wants, it seems sensible to take the hand. If I were asking my mistress for help or leniency, I imagine I'd kneel before her and kiss the hand she offered, so that's what I do.

The followers are nodding. Their chief's eyes are locked on me; I don't know what he sees, but somehow I have a horrible feeling he can sense the fear I've been trying to hide. Is it one of his men who'll chase me in their checked trousers and spit me on their sword? Which one might it be? None of them look straight at me as he does. His mouth twitches in an expression of regret, and he puts his other hand on my head. It's heavy and warm and comforts me; my death won't come from him.

I wave the tankard I've brought for ale, and he takes his hand away, allowing me to leave. At the keg of ale I find Secundus filling his own drink. Isn't he on the strong stuff, like the wine? I was sure he was a bit of a drinker. As Naasir instructed, I don't talk to him; he's looking round for someone else, anyway, and behind me is Achlus. Of course he has no trident tonight, although he's flexing his hands as if he wished he had one for security. Instead of saying 'hello,' he can only manage; "Er..."

"Achlus," I nod. "Good food?"

"Not bad," he tells me. He clearly has more to say, because he doesn't move away.

"What's up?" I don't want to be rude, but I wanted to reach the augur and nod in his direction, just in case it helps, and Achlus is getting in my way. "Time's short."

The gives him the impetus to carry on. "Aysel.... Have you ever thought about marriage?"

"No, not really. I've always been a slave, I wouldn't get a choice. And now, with the games tomorrow... There's really no point thinking about the future." A daft conversation to be having tonight!

"But if you did...?" he prompts. I can't see any sense in this. He's just a newcomer, he won't be able to beat seasoned gladiators, why would he bother talking about the future? Ah, yes, I do see what he's getting at, though it's hard to believe. What can I say? Nothing offensive. But I shouldn't lie.

"I... erm... I'm thinking of it now." Oh no, he's smiling, that's awkward.

"You are? I've always been a slave, too, but I'm trying to win my freedom."

"Good for you. Erm, this breastplate isn't my real shape, you know!" That's enough to make his eyebrows rise. I sip some of my drink, unsure how to escape him without causing offense. I don't need to; four more men are waiting impatiently to get to the drinks table. They're some of the damnatii, criminals turned gladiator, unwashed and growing angry.

"Oy!" one of them butts in. "Get out of the way, kid!" Achlus tries to protest that they should treat me politely; their sneering laugh's louder than the shawms blaring out their music across the room.

"Think you're hard, Achlus? I've got a spear with your name on it!" He pushes his comrade forward, jeering; "Look who you're fighting tomorrow, Achlus! Might as well lance yourself through right now!"

"I'll help you!" the opponent suggests. "Doubt you'd manage it!"

"Leave him!" I venture; I'm good at saying that, particularly in my sleep.

"Shut it, little girl!"

"Yeah, you're in a man's world now! Did you ever think you could fight with us?" No, of course I didn't, I'm trapped. I could try to fight my way out of their threatening circle, or duck under their legs. I'm shaking already, torn between fear and the urge to lash out. "Nothing to say? You know I'm going to spit you on my trident?"

"No, give her a proper man, me! After that, you can feel my knife…" The ringleader has a real iron knife in his hand, he brushes it across my neck. What if I fight back and he accidentally kills me? That'd save Naasir some worry. I raise my hands to fight, and clear my throat to scream.

-Tell them where you're going if you die.

Hm!

"I was forced to come here and fight, just like you. When you kill me, I'm going to a beautiful Heaven where I'll see God face to face and I'll never die again."

They're stepping away.

"Tonight I'll pray that God'll let you in to Heaven, too."

One of them's still brandishing his knife.

"God never made us to kill, death robs you of the people you love. This isn't a man's world, it's an evil world. This world is what we should be fighting, and I don't mean with weapons!"

The damnatii are gaping; the augur's there, too, and that Flavius, our lanista's wedding guest. I give each of them a nod, which they both answer respectfully. In the sudden silence a hand reaches through the crowd to grab mine; Secundus.

"They're here!" he hisses. I don't get it, but I follow him. I'm very to escape. "Come and meet them."

"Who's here?"

"My family, all of them! They heard I was in Rome, so they came over from Pompeii just to see me! You have to meet them!"

Chapter 24

I can see how the play-acting runs in the family. Secundus'
father stands in the large doorway to the outside world, with
the dramatic peach of the twilit sky behind him, as if he's
about to open a scene in a drama. He wears a well-draped and
well-worn toga and stands in a classic Roman pose. Beside
him stands his older son, bare legs astride, in tall red boots.
Before moving forward, he surveys his audience, turning his
finely-chiselled face towards the candlelight.

Secundus' mother holds her husband's hand and looks up at
him, afraid of the miserable setting and the rough company.
Now I can see where he gets his good looks. His mother's
hair isn't piled in fashionable curls, it just hangs down her
back with the sides tied up roughly; her stola's of plain wool
and she wears no make-up at all; but I think she could knock
spots off Lucina, or Drusa, or even my own Mum... I wish I
could have had one last little hug from her before I left
Ephesus.

Secundus has already greeted them, and now he introduces
me, friendly as always. "This is my Dad, my Mum, and
Primus. Everyone, this is Aysel, the Unwilling Gladiatrix."

I try to throw off the horror of the damnatii mocking me, to
grin at all the family. Again I get to see citizens treating me
as an equal, I may never get used to it. Here I am, being
introduced like the hero in a play, and they're shaking my
hand as if I'm much more than a plain slave.

Primus takes my hand and kisses it; he's a hand shorter than
his brother, his eyes are darker, and flash playfully. He makes
no pretence of looking over my outfit with the stupidly short
tunic that shows most of my legs. His eyes rest on the new
panels of leather hanging like a skirt to give me a hint of
protection, then on the breastplate that's ornamented in
embarrassing places and several sizes too large. Today the
shoulder plates were taken off, so it's easier to move in, but

leaves me feeling more exposed, particularly under his admiring gaze.

"Ha!" he laughs, trying to whisper; his voice projects easily through the talk and the music. "I see what you mean, Sec, quite impressive! Do I get first refusal?"

His father brushes him away, pretending to cover his eyes with a chuckle. "Excuse him, my dear. He was born with natural charm; I can't think where he gets it from." Primus' laugh tells me that's a family joke that doesn't offend him at all.

"I didn't get it from you, Dad! C'mon, Sec, where's the food?" Now I'm trapped in their little group, and it's a much more cheerful group than the damnatii make. They're all so clearly delighted to be back together, his family have missed Secundus and aren't afraid of showing their affection.

Secundus passes his brother a duck's tongue to chew; it doesn't stop Primus from talking out of the side of his mouth. "Woah, they've gone a bit over the top here! A whole goat? Mind you, look at the size of these guys, they'll murder it. Excuse the pun." He looks expectantly at Secundus. "I suppose you'll say it's not murder in the arena, just a contest. Heh?" When he gets no response, despite his prompting, he appeals to me; "How's the goat? Have you tried it?"

A quick shake of my head and he's loading my bowl with slices of meat. After years of cooking goat in our kitchen, basting it, smelling it, then handing it over for the master's table, I finally get to taste it. It's good, much better cooked than those bull's things that must have been done by an apprentice. One glance at the blood still oozing from them, and my stomach wrenches.

Secundus is thinking about something tricky. His father exchanges a glance with Primus, looks suspiciously back at me for a second, then presses on with the cheery banter.

"Brains? Lovely, did you try them?"

"They're chewy," Secundus replies. "Supposedly they enhance your reactions in... in battle. Mum, try the omelette, it's fresh, I think you'll like that." He passes her a plate, and absently watches the women who thronged him before, now surrounding Primus in curiosity. Primus is quite comfortable with their attention; he pinches their cheeks and wraps his arms round them, complimenting their gowns and letting it slip casually that he's an actor. That's enough celebrity for them, once they know he appears in public they won't leave him alone. So he willingly sits down to tell them stories about an actor's life in Pompeii, the most beautiful town in the Empire.

That leaves Secundus to talk to his parents more quietly, and he loses no more time getting down to business. "Dad, I've settled things with my lawyer. There's nearly enough in my account to buy the Odeum, if it's still for sale. I've been away a while, I suppose it..."

"It's still for sale," his father assures him. "With you raising all this money for us, we were thinking of renaming it The Secundeon... But we don't want our patrons to think we're second-best to the Pompeium!" He's about to make another cheerful quip; instead he puts a hand on his Secundus' shoulder and asks; "What's wrong, son? Last time we saw you, you were raring for the next fight."

I want to know what's wrong as well; I want to be the one comforting him, but it's not my place. So I shove a heavy bench closer to them, allowing them to sit down and talk. It's not much in the way of protection, but I stand behind them and cross my arms over my chest, watching so no-one disturbs them.

"Come on, son, what's changed?"

"A lot's changed," Secundus tells his parents. "It's different this time. You remember how it was. I didn't care much about my life, after Tertia died." Who was Tertia? I see his parents bow their heads, and his father wraps an arm round his mother's shoulder. Her name means Third, she must have been his little sister.

"I know," says his father. "We all took it differently, but you were very angry. You didn't need to run off and do this..." He pauses as his wife nods at her younger son, showing she understands how he must have felt. His father raises his hands and waves them up and down, stuttering; "But now, you look... well, you almost look afraid! What's the big difference?"

"Hush," whispers his mother. "Give him a chance to speak."

Secundus is silent for one more moment, then he confesses gently; "I've found something to live for. Two reasons, actually." I try not to listen to his voice right below my head; I sip my ale and study the bright costumes of the musicians at the other side of the room. His voice is the only thing keeping me awake, I never want to stop hearing it, and I wonder what he's getting at. "I've written you a letter, the lawyer's got it, in case I... you know... Are you coming to watch?"

His father looks questioningly at his mother; her eyes widening in fright are the only clue he needs to read his wife's mind and reply;

"No, son, not this time. Maybe another..." There's unlikely to be another time. "Tell us your reasons to live, it might help your Mum feel better about the fighting. Can I guess one reason?" Secundus shrugs and opens his hands. "Is it your little guardian, standing behind us?"

I'm saying nothing, pretending I'm not there. I can't see Secundus' face, I don't know what message it conveys to the father who's known him all his life. I've only known him two weeks, I can't mean anything to him, he can't think I and my frosty friendship make up a reason for life. "Dad, you believe in fortune tellers and soothsayers and stuff, don't you?"

"I'm not sure about them, the gods never did anything for me..." he answers cagily. Here we go, Secundus' beliefs are exactly why I have to keep my distance, emotionally at least.

"Good point. Well, we went to make a sacrifice at the temple, and we met a soothsayer. He knew all our names; that was something unusual, a bit of proof, maybe. Anyway, he told me that they nicknamed me 'The Lover', but my love was misplaced."

At last his mother speaks up. "Son, if you've found love in this horrible, horrible world, you shouldn't let someone like that stop you." He nods quietly.

"Mum, I knew you'd say that. You're right, I had to think about it for a long time, then I realised he wasn't talking about regular love, he meant following the gods."

"You never did follow any gods!" his father retorts, hopefully.

"I sort of did, when I realised in Ephesus that I was likely to die. But there was an old gladiator in the cells- that African man over there, pouring wine for our lanista. His name's Naasir, and he follows a new God. No, make that an old God, the one that made the world, the only One."

"Funny idea!" his father laughs. "A god with a monopoly on godliness! Who made this one up?" His Mum's more serious, she's watching her son's face and mirroring a reverent expression.

Secundus points at Naasir again. "If it wasn't dark as sin in here, you could see Naasir has a scar that runs down his head and neck. When he first learned about this God, he realised murder is evil and he had to stop killing. Unfortunately that was in the middle of a fight. His opponent dealt him the death blow."

"But he's still here," his father splutters. He's glad to take the cup of ale Naasir passes him on his way back to talk to Corinthus. "How in the name of Juno…?"

"A servant of God put his hands on him and prayed. Now he lives to serve God; you know that's traditional when someone saves your life." His mother nods again, and squeezes his hands in her own. She shivers slightly, and Secundus holds her waist beneath his father's arm. I like how their family works, it reminds me sharply that there's real life and love going on outside these gates. If I keep quiet I might hear more of Secundus' incredible news. I concentrate on the door we came in, and the door they came in, could there possibly be a way through here out of the circus? The doors are thick...

His mother wants to hear more, too. "So if you're injured, and you leave the old gods for this new one, will you be miraculously healed?" she inquires.

"I don't know, Mum. It'd be good to think so, but I doubt it. The point is, if I die I'll go to be with God. With God, Mum! I can't describe it. Dad, I'm not kidding. How many times did the Roman gods ever speak to you, actually speak to you?" His head's swishing from one parent to the other, as if to include them both in his excitement.

"But they're not real!" his father insists.

"Never," his Mum answers. "They don't answer, it doesn't matter how you plead. I never wanted you to choose this way of life, I sacrificed to Mars and Jupiter and Vesta and Mercury... and nothing changed."

"God speaks to us all the time, every night, every night!" I can feel the thrill, the same I feel when I close my eyes in my grim, lonely cell, and feel the greatness of power and know it'll be all right. And one thrilling thought hits me now; he says he believes the same as I do. Am I allowed to love Secundus now, not that it'd be any use? I can't pursue that train of thought, it'll overwhelm me, I'm sure. "Mum, I've put it in the letter, in case I don't get to tell you all about it."

His father's looking at him through the gloom of the candlelight as if he's gone crazy and he's talking gibberish. His Mum's looking at him with a loving smile, which fades slowly into an image of pure pain, as she realises what Secundus is saying.

"This God doesn't permit you to kill."

"No. Sorry."

"So you're not going to kill your opponents? You won't fight back?" She can't say anything else; her eyes squish and before she can stop it tears trickle down her cheeks. "I don't want to lose you!"

"I want to live for ever, Mum, who doesn't? And this is the only way, I know it." He tries to comfort her, but it's no use. Of all the people I've met in these two weeks, she's the only one who's responding properly to this horrible situation. All the rest seem to be blanking out the moment these men around us start disappearing from the world for ever, vanishing from their loved ones. Only she and I want to scream out the horror of it.

Secundus is alarmed, for once he doesn't know what to say. "Get the letter from my lawyer, I've tried to explain everything in it. Read it now!" She's crying aloud, careless of who hears her; it's stopping conversations all over the room, as men turn to hear the mother pleading with her son.

"You have to fight! Give yourself a chance!"

"Look!" his father growls. "You've upset your Mother!"

"Read the letter!" the gladiator begs.

"Stop it!" That bellow is so forceful it could reach the other end of the Circus Maximus. "If you're going to believe a load of claptrap, you needn't come home again!"

His mother screams out; "No! Do come home! Secundus, do everything you can to come home!" And her son promises he will, he'll do anything he can.

"I'll try to help him," I vow. "Anything I can, but that won't be much." She's immensely grateful for my offer, and my understanding. I'm wrapped in her arms while her tears of panic cover my face, and she whispers;

"You take care of him!" She understands a lot of things without having to hear them. I nod into her chest, and she's reassured. If she knew how pathetic a warrior I really am, she'd be in a worse panic than before. Secundus pats his mother on the back, adding;

"Go and get the letter. I love you, Mum, I do, all right? Just remember that. I'm going to say goodbye to Primus." His angry father's leading her away already, in the direction of the lawyer. At least he's listened, and is going to get the letter.

Primus is at the other end of the food table; as we dodge through half-drunken gladiators towards him, I can only send Secundus a stare of disbelief. He's just left his mother in tears, and he has time to grab some more of those disgusting bits of bull for later!

"Surprise!" he exclaims, his grin shaken by his mother's concern. His comic timing's great, that one word gives me a weak laugh.

"Yes, that was a surprise. You could have told me!" Looking back, I could have guessed Naasir wouldn't have been idle in the cell next door to mine. I already knew he'd been talking a lot to Takis, why not to Secundus? I knew he'd stopped drinking, and cursing...

"I couldn't tell you, I've hardly seen you." No, not since we came to Rome. And since then, one thing has kept bothering me.

"I'm sure that soothsayer was talking about... you know, worldly love."

"No, he couldn't be!" He stops in his tracks, turns to me in the middle of the party chaos, and says plainly; "I'll tell you the truth; I love you the way my Dad loves my Mum, there's absolutely nothing misplaced about that. It's just a pity it's not returned, coz you won't escape from me now, even by dying!" That's a romantic way of putting it.

But now I discover Primus' comic timing isn't half as good as his brother's. He's advancing, waving a poster, an advert for the games. Just as I begin to say;

"It is returned," he interrupts me by bellowing over the racket;

"Heh, Sec, who's this Naasir Bestia you're paired against?"

Chapter 25

Here's yet more proof that I'm no gladiator; gladiators don't faint. I assume that's what happened, because I'm back on the sandy floor of the arena in the black of night. On the little temple the torches which seemed so pale before are blazing brightly. I'm being led slowly towards the light: my fuzzy head wonders if I'm to be sacrificed again. One of my wrists is tied to someone else; I glance sideways, into a useless eye.

"Kiral? Where are we going?"

He looks down at me; his good eye's trembling and red, he's probably drunk a lot, but he's as friendly as he has been since we arrived in Rome. When he speaks it's clear he's still eating a mouthful of party food.

"Naasir and Secundus thought you could do with some air." You'd think one of them could have brought me, we all have plenty to discuss. "The boss wouldn't let any of you out alone, so you got me."

"That's fine," I mutter. It's the most polite reply I can find. I've seen more than enough of the other gladiators, the ones trained here at the circus; they behave like animals, most of them can hardly be described as human. I soon discover why he's taking me towards the temple; there's a ladder left there, for someone to climb up and light the lamps, and on the flat roof it looks quiet and private.

"Sometimes people come up here to watch the racing," Kiral tells me, waving for me to climb up. "I've heard there's a good view across the valley." It's tricky climbing the ladder while we're tied together, he has to come up on the step right behind me and stretch round me as I reach up. If he's not bothered, I needn't be; it beats being pawed by the contestants in Ephesus.

We're up on the roof, and it is as quiet as it looked. We can still hear the noise of the party and see its light glowing out of the door near the Circus gates, but they couldn't hear us at all at this distance. It feels good to be out of the chaos. I can see the whole length of the race track, and the wooden seating. Far beyond that, the glow of other torches lights the city on its seven hills. The Emperor's palace towers above the Circus, flickering and smoky, and wisps of blue smoke twist up from all the temples around us.

"Do you feel better now?" The heat from the torches is comfortingly warm, and I lean against a large jar of oil that they've left here to fill the torches later.

"Yes, thanks, I'm better. Kiral, how could they do that? Setting up Naasir and Secundus to fight each other?"

"That's the name of the game," he points out, resting his hands on the low stone wall, beside my own. "Naasir's been driving Corinthus mad with his preaching."

"So he did this? To two good friends?"

I have to talk to my God about this. He has his own son, Jesus, he must understand, and Jesus has many friends, some who've never even set eyes on Him. I can't talk in front of Kiral, I don't want to drive him mad too. It's more of a scream inside my head; "Dear God, I can't believe how depraved they are! Please take care of... well, one of them has to kill the other, and I can't choose between them. It seems useless and hopeless. But Naasir says You always have a plan, so You choose." If I were God, I think I'd choose both, but what do I know? "My heart's aching for them both. Help me accept what's right..."

Kiral's standing patiently beside me while I'm silent. That's not polite of me.

"You've been very kind, taking me places."

"Yes, I have." That answer surprises me. So does the hand he places on my shoulder. "It's time you thanked me, isn't it?"

"That's what I'm doing!" I smile, trying to wriggle away. His hairy, scarred chest's rubbing my breastplate. "I came back, and saved you from being flogged, remember?"

210

"Hm." We're up on a roof, far away from everyone, and I'm tied to him. He planned this. Secundus and Naasir sent me, he says. As his lips brush my braided hair I recall all the things my Mum said about men; what happened to her to make her warn me so desperately? Was this how I was born? His alcoholic breath's on my forehead, and his body presses against my cool breastplate. I scream at myself in my head; 'Come on, Aysel, you've been through some training now, you should be able to think quickly!' I'm not responding to him, so he grabs my arm with fingers strong enough to leave a large bruise. Mistress Lucina often suffers bruises; now I see, she gets this kind of rough treatment all the time, from her own husband. How does she deal with it?

I've seen her once or twice, pacifying Master Panaius, pretending she wants him to hold her, so he treats her more gently. So I let Kiral kiss my lips, and I kiss back. My stomach's churning.

"Hm," I echo him. He thinks I liked it; his grip on my arm loosens. "I'd feel better without this breastplate on." He must be drunk, if he thinks I like him this much! He moves away, steps behind me to find the straps- and I throw him over my back.

I'm dragged against the low stone wall; Kiral's gone over the side, now he's dangling against the wall, hanging from my wrist. With my other hand I grasp the rope, to stop it snapping my hand off; he's heavy, and my eyes are misting in shock. I scream for help, over and over, aiming my screams in the direction of the party hall. Between each scream I hiss to myself;

"Liars! They're all liars! I can't trust any of them!" It seems as if no-one will come past. Some men are walking round the stalls away from the party, but they're too far away for me to be heard above the music. My arm and my heart ache so much, I'm staring out over the arena, remembering that everything I see tomorrow and the next day will be much worse than this.

Just when I think my wrist will break from Kiral's weight, the music stops. Corinthus comes out first; he hears my cries, looks over at his most experienced gladiator, dangling with one foot on a little ledge, and laughs as if he'll burst.

There's some commotion in my cell, I think they're bringing the noxii in. Tonight I'll be in the company of hopeless prisoners, criminals due to be executed in front of the crowds for their entertainment. Soldiers chain me in the corridor instead. I can live with that; the cell next to me looks totally overcrowded and the gladiators are moving about however they like for one last hour. Now the party's over, the men are streaming back down here, some of them look suddenly miserable at the thought of tomorrow's carnage. It looks like someone's engaged a bit more entertainment for them; there's a small table in the middle of the cell, and they're gathering close round it.

At the table sits a short man in a robe made of scraps, colourful and crazy-looking. Only one candle lights his table, so it's hard to see anything. However, when he speaks I recognise the voice of the soothsayer we met outside Julius Caesar's temple. The men must want to hear what they missed last time, although that proved so disturbing I can't see why they'd go hunting more spooky foretellings.

"Place your hands on the table," he orders the front row of men. They obey. It's strange that such a powerless person should command this fierce crowd. "If you would know your fate, move your hand forward." I can make out the stout gladiator who's an augur in his spare time; he's the first to put his hand out, so if he has faith in the visitor, his followers will too. "I call on the spirits of the dead," the soothsayer begins, rolling his eyes up to the cell window.

He's only just begun to cast some dubious spell, and I feel sicker than before. Despite all I've lived through, despite the horrors I've witnessed, there's been a sense deep inside my soul of peace, a sense that nothing can really hurt me eternally. Now that man's casting a cloud over my peace, threatening to disguise it. If he succeeds, I think I might give myself up to despair.

The violent warriors are still, watching the augur and the soothsayer; his face has become glazed and he talks to the empty air. "Are there any messages from the spirit realm for this gladiator? The birds tell him he will have success in his fight. Is that the whole truth?" As he waits, and the men listen anxiously, I study their faces, trying to remember which ones may be my allies.

Secundus is there, lounging against a wall. If he served my God, as he said, he wouldn't want any part of this blackness. He was lying, he must have been, to get me on his side. And even Naasir's there; now the eve of battle has come, he must be hedging his bets, listening to advice from the old gods. He told me they weren't real, so who's talking to us now?

The voice has changed, it's grown high-pitched and eerie. "I am his aunt. I come from beyond the grave to bring him a message." Some eyes widen. The soothsayer asks himself; "What is the message?" and answers again in the quavering woman's voice; "You will win many a victory for your men, but I will see you soon."

Silence reigns; only briefly, before his men lean over the augur's shoulder to growl at the messenger;

"He's not going to die! Master, we'll protect you! He's talking rubbish, don't listen!" The soothsayer doesn't care if they're sceptical or not. He appears to be in a trance, staring at something they can't see. It's enough to make me shiver.

He's faced with a big challenge now; the chief has put forward his hand. The gladiators trained in Rome begin to murmur; this barbarian can't speak Latin or Greek, so how is he expected to understand any message?

Their scepticism vanishes quickly; the little man's voice has altered again, and he's speaking fluently, but it makes no sense, except to the chief and his men. He's no happier about his message than the augur was, yet what did he expect?

There won't be a lot of survivors the day after tomorrow, they can't all be winners.

The Soothsayer moves on, reverting back into Greek to speak to his astounded audience. The youngest of the five velites happens to have his hand on my side of the table. The rest are arguing that he should let the leader of their team take his place so they can discover how successful their spears will be. The leader's not so keen, though he doesn't want to appear afraid of the unknown in front of all his opponents. So he kindly waves for the young spearsman to reach out to the soothsayer.

The little man remains in his trance-like stance, yet he stares directly at the veles. "Wielder of spears!" he proclaims above the rumble of gossip from the growing crowd. They no longer need this proof that he knows who he's addressing for them to believe his every word. "I tell you truly, your spear will strike the final blow of the festival."

What? That comment sends shockwaves through the gossip. As the news spreads they all begin to stare at the youngest veles with his spiked hair. In virtual silence he's pushed away from the table in their fear of hearing more good news for him and worse for them. Half the crowd's clammering for news now, from the spirits who ought to be left to rest.

In the quiet I hear a loud cough. The soothsayer turns into the darkness, to the bright eyes of Naasir, then back to the young veles. With a hint of guilt, he mutters more to the spearsman, though I'm not sure he hears it;

"When you die, you will be in Elysium." That's nice to know, but why talk about his death, after telling him his spear will be the last to strike, so basically he'll be the last man standing? Naasir coughs again. I'm surprised he hasn't stormed out of there, since he clearly disapproves of all the fuss.

The visitor's angry, and confident enough in the admiration of the mighty gladiators to face up to any sceptics. "There is one in this room…" he begins. Heads turn back to him; he hasn't faltered so far. "There is one in this room who doubts the truth… The truth!" he insists. "Before I continue, I must ask him to leave."

"I can't," Naasir replies calmly. "I'm chained to the wall. And you're not telling them the truth." There are a lot more murmurs, a rising growl. A fist hits Naasir in the stomach. I would try to help, it's a natural reaction, but of course I'm chained as well.

"And what do you call the truth, African?" the visitor sneers.

"He's not going to Elysium, is he? Tell them about Hell! We call it Hades, tell them what it's really like, give them the chance to change before they face death!"

"They don't want to hear that," is the soft reply, laced with panic. "Don't ask."

"Tell them, go on."

All eyes are on Naasir, straining closer to the table, and on the cowering soothsayer. His fists clench, yet his eyes roll up, and in a moment he's engulfed in the panic. He tries to keep his voice calm, as if his revelation's just another prediction, nothing to worry about. As he talks, his voice fails him.

"There is a world of darkness, a world of fire. People are there, in the fire, men and women of every nation, covered in fire. They cry out, they scream, they're never consumed. I see you, spearsman, and you, augur… I see myself, covered in flames. I'm in pain, I'm afraid, why can't they let me die? Darkness, terror, dying endlessly! Let me go!"

"That's enough," Naasir calls out. He's concerned for the smelly little man, trapped in his terror by the spirits he consults. "In Jesus' name, stop talking for a minute!"

He does, in the middle of a word. Gradually his expression of terror eases, his eyes lower, right down to the table. Then they widen as he tries to curse Naasir for asking what he did. His mouth moves, but no sound comes out. He shakes his head and rubs his throat; there's still no sound. He's offered a cup of wine, it doesn't work. He shrugs weakly and raises his eyebrows in amusement instead of anger. Then he stands up, straightens his robe of scraps and pushes into the crowd, leaving his table behind.

For a while men stand, staring at Naasir, though all they can see are his eyes in the darkness. It looks as if some of them want an explanation for what just happened. What would happen if he told them how to escape that vision, and they all repented? But they don't. One or two jab others in the ribs to jolt them back to normality. The edges of the crowd peel away, men return to their own cells and possessions what few possessions they keep. At last only the augur and the chief are left, staring at the chained Mauretanian prisoner in curiosity.

My pathetic faith's restored; not my faith in men, I think that's pretty dead, but the cloud vanished from inside me the moment that man stopped talking. And I need all the faith and courage I can get, because the men are slinking back to their cells and I'm being unchained and taken back to mine. A crowd of ten strangers meets me; the noxii have arrived.

I'm shoved into the cell; there's an instant cheer at the sight of a woman, however young. They're like ten Kirals at once. Some are chained back, so I can avoid them. None of them look kindly at me, like Takis or Secundus. If Secundus were here... he's in with the hunters of spirits, preparing to kill Naasir in the morning. My first instinct is to give up and cry.

Naasir wouldn't think that way. He'll be in the middle of his cell, telling his message of life to anyone who'll listen. Every time he tells that message, he seems strong and fearless, the way I'd like to feel in the face of these bitter-looking criminals. He told me that there was a criminal on the cross next to Jesus, who believed at the last moment. So could these.

I stand in the middle of the group, breathe in a huge, prayerful breath, and ask clearly; "Are any of you afraid? Would you like to live for ever?"

Chapter 26

It's the first day of the Volturnalia Festival.   Across the
city of Rome, across its Empire, slaves will be waking at
sunrise to cook their masters a filling breakfast, to put a final
polish on their mistress' jewellery, to braid wreaths for rich
young girls who are allowed to attend the gladiators' contest.
They'll be accompanied by chaperones, of course; it wouldn't
be appropriate for a young lady to watch half-naked men fight
to the death on her own.

Far away in Ephesus, Panaius Celerus will be woken by
Aunt Yildiz, or a new male slave, and will hopefully be
welcomed by a serious headache.   It was his job to plan the
Ephesian games, and I can't find it in my heart to wish it all
goes well for him.   He sold Naasir, and gave the soldiers
enough money to take me away too.   He was never kind to
me; whatever should happen in the next two days, I never
intend to see him again.

I wonder if Lucina will accompany him to the games,
wearing her usual garland of rosemary and lavender from our
peristyle plants.   Will she think of us, so far away, and
whisper a secret prayer for us, well away from her bullying
husband? Or has her belief faded in Naasir's absence?   She's
probably too soft to walk into town among the crowds, let
alone to sit through the displays at the stadium.   I'm unlikely
to see her again; what a crying shame!

I wake in a cool cell, after a couple of hours' sleep.   Ten
rough men share my cell, and I'm still alive, untouched.   We
wrangled a long time last night, they were quite fascinated by
the case I put for Jesus and his saving love.   Some said they
found it mind-blowing; well, so did I.   None of them took up
the offer of eternal life; I don't know why not, I made it clear
enough, like Naasir did when he first spoke to me.   He said
people harden their hearts to the truth.   But they started to

respect me and the jeering at a girl gladiator disappeared long enough for me to sleep.

This morning the reality's sunk in for the more fearful prisoners. I've heard they're to be hanged, a much quicker option than being crucified, they'll suffer for minutes rather than hours. There's chanted praying, and wailing, and the stinking sweat of panic. I won't have to watch them die; I'm being called to Corinthus' room, where I'm to be dressed for the morning's procession.

I bathe for the third time in two weeks! I'm a bit surprised I have any skin left, after so much scrubbing. Fortunately there's limited time, so I don't have to put up with other women washing me, or having my feet scrubbed and my nails filed. I'm not sure I could sit through that pointless exercise again without grabbing some girl round the throat accidentally.

A red tunic hangs on the wall, as red as a legionary's cloak, nearly as short as a man's. The neckline's unusually wide, when I put it on, it falls off one shoulder. Surely that must be a mistake, but there's nothing else, apart from a good pair of shorts; I'm very glad to put those on. A tailored leather waistcoat protects me from chafing by my bronze armour, while a skirt of leather strips makes me look more like a legionary.

After that my outfit goes wild. The breastplate's decorated with swirls, crossed tridents over my stomach, and straps with girly tassels that are bound to get caught on something. My hair's washed and freshly braided by a terrified slave girl. She watches my raised eyebrows and disapproving face in intimidated horror. She piles the braids round a cone, just like the style Corinthus' daughter wore on her wedding day, with curls streaming from the top. My sandals have been trimmed with gold, and they're strapped all the way to my knees so my calf muscles can only just flex.

Then come the wings. Who dreamed up this fantasy? I understand for every games they're supposed to think of

218

something new. They are beautifully made, a willow frame with white swan and ostrich feathers- a nod at women's purity, Corinthus says. I can't comment, looking at how he's tried to ruin me. I wish I could fly away from him with those pristine wings. But once they're slotted into the back of my armour, they're heavy and unbalanced.

Wearing them is my only physical challenge today, after I've climbed onto the back of my elephant. Mine? She feels like mine, she likes the way I smell, she carries me easily and doesn't have anything to worry about. Naturally she's been dressed up, too. She has a pink, jewelled blanket and a matching headdress of ostrich feathers, larger than the ones the other elephants wear. Her trainer gives her an elephant snack before he passes her a burning torch to carry in her trunk.

On my way outside, I catch sight of a wooden platform on the sand behind the central temple, with ropes dangling from a frame, for hanging. Beside it the gladiators have gathered, surrounded by soldiers to prevent any danger to the people of Rome from these violent monsters- the monsters Rome created. Usually we slaves are dressed in plain, worn tunics, but today the gladiators make the soldiers' red and white uniforms look dull.

The velites are dressed as a team, although they're not allowed to carry their spears in the procession; they're in rich blue tunics, trimmed with yellow and white braid. The barbarian chief has got hold of a thick collar of fur, while he and his men wear the bright, checked long trousers they need in the North to keep them warm. They must be sweltering in the Mediterranean heat of summer. The augur, the most fearsome of all the gladiators today, has an animal skull on his head and a leopard skin across his shoulders; I wonder if he killed that leopard himself, in the arena?

Among the others there's a surprising amount of gold flashing in the sunlight, and another mass of feathers on the gladiators' heads! Some of them will do anything to attract attention; I suppose this is likely to be the last day of attention they'll get. But some of them have bad headaches from last night, and they're trying to pull the other men's feathers down out of their eye line. The soldiers have to step in.

Corinthus' men have been given red to wear, like me. It's the right colour for making Naasir look intensely striking, but wrong for Achlus today; he looks exhausted and white-faced, sicker than I feel, his head hangs low as he's shoved into place by a legionary. "Achlus!" I call down. "Walk by me, Chica won't let you fall." He brightens at my invitation, so I think he'll manage the parade. What then, no-one knows.

Secundus marches further from me and my elephant. He hasn't bothered to say 'good morning,' which would hardly be true. He only gave me a glance, and he ignores Naasir completely. Takis marches between them, still with his flame-coloured scarf round his neck. From his far-away look, I guess he's thinking of his new wife, and wondering whether it's true that he can escape death by avoiding battle, as the Soothsayer said.

The moment we leave the Circus the crowds are there. They clap with the musicians who lead the procession, laugh at the jugglers and tumblers, jeer if they're distracted and drop any of their coloured balls. They cheer for the actors, and the paegniarii who stage unlikely street fights each time the parade slows. We make slow progress at first; the weight of people presses them into the streets so we can't pass. So they order Chica and the other elephants to the front; the crowds soon clear before her and her flaming torch.

Behind us there's a sudden panic; a woman has squeezed past the soldiers and slashed Achlus' arm with a kitchen knife. She runs along beside him, pulling his hands away from the wound, holding a cup up to it. So the stories I heard are true, they really believe the warm blood of a gladiator will cure diseases, epilepsy, I think. The soldiers level their spears and herd the woman away; there's a loud discussion about what to do with her, but she gets away with it, scurrying into a shop- and hopefully straight out of the back door.

A doctor steps up to treat the gladiator, and the procession continues, relentless. I don't want to be impressed, but I can't help it, the city is beautiful in the bright sunshine. Columns tower over us, topped with painted marble statues. Trees grow to mask the dullness of paved streets and high stone walls, bushes grow green and flowering outside brightly coloured house doors. Children play, and cheer us as we pass, excited by the music and glamour. From here on the back of an elephant I can touch the top bricks of the arches as we pass beneath tall aqueducts. High up here it seems safe, peaceful, a wonderful place to live.

I turn my mind back to my only concern; who will win, Naasir or Secundus? That wipes the growing smile from my face. Sometimes, if a gladiator fights well enough, he's excused the death sentence even if he loses. Could Secundus do that? Or will Naasir sacrifice himself for the young man? Did I misjudge Secundus? He doesn't have a lying face, in fact he has the kind of face I could look at for ever. The thought of it's threatening to make me smile again.

We pass the Senate House, and the temple of Caesar, and progress down the path they call the Sacred Road. Most of the traders stop their bartering to watch us pass, shouting out to the men they've betted on to do well or they'll be in trouble. They haven't thought that one through. As we pass the arches of the Forum, a lone voice cuts through the cheers, crying out; "Aysel!" just once.

Typically, the masses take up the cheer, and in an instant they're screaming my name all over the hill.

"Aysel Pulchra! Gladiatrix!" Glancing back, I see striped robes and a dull hat, then the short beard of Abram. He tries to shout me a message, or to mouth it, but we've passed by and I can't understand his signs. Soldiers step up to push him away roughly. I see why he hasn't been able to visit us; he's brave calling attention to himself right here. He must have had some important news that I'll never discover now.

Once I've ridden by, the cheers become roars. The paving stones resound with the thunder of hooves and wheels; the real heroes of the festival are riding behind us, famous charioteers from across the world, heralded by long brass trumpets, thronged by their teams. Flags wave for them, they wave back at thousands of adoring fans. Surely they could entertain people well enough, without the need for our deaths to warm up their audience.

Back in the arena I ride with my head lowered past the grim scaffold greeting spectators as they crowd into their seats. I'm glad at least that I kept my promise to pray for the victims there. Chica's jumpy after the procession, ready to lay down her torch and eat in the relative peace of her stall. I assume my task for the day is done, and the animal trainers help me take off the cumbersome wings so I can stretch my back once more. In the back of Chica's stall I ignore the stench and turn my mind to remembering Naasir's plan of campaign. I can hear names announced, trumpet calls, the distant clash of weapons, but I can blank those out for now, if I try.

Less than an hour later, Corinthus' deputy discovers me. He drags me away, brushing straw from my tunic, shining up a mark on my armour with his thumb.

"I didn't think I was fighting today," I protest in surprise. He pulls me faster. I'm not taken to the Gate of Life, but up into the seating, close to the Emperor's box, next to the white-robed, stern-faced Vestal Virgins. The deputy sits down beside me with his knife on his knee; his message is plain, 'Don't cause any trouble!'

The editor of the games stands close by, on a platform placed so that his voice can be heard almost all the way round the arena. The crowd hushes long enough for a body to be carried away, and for him to announce;

"And now, for the delight of our young ladies, we present to you a pair fresh from the games in Ephesus. They fought as a team then, and now they must fight each other; I give you Secundus Amator and Naasir Bestia!"

The crowd have read the hype, spread the gossip, placed their bets. They cheer the two men on; I watch, as I'm forced to, bent half over by the pangs in my stomach. They've both chosen more armour than usual; Naasir even has a helmet on his deep brown head. Secundus' hair is bleached and already spiked in the air with sweat. He gestures to Naasir, who shakes his head, telling him something no-one can hear. Secundus shrugs, and lays into him straight away.

They spar well; after all, they've practised together hour after hour. To the inexperienced watcher the fight is fast and tense. To the better-educated it's dull after five minutes. Behind the purple curtain, in the royal box, I hear a groan, and a voice yells;

"Get on with it!" The fighting speeds up, they're unlikely to escape accident at such a pace. Secundus' sword nicks Naasir's arm before his axe can parry it.

"Use the net!" someone yells from the front row. Naasir tries, but it'll prove too dangerous to do that, he may injure his young opponent.

Their referee is unhappy. "Consul Nero commands you to fight!" he bellows. Then he gestures to two other men hanging on the edge of the fight; lorarii, marshals with whips to goad unwilling men to fight harder. They beat Naasir, although he's already injured. He throws in a few heavy blows which just look clumsy, and hit nothing, and one which draws blood. Now the whips rain down on both the men. My fingers are clenched so tightly the nails will leave scars.

Naasir's back is bleeding from the whip; he does little to change his tactics, he's determined not to harm anyone. I know the only important thought in his head is of being right for Heaven, he sees that eternal gate whenever he shuts his eyes now. Secundus' face is angry, the whip has stung his pride as well as his skin. "You want me to kill my friend?" he growls.

223

"Nero commands it," the referee returns, beckoning for the lorarii to lay on with their whips again. Nero, Caesar's nephew, the same one who Flavius promised me would restore justice to the world? Does comradeship mean nothing to him? He's giving the friends no chance. Secundus slices at Naasir's leg; the blade catches in the greave and draws a trickle of blood.

My friend is wounded, his leg trails. He flails out with his axe against Secundus' breastplate. He's also drawn blood, and flesh! It's the first wound I've seen him make. It angers the young man, who closes in on him as his leg weakens. Another stab to Naasir's leg brings more blood, and throws him to his knees. He's at his opponent's mercy.

"So, I've beaten him!" Secundus screams at the box. "Are you happy?" A hand reaches out between the royal pillars hung with garlands, a hand with the thumb turned downwards.

"Continue," orders the referee. Corinthus' deputy puts his grubby hands firmly on my knees so I can't go anywhere. His face is amused by my pain. In my head I'm vainly whispering;

'Save them both, just for today! Let the people show mercy.'

Naasir stabs at Secundus' waist. Why is he attacking? Now his life's in real danger, has he given in and chosen self-defence? Who could blame him? Secundus grasps his stomach, something fleshy and oozing falls between his fingers, and they stain at once. When he rubs a hand over his sweating brow it turns scarlet. He's a mess, and he's very tired after their athletic sparring. He looks down at Naasir, bent at his feet, then appeals to the crowd once more.

"In the name of the gods, what more do you want?"

I venture a glance behind me, up at the thousands of cheering faces towering above me. Many of them have their thumbs up, they want Naasir to live at least until tomorrow. Others are grumbling and shouting out; "Lance him through!"

"He doesn't even believe in the Roman gods! He follows Jesus, the Christ!" I have no time to wonder why he's saying that, after all he told his parents last night. It sounds like advertising for our way. Nero's ringed hand appears again; he agrees with those who want him dead. The lorarii close in on Secundus; before their whips reach him, he screams out; "Naasir, they force me! Only your God can save you now!"

He raises his sword and stabs at Naasir's stupid, tiny breastplate. Blood and flesh spatter his sword, and my best friend hits the ground.

Chapter 27

This time I definitely won't faint. In a desperate moment of strength I push the deputy off me and kick him down. It's only a step over someone's lap to the front seats; spectators yell at me, I don't care. Bracing myself, I jump across the moat onto the hot sand.

The stewards are unimpressed, though one of them recognises me and signals for them to allow me through. Secundus is raising a hand in triumph when I shove him on his back, out of the way, and throw myself at Naasir. He's still breathing, so gently it's hard to see. Maybe there's hope; the crowd are cheering the bloodthirsty murder of friend against friend. All their attention's for Secundus, the winner, so if I could get Naasir away, to a doctor…

Secundus laughs grimly at me. He grabs my hand, forcing me close to him. The crowd laughs with him.

"To the victor the spoils!" he calls out, still the actor he always was. Is that the truth, I'm part of the spoils to him now? As if it's no weight at all, he throws Naasir onto his back. He hasn't given a second thought to the damage he may cause, he just assumes, like all the rest, that my friend is already dead. Then he grabs at me again, shouting back so those in front of him can hear; "I'll bury your friend for you!"

We head for the arch they call the Gate of Death. It's hard to move my feet, I can't even cry, my despair's too great. I fight against his rough grip until I realise that's what the audience like, then I give up and let him pull me. It's not as if I can see where I'm going anyway, through my tears. I don't even care.

There's nobody here, the men who deal with the bodies are out watching the show to see who's next, since Secundus is dealing with this one for them. There's only a cold, empty cell full of bandages and cloths to drape bodies in. Live gladiators aren't supposed to come this way, and neither could we, if our tale hadn't been so widely spread through this vicious city.

Secundus lowers Naasir's body onto the blood-stained wooden table, more gently than he carried him out. I try to feel for my friend's heartbeat, but Secundus takes my hand, and the wrist he dragged me with, and murmurs in a much softer tone than before; "Sorry about that. It was part of the act."

Act? He calls that an act? And what else was just an act? He peeps out of the cell, and murmurs again;

"There's no-one coming. It's all right, you can get up." I'm standing up already, reaching for a bandage. I stop with my hand in mid-air as I hear;

"You made a fool of God, Secundus!"

"No, He's too big to look foolish! But what'll they think when you appear again tomorrow? They'll call it a miracle." He's helping Naasir sit up. The African eyes are bright and very much alive.

"That was a huge risk! You could have been..."

"Yes, I could have died. I think you mean to say; 'Thanks for your quick thinking, Secundus!'" He reaches into his shorts and pulls out bloodied flesh, with no pain at all. He simply throws it out of the window. Naasir's on his feet, doing the same. There are bits of flesh behind his greave, under his breastplate, beneath his helmet.

"You must admit, I've got balls!" Secundus jokes, throwing all the evidence through the window bars. "Some dog's going to be delighted with all that."

"You've got guts, all right!" That's the first joke I've ever heard Naasir make. He throws the last stinking glob out of the window in the nick of time; Secundus is keeping watch, and hisses;

"Lie down, it's Corinthus. Aysel, start crying."

The lanista storms into the cell, raging. I'm almost getting the hang of Secundus' ways; I throw myself on Naasir and

227

weep tearlessly; I'm so mixed up now, my lungs need to cry out for a while.

"He fainted," Secundus explains. "I seem to have missed his heart, sorry."

Corinthus has a glob of flesh in his own hand; he's tossing it up like a juggling ball. He saw those uncooked bits of bull at the party, but failed to realise their potential. "Dumb paegniarius! You'll make me look an idiot!"

"Not if you don't tell. It's a miracle!" The lanista's well-aware that he daren't tell, or his career will be in the dirt. "Like I said, you forced me, setting me against him. You took me on; you wanted me to put on a show!"

"Then keep it up," Corinthus hisses. We all nod in understanding. "I swear, only one of you's getting out of here tomorrow!"

Once he's gone there's nobody around, until a doctor is sent for to dress the real wounds the friends inflicted on each other. And what about me? I was sure I'd witnessed Naasir's murder.

"Sorry," Secundus repeats, although I haven't said a word.

"I get it. You needed me to react properly. What's real now?"

"This." He puts out his strong, red-flecked arms, and folds me in them. How can such strong arms be so careful? My arms just fit round his waist, since he's full of feast food. He rests his chin on my head, and whispers; "Cry if you need. It helps."

And I do, from horror, from relief, joy to be in his arms, pain that this'll end tomorrow, fear, longing for my Mum, love. Does he understand I love him and his funny ways? Words seem pointless. He holds me the way his father comforted his mother; for a slave like me to have had a marriage like theirs would have been a miracle.

So mercy is real. They're both alive and we've been undisturbed all day, apart from the doctor's visit. Corinthus told people I was nursing Naasir back to health. Instead, the three of us have talked and talked, about tomorrow, about Heaven, about what we would have done with our lives, had we been given the chance. Naasir would have preached before Caesar himself- he laughed at that dream. Secundus and I would have made our home in Pompeii, near his parents, helped run the theatre, set my Mum up as a baker and started a group of Jesus' followers. We didn't dare dream any further.

Naasir broke into our cosy daydreams by announcing; "Corinthus was quite drunk last night."

Oh, and...? We hardly wanted to hear that, but he wouldn't bring it up except for a good reason.

"He accidentally told me a few things he learned in the arena about lions. There are two lions, three lionesses and a cub down there; the cub's there to look cute for the children. The lions would rather scavenge than hunt, we've seen that already. Corinthus used to fight them with flames."

"That's no use," Secundus corrected him. "We common gladiators aren't allowed to fight with fire."

"He says tridents are best against them, and if you're very lucky you can knock them on the head."

"Yes, but usually they'll have your leg off first, I've seen that happen." Man, they're a cheerful pair! "They're not fans of elephants," he added, throwing a meaningful glance at me. I reminded him the elephants were only for the procession, they're not going to be part of the contest. Naasir reviews everything else Corinthus let slip, in case we find any of it useful, and makes me repeat it back to him.

By evening Naasir's bandaged convincingly, and Corinthus is so fed up with him, he sends him into the same cell as me, to stop him 'corrupting' the other gladiators. The noxii I spoke to last night have gone. But visitors have arrived and are waiting in their place. The little barred window lights up three heads, one in a modest veil. As my eyes adjust to the light, I burst out in delight;

"Abram, you came to visit! All of you came! Naasir, this is Abram, who I told you about. This is his wife, Persis, and his son, erm..."

"Nathan," says the young man, waving a hand. It's chained. They're all prisoners.

I lean against the wall, too ashamed to sit with them, convinced I've brought them here by following Abram home the other day. Nathan crouches in a corner, silent now, with his face hidden on his knees. Persis is cuddled as close to her husband as she can get. She sniffs now and again, or gasps in a frightened sigh, something like me when I was captured and dragged out of my home. Only Naasir's calm enough to speak.

"Abram, you're a follower of Christ?"

"I am. We are." He tries to sound bold, yet his voice trembles worse than it did in the Forum.

"Then don't be afraid. We know where we're going; to die is gain, remember?" Abram nods, too afraid to let his voice betray his fear again. "What are you here for?"

"They're accusing me of marrying my sister," Abram whispers. "Only because we all call each other 'brother' and 'sister.' Maybe we should be more careful. A man came to the Forum this morning, a man with a strange eye, and some soldiers. My wife and son came looking for me..."

So it's not my fault? "Kiral!" I hiss. "I hate him!" A few days ago, in the safety and comfort of his own home, the old man would have graciously told me what he thought of that remark; now he speaks up in nothing more than a respectful whisper;

"My child, we have no room for hate in our hearts if we are preparing to meet our God."

"Well, I hate him!" I repeat. ""You're surely not going to ask me to forgive him and pray for him, are you?"

Yes, he is, I can tell by his face.

"He's just hateful, a liar! He was horrible to me!"

"Worse than Master Panaius to your mother?" Naasir throws in.

"What? He never laid a finger on her!"

"Oh?" I've no idea what he means by that 'Oh!' And Abram chimes in;

"Love your enemies, do good to them that hate you..."

Surprisingly, Naasir almost snaps back at him;

"Leave her for a minute! Leave it to her conscience." Yes, yes, I'd really missed hearing him say that! But I've never witnessed his next comment; "Aysel always choses the right way."

Our little disagreement fizzles out as we hear Nathan's voice rise from the corner of the cell, singing weakly, between sniffling tears;

"I will praise you, O Lord, among the nations;

I will sing of you among the peoples.

For great is your love, reaching to the heavens,

Your faithfulness reaches to the skies."

It's like the sound of a Heavenly angel, showing us a bigger picture of creation, reminding us how Heaven is the goal. Kiral's the least of my worries, he's just a man like any other. Nathan sings on, growing slightly braver as he concentrates on his breathing, and the words of the psalm he's translated into Greek for us. It works as a lullaby, sending his terrified mother to sleep.

We've all been keeping fairly quiet so we didn't worry her too much, but now she's asleep I can ask what I wanted. "Where's Gaius?" I wonder. Will they drag him in here next? I wouldn't wish that on him, though at least he had some body strength, unlike these three. Abram whispers back;

"He left this morning to meet someone arriving from the port, someone from Ephesus, I believe. I'm glad he was well out of the way when the soldiers came..." He tails off, looking at his son, probably recalling that moment and wishing Nathan had been far away too.

"You met Jesus, here in the world, in the flesh?" asks Naasir. "What was that like?" That helps distract him. The old man tells his tale as he told it to me, adding other tales and experiences and new wisdom that Naasir hasn't heard before. For a while it seems that they've thrown off their ties to this world completely, and it counts for very little while they already walk in the world of eternity.

I listen in wonder to a lot of it, but my weary mind wanders, and Nathan's no help; in the middle of his father's story he strikes up another soft song. It's a popular love song, the sort people might hear sung in the theatre or whistled in the street.

"She's bright as a dove, and she talks like an angel,
She's all I could hope for, more than she seemed.
The moment I saw her I loved her for ever;
She rose like a dove, and flew out of my dream."

It's sweet, his voice suits easy music. The tune's catchy, and I'm sure by the relaxed way he sings it that he's written it himself. I may only be a slave, but I reckon he could make a career out of his singing.

"I'll fly up and find her, and catch her and hold her,
The bird with the white wings, and shimmering heart.
I don't fear her weapons, the net or the trident,
No power of this world can tear us apart..."   Oh, man, that could be a problem! I have to get this boy out of the arena alive, or die trying; putting women in the Circus is bad enough, but they ought to draw the line at innocent boys of sixteen!

Naasir heard the song; Nathan's been whimpering it to himself several times over, perfecting it as Secundus would practise a stage oration, imagining in his misery that no-one can hear him. My friend draws me away into the far corner, and asks me quietly; "Remember how you use the net to pull the sword out of my hand?" I nod; that was a mistake I kept making when I was tired out. "Can you teach me how to do it?"

"Me? Teach you?"

"Yes, we don't want any more trouble from loose whips. Aysel, I think our plan of campaign needs to change."

"I thought so," I agree. "We've got to get these people out. It might be possible. I've seen a couple of things..." I have to think them through first, though.

He squeezes my arm with invisible appreciation. "With God all things are possible. Although we might have to..."

"To sacrifice some things? Like our own lives?"

"Maybe just mine. We do have a secret weapon."

"Do we?" I grin, with a sudden flash of hope. "We'll need it. What is it?"

"You!" he whispers. Oh, man!

Chapter 28

Volturnalia Games, Day 2, Circus Maximus, 543

Thirty-eight surviving gladiators.
Five of them velites,
One of them a seasoned, one-eyed villain,
  one a revered augur,
  one a fallen chief of men.
One of them newly married,
  one scared of tridents,
  one a foolish play-actor.
Three innocent Christians.
Six starving lions.
One single gladiatrix (untrained.)

It looks bad, very bad.   I took special care this morning to fix a vision of Heaven in my head. It shines brighter than the sun when I shut my eyes, and fills my heart with warmth which eases the horror of waking.   In my master's room a poster shows a list advertising the entertainment for this morning. I can't read it, but I can make a list of my own.
  Bath, yet again, waste of time.
  Hair and nails preened like a rich lady.
  More clean underwear, waste of money, at least it's not mine.
  New white linen tunic, leaving bare, unprotected shoulders.
  Gold trim, probably rich enough to buy my own freedom.
  Shimmering breastplate, may dazzle some opponents.
  Gold-trimmed sandals, slippery but beautiful.
  Wreath of leaves, to be torn to pieces.
  Towering wings, clumsy, constricting, uncomfortable.
  And finally, gut-wrenching fear that shakes every part of me,
    at least the trembling brings life to the wing-feathers.

Today I'm no longer a sacrifice, I'm a contestant. With trembling hands I strap on my sword-belt. My lanista takes out the broken sword and replaces it with one that's full-length and razor-sharp. He slams a net into one hand and a trident in the other.

"Give 'em hell," he says. My mind responds calmly before my angry heart can interrupt;

"I'd rather give them Heaven."

"Not another one!" he gapes at me. "You're condemning yourself to death, then?"

"No!" my heart snaps at him. "You're condemning me. Tell your daughter I said 'Goodbye.'"

He stares at me, then tucks a knife into my belt. I don't know what category of gladiator I come under now. I hear there've only been a couple of female gladiators, so there are no rules. "You will kill, when the time comes."

"I won't."

"You know nothing about it," he insists, as if trying to convince himself. "When a man actually does die for his god, *then* I'll listen!"

"Watch me," is all I can say, or I'll cry. I've never felt as sure of anything as I am of our God right now, that love's wrapping me round tighter than armour. The lanista kisses me on the cheek.

"May your gods... your God defend you, and... make me some money."

Soldiers close in on either side of me, careful not to touch my wings; we march together to the Gate of the Living. From there I can see the giraffes, loose on the sand. They're taller than they seemed in their cells, elegant even when they're running. They have to run, from the velites and their spears. Some of the spear-tips are wider than usual, I imagine they could cut a terrible wound through one of those tall yellow necks.

The velites chase, they spread out round a towering victim, the crowd cheers with laughter. Poor giraffes, they're too delicate to be hunted to death, they don't deserve it. They have no claws or huge teeth like lions, no way of fighting back. One escapes into an archway, while a dimachaerus is introduced to the arena, whirling two matching swords. The velites need to turn their attention to him now, so the giraffe stands shivering but safe for the moment.

Gladiators are being introduced, in pairs, at intervals over the morning; a body's being taken through the Gate of the Dead already, and several men are left in the arena, turning from one victory to the next fight. Every few minutes someone else salutes Caesar's nephew as they're due to die. Trumpets sound, the crowd sits up in expectation, the editor calls out from beside the royal box in Latin I can't understand, then in familiar Greek;

"We present to you Blandinus, wielder of spears from Sicily, our youngest contestant!" Polite applause runs round the stadium. "At least, our youngest *male* contestant. Fighting against him, please show your appreciation for Aysel Pulchra, the Gladiatrix!" Grumbles at the appearance of a woman are drowned by cheers. I stand like a statue in an arch on one side of the sand, thinking;

'Blandinus, Blandinus, I must remember his name, remember he's a man, not just a contestant.'

I can see him close by, framed in another arch, tall and strong, with a sharp spear in one hand and a sword at his side. I force my legs to keep pace with his as we come before Consul Nero.

"Moritori te salutant!" we cry in unison. I'm telling the truth, if this man's spear will strike the final blow, then I really am about to die. I launch into Naasir's first stalling trick, walking away from my opponent as if to brace myself for action. Blandinus takes my example and mirrors my movement. A sharp hiss of sand under his feet, and he turns back. We walk straight towards each other; the walk becomes a run. He meets me with his spear full-tilt. I dodge and race on. He turns and tries again; I play the same trick, dodging in a different direction. If I keep up the variety I could get away with this for a while.

Achlus is in the battle already; he watches me for a brief moment after a kill, tilts his head, then backs away. I'm carrying a trident, and he's been warned to avoid tridents or die. Blandinus comes back at me; I duck, and he slides over my back. I stall long enough for Naasir to be announced, against the barbarian chief in his checked trousers. He has a hammer; I can't see what use that'll be against an axe, but he lays into Naasir keenly with it.

I must survive long enough to help Abram and his family. Blandinus and his racing spear are starting to bug me; besides, he's losing energy after a few runs at me. Hovering around us both for a minute, like human vultures, come the lorarii. They aren't convinced we're fighting properly. The whips appear, and Blandinus gasps with the pain of the blow. My breastplate may be heavy, but I'm glad to have it now; it catches the force of the whip, my leather skirts deflect it and it only catches my legs. I feel why he cried out aloud; Secundus and Naasir suffered this yesterday. I wouldn't like to feel that whip again, even for the sake of a friend, let alone an enemy.

No, Blandinus is not my enemy. If I think so aggressively, I'll be my own enemy. Naasir's disarmed a lorarius already; I could try that, if I get a break. The young veles comes at me again, I can't keep throwing him over my back or my hip or tripping him, I'll wear myself out and the audience will get bored of us and turn their thumbs down. His spear aims for my chest; I twist the trident at it, and the wooden shaft snaps in two. I've never managed that before.

He dashes in past the sharp forks of the trident, and grabs my shoulders. I look into his eyes, he falters. He's remembered I'm human, a woman. Still, he draws his blade, so I draw mine. It shines silver in the morning sun. Blandinus' is a

237

strange colour; it's bronze, he's been set up! I parry several blows before he realises the clang of his sword's ringing false.

The sword's breaking. I suppose the spear was sabotaged too, to give me a chance. He knows it, there's genuine fear on his face. He strikes out in panic, scraping the bronze blade down my cheek; it stings horribly. I kick him, he falls, I kick him in the jaw, he lies flat.

I'm not supposed to be injuring people. But as I back away he throws down the useless sword and virtually sobs; "Go on, kill me!" The referee approaches, appealing to the spectators to show their opinion. Their thumbs turn downward, they want to watch me kill. The lorarii and their whips are a few paces away. "Do it," screeches the veles. I raise my hands as Panaius did, and my trident, and shout as loudly and clearly as I can;

"NO, I WILL NOT!" At the same time I brace myself for the thrash of a whip, or the death blow. Blandinus' fellow spearsmen are also marching on me. Nine of the surviving damnatii are massing behind me.

The lorarii can't reach me; suddenly I'm surrounded by spears, sheltered by Blandinus' comrades, as the damnatii descend. At their head of the spearsmen struts the augur, a mighty dimachaerus, flashing both his swords so fast the blades are a blur. He calls for Blandinus to get up and join them; the young man rises, reaching out for his spear- and the three prongs of a trident appear through his chest. His reactions were no match for desperate criminals. It seems that the soothsayer got something wrong; when the poor young man walked into the arena, he was expecting to win.

The velites surround me, in thanks for my kindness to one of their own. In a brief pause for breath, I glance across the sand. The barbarians have also grouped against the damned; Naasir's among them, they're protecting him. He's gathered up the whips that goaded us, and passed them out to the barbarians. They've shown him some reverence ever since that incident with the soothsayer. They know he has some power they can't measure.

Of course he has power within him, so do I. I have the will to fight on, to defend my unexpected comrades, to survive until I can help Naasir rescue Jesus' followers. His spirit is inside me, guiding me, subduing my urge to lash out aimlessly at anyone.

For a while I'm safe from injury, until two of the velites fall. The damnatii break through the spears and it's an all-out battle. Takis and Secundus are nowhere in sight; they volunteered for a special task, no-one knows quite what's being prepared. But I find myself a companion in Achlus; there's an awkward moment when he throws me to the floor and tries to stand over me to protect me. I have to kick him away so I can bounce back up and persuade him to share the burden. Then we fight back to back, he fields the sword-blows while I do my best to keep the tridents away from him.

We're trapped deep inside a nightmare; the stadium, the audience, the summer sky shrink away, all I can see are bare legs and flashing weapons. My mind's consumed with fielding blows, no room for any other thought. My weapon thirsts to bite into flesh, which crowds on every side. I see what Secundus meant, you get used to it; I'm only seeing targets, not people.

My legs brace, and twist against the targets; my hips throw my weight into the swings of the trident. It's a bad weapon for stabbing, but good for disarming; it can strip swords away with little blood shed. When I wrench the shield from the arm of a hoplomachus, Achlus stoops to pass it to me.

"Where are you going?" he asks, suddenly.

"I'm not leaving you." It's a struggle to talk, to think of words when our lives are so threatened.

"After death?"

"God's taking me to Heaven. Like Naasir said."

"Would he take a...?" He never finishes. His full weight sags onto my back, and he slides down to the ground. I turn

239

to see how carefully he's been protecting me; his arms and legs are cut to ribbons. He rolls onto his back; his chest's invisible under blood. I stoop down, put my hand on his head, and whisper;

"Yes." I hope that answers the question he was trying to ask, although I don't know what it was. After avoiding the tridents, he's dying from loss of blood.

Three blades at once scrape down my arm till I can see my own muscle. I'm driven out of the tight circle by the points of a trident. I'm on open sand again, and under attack. This opponent strikes heavily, I'm too weak to parry, there's no mercy in his face. My arms ache, my feet slip, but I can still run. The trident slices down my leg; I'm bleeding again, though the thump of adrenalin drowns my pain. He chases me to the central barrier; I could squeeze between the pillars and statues, if I wasn't wearing fake wings. He's gaining, and I don't have time to think.

The editor of these games has made a foolish mistake; he's ordered garlands to be wound round the pillars of Jupiter's temple facing the royal box. They're strong garlands, made with rope to withhold the rigours of the two days' events. I've been climbing our garden wall since I was small, with nothing to grip but the bare brick, and this temple's hardly taller. Even with white wings waving heavily behind me, I can easily scramble onto the temple roof. The wings get in the way of my desperate opponent, and at the top I turn with my sword to slice through the garland and let it fall.

I'm too slow, his hands appear over the parapet; I could slice at them, if I were cruel enough, but the pain in my cheek and leg remind me not to. I wait for him to climb up, then put my sword to his throat. I can picture the sight if I cut into it; right now my other hand's tightly clenched to keep me from stabbing. He elbows my sword away, aiming for my throat in exchange.

He stands behind me, pressing me against him, looking out to the crowd to see who's watching the moment when he finishes me off.   I struggle with all my strength to pull down his arms.   Standing high above the rest, in my bright, spreading wings, I'm a target for anyone who can throw.   No matter how hard I try, I can't tip my opponent over the edge.

A spear whistles through the air, under my armpit and into the damnatius.   He falls heavily, I'm trapped beneath him, feeling warm dampness seep into the back of my tunic.   No-one can see me once I'm down, I may as well be dead.   So I wriggle my chest free to gasp in a few deep breaths, and rest.   He's lying on my wings, if I wriggle downwards they'll slide out of the sockets and I can finally escape them.

Below, I hear the trumpets heralding another announcement from the editor.   "There will be a short break, while our gladiators take some water.   Meanwhile, courtesy of the … what's that word… of the Christians in Rome, I present to you a classic tale, of the Abduction of the Sabine Women.   Bring in these… Christians!"

Chapter 29

Five women in long, draping robes are shoved through the gate into the arena. Five! The last seven gladiators emerge opposite them; the women don't stand a chance. But where did they find five women? Peeping one eye over the parapet of the temple roof, I watch them advance in terror. I recognise the flowing hair of Persis, wringing her hands and staring around her as she staggers. Clinging onto her arm comes a young lady in an unrealistic wig of wool; it's Nathan, they've put him in a dress so the audience can laugh at him.

Now I get the idea, I recognise Abram, with his beard shorn, and Takis; he's gone to some lengths to avoid battle! They've taken his scarf and forced him to wear it on his head, as his bride did on their wedding day. And lastly comes my Secundus. He makes a tough-looking woman, and he shows no embarrassment. In fact he plays to the crowd, blowing kisses at the referees, walking with a swing. He told me he used to act women's parts when he was little.

It's clear why he volunteered for this assignment, it certainly wasn't out of cowardice; he's protecting the victims as they walk, shepherding them towards the temple, the way I suggested yesterday. That's good, they're coming close to me. Now I notice they're completely unarmed as the seven gladiators advance.

I hear the Romans many years ago held a party and abducted the women they'd invited, so they could marry them and continue the family line. It sounds like the kind of thing Romans would do. Sometimes they recreate the story during festival parades; occasionally they have real women, dressed in colourful gowns with flowing tassels and veils. This display isn't going to be a cheerful wedding scene with veils and cake, it's meant to be a show of pillage and carnage, unarmed men and a woman against total brutes.

From my place of safety on the temple roof I can see how Nathan gapes at the seven gladiators. There are bare chests, leather straps and breastplates, metal plate armour on legs and shoulders, two fierce helmets designed like bears' faces. And they carry the sharpest weapons, long swords, short ones and curved ones, spears, an axe. A sensitive boy should never witness a sight like that.

I have two swords, two knives and a spear up here. "Psst," I hiss. Secundus looks up in sudden, strained delight; like the rest, he thought I'd been killed. He's more delighted when I throw the weapons to him and clamber down a garland to his side.

"Our secret weapon!" he grins through thick red lipstick, holding a sword out to show his audience. I pick up a loose trident and shield for Takis; he blankly refuses the weapon, though he grabs at the shield. "For the lady?" Secundus presses, with a friendly smile at Persis while she throws up on the ground.

"Don't trust myself," Takis whispers. But Abram stares at the trident.

"Pass that here," the old man suggests. "I'll protect my family." He knows how to brandish a long weapon, that's a start. "No, give me the sword."

"Are you sure?" asks Takis. He can see Abram's hands trembling already. "These are dangerous men. Once they see you're armed..."

"What if you kill ...?" Secundus begins. Abram guesses quickly;

"You don't have a wife or children. I'll defend them!"

"Right!" Secundus agrees. "Strange place to defend them."

The irony of defending a group of Christians inside a temple to Jupiter hasn't escaped him. Nathan tries to disguise his worry by struggling out of his costume and using the dress to sponge the feminine chalk from his face. But I understand; there's a strange air in this small space beside the statue of

Jupiter, it seems to enclose us and encourage our fear. I have to get out.

Not far from us, Naasir's with the two surviving barbarians, the Chief and one of his advisors. They appear to have developed a bond, fighting in a tight triangle against Kiral and the last veles. Picking up my trident again, I run to see whether I can help; we need our allies to fight nearer to the temple. Naasir chops through a spear and disarms one of the velites, while the Chief dives in towards the other.

I look away to avoid the terrible moment the Chief kills the spearsman. When I look back he's still there, alive, kneeling with his companion before the Chief. Placing a regal hand on each of their heads, he adopts them into his tiny tribe, and they take their places beside him. Naasir's trying to follow Kiral with his net, and struggling.

"Naasir!" I scream as I run, thinking as quickly as I can. "Abram!" He can see the situation, but he can't run as quickly as usual, his foot's bleeding from a stab-wound. Secundus calls me back, Takis begs me to take shelter and preserve my own life, a veles skids to a halt at my feet, on top of his own spear. An axe protrudes from his back.

The Chief has one man left, and Naasir. The augur's rushing to help us with his two followers, if they can cut their way past Kiral's whirling sword and whip. Kiral threw that spear which killed my opponent on the top of the temple; does that make us allies again? If we all fight the seven together, it looks like we have a chance of survival.

For a moment I seriously believe that the battle's coming to an end, that we've achieved our goal with only a few injuries that will probably heal quite soon. Am I still so innocent? And forgetful? In the comfort of the curtained royal box, Nero waves his hand. The animals' gate opens. The lions have arrived.

"Inside!" Takis yells. The civilians obey at once.

"Get on top!" I yell back to him. He sees the point, and hurries to stand at Persis' feet, goading her to scramble up.

Now Secundus is armed, he slits through Abram's ridiculous gown so he's down to his tunic. Once his legs are free he can scramble up the ropes twisted round a stone pillar, with help from Takis.

Soon four of them crowd on the roof; the old preacher has his sword tight in his hand, the shaking seems to have stopped and he's ordering his wife and son to get busy taking my abandoned wings to pieces in case they can be used as weapons. Takis tests which tiles or pieces of plaster may come away to be thrown down at the lions.

Both the men wait for the order of the one on the battle front; Secundus stands below them on the little temple step, robed like a noblewoman, but armed with the spear and sword.

The seven Roman gladiators turn unwillingly away from their pursuit, to follow the progress of the lions. Two have gone round the far side of the barrier, chasing the last giraffe. Three are advancing on us in a relaxed walk, confident none of us humans could outrun them. The male pauses to sniff bodies, but two lionesses make directly for the line of seven men, with the cub trailing his mother.

One of seven Romans is whispering to the young man at his side, who's hopping about on his feet. He'll be warning him to calm down and, above all, not to run. He doesn't listen, he can't, he's too concerned by the lions, who wouldn't be? I will him not to run.

Two lionesses have reached the temple; Abram and Takis pull Secundus to the top just in time to avoid the snap of powerful jaws. The lionesses pace in front of the step, menacing. Abram and Persis peep down; I hope they haven't heard that lions can climb, the roof's not even that high.

Out of the chaos I hear a voice, echoing through the arena to the hills either side of us. It's a tune I know well, the same one I sang in the stadium in Ephesus. This time it's Nathan singing, and he's changed the words.

"Jesus is Lord, His angels will guard you;

Trust in his Word, no lions will harm you.

He'll keep you safe, whatever may come,

Wrapped in eternal love." His mother picks up her trembling voice to sing with him. His father's baritone is added to the music; he swings his sword gently, in rhythm. They sing it over and over, while the lionesses pace; their desperation has eased, their ears are pricked up, they don't bother trying to jump onto the roof.

There's nothing for Persis and her son to do but sing, so they carry on. I like the words, particularly the eternal love bit. Many of the audience know the tune, and hum along. It's far too beautiful a sound to accompany the clash of the seven gladiators' swords as they meet the lions.

A massive trumpet-call hushes the audience. It trips me up on my way to Naasir; sand rubs deep into the wound on my leg. Well, there's no time to think about that. Out of the corner of my eye I notice the silk-robed palace guests in the royal box are fidgeting, shifting their seats in the middle of the show. I suppose they're too rich to be polite. A new guest comes to sit at the front of the box, in a deep purple toga embroidered with gold. The editor stands to attention and orders the crowd;

"Hail, Caesar!"

"Hail, Caesar!" The cry whips in a wave across the arena. From here I can look straight into the face of Claudius Caesar; I've come a long way! He's muttering something to the editor, who nods obediently and raises his hand. Once the clash of weapons grows quiet, he addresses the audience once more;

"By order of great Caesar, the chariot racing will begin as soon as this fight is done. Caesar requires that you give him a show, give him everything you've got!"

What more can he want than he already has? Bodies sprinkled in every part of the arena, innocent people waiting to be torn to pieces by hungry lions? Maybe there is one more thing.

One of the group of seven has lost control; he was struggling to stand strong, as the lions approached he grew visibly fearful; now, against his own will, he runs. The crowd laugh, the lions chase him. That's my chance; I race in the other direction.

"Don't run away!" Nathan screams after me. I've gone out of his sight, back through the arch into the cool tunnel near the gladiators' cells. I drag my leg on, to the menagerie.

"No gladiators are allowed in here," snaps a trainer. I lower my sword at him, hissing;

"GladiaTORS, not me! Get the elephants! Caesar's here, he wants everything, now!" I slide open Chica's door myself, stroke her between the eyes, and lead her back to the arena. The trainers are convinced, so the other two elephants follow us. Once through the gate, Chica lifts me up onto her back.

Across the sand from us is the door to the party room. It's heavily-barred from the inside, of course, but I think Chica could fit through it. And the door to the outside is much larger. The door to the outside! I'll never see that again, but Nathan must.

One of the lions is dead, so is one of the seven gladiators. The sight of them lying there is too awful to look at. I can't explain it, but the lionesses have stopped pacing at the temple step. They move away, still pacing ruthlessly, looking for a different way to climb up, or easier prey. While they circle the central barrier I drive Chica and her friends to the group of my friends trapped on the roof.

There's another of those last seven men hanging over the low wall, dangling his mace in his hand. Abram stands over him with a reddened sword. He's clutching at a rip in his shoulder, where the mace must have caught him, but his eyes are fixed on Persis and Nathan. He jolts back when he sets eyes on the elephant.

"Nice one!" Secundus laughs in relief. "Our secret weapon. Listen, Takis, remember the party? The doors are big..." He needs say no more, Takis' eyes widen in appreciation of our brief plan. He slides down onto the back of an elephant, waving for Nathan to follow; the boy's face is terrified, though his singing never falters.

"They'll be back in a minute!" I remind him quickly. "What next?"

"Cut my dress off," Secundus suggests. "It's tied like the Knot of Hercules." I slash at the tangle he's made trying to get it off. Corinthus was right, it would have been much easier to cut through his daughter's belt at her wedding instead of rearranging it for her groom to play with.

"If only we had fire," Takis sighs, "we could hold the lions off. If only…" I point out to him;

"There are amphorae of oil up there." Without a flame, they're useless. But Secundus hisses in a breath, followed by an alarming chuckle. We both stare at him. His next announcement confirms his madness;

"We'll get married!"

Chapter 30

Has the world stopped in its tracks? Yes, one day we could have been married, and not in haste. I'm fairly sure I would've said 'yes'; but here, now, with lions circling and damnatii throwing spears? What in the world can Secundus be talking about? In the heart of chaos, he's *still* having a chat!

"Caesar wants a show, and a wedding needs fire! Takis, give us your scarf." I can tell by his tightened lips that he's writing a script in his head; nothing can stop him.

"All right, let's get married! Don't worry, it's meaningless. What's that face?" What face does he think I'm making? I don't know! Why's he still talking, in the middle of all this?

"Fine, it's real."

"Fine!" I snap.

He sits behind me on Chica's back, tugs off the scraps of wreath that still cling to my head, and spreads the flame-coloured veil beneath them. Takis hands him two amphorae, one in each hand, and Secundus orders me to take us to Caesar. He's not too careful with the oil, it drips behind him in a thick trail.

Caesar sits in his box before us, almost on a level with the elephant's head. It's pointless being scared of the purple-robed man now, but I still am. And I'm hallucinating in the heat, I see a woman moving along the seating in a woollen stola, and convince myself it's my old mistress Lucina. The gladiators had something to drink, but I missed out, now I'm dehydrating and going mad.

"Hail, Caesar! I have captured my Sabine woman; do you mind if I finish off the tale by marrying her?" The audience laughs, he smiles at them, sweeping his gaze across them to draw them into the action.

The editor rises to stare at him incredulously. "A wedding? Here? Is she willing?"

"I am, sir," I shout, trying to project my voice. I may as well try the sweeping glance thing as well. How do all the audience feel, to be looking death in the face?

"Get on with it, then!"

"Sir, we need cake!" Nero rises; he may be a powerful Senator, but he's no older than Nathan. He holds out a whole cake that was going stale on the table in front of him. Chica stretches across the moat which divides us, takes it in her trunk at my command, and spares us both a chunk once she's tasted it. Food! It tastes like ambrosia. With elephant-spit.

Secundus continues to work the crowd, calling out cheerfully; "Anyone who has cake, please eat it with us! And wine, if you don't mind..."

Again Chica reaches her trunk over the moat to the royal box; the audience roars as Nero's rich goblet of wine splashes over us. Secundus is unfazed;

"An offering," he shouts. "Thank you very much, elephant. Now, Aysel Pulchra, Gladiatrix..." He turns me to him, and holds my hands in his. I bet he knows he's turned my back on Caesar, a deadly sacrilege. And he cares as little as I do. "Repeat after me," he smiles. "Ubi tu Gaius..."

I remember the words from Corinthus' daughter's wedding. I cry them out across the bloodied arena; "Ubi tu Gaius, ego Gaia!" and hiss under my breath; "Hurry!"

The lionesses are nearing the front of the temple again. Abram struggled to slide down onto the elephant with his wound, but now he's waving his sword dangerously at the lions. Naasir's trying to reach them, but Kiral's engaged him in a fight. So Kiral's not on our side at all.

"Well done! Isn't she beautiful, everyone?" Secundus rolls on. They cheer back, yelling grim congratulations. "Now, my bride needs to carry a flame. Senator?" Nero's amused; he reaches for a torch, but his uncle holds up his hand in a stern warning, and glares. Nero fixes him with a look of hatred; then he nods angrily to a blue-cloaked guard.

250

The guard places the torch in the waiting trunk. Chica's trained to carry torches; she puts it straight into Secundus' hand. He glances behind him; Persis is scrambling onto an elephant. "Now I ask my bride to light the fire... and free the rest of the Sabine Women. Drop it now."

Guards leap forward; they can't reach us, it's too late. I drop the torch onto the trail of oil. Flames leap up beside us, searing across the sand to the temple. The lions are trapped by the fire, the two elephants storm over the clear path across the sand and charge at the arch in the gate of the arena. The door breaks with a crash and a trumpet of rage. Takis, Abram, Persis and Nathan are gone, to safety, I hope.

The battle isn't over. The lions are gone, so are the rest of the seven fresh gladiators. Naasir's battling a lioness; he's trying to stun her with a hammer instead of killing her! Seriously! The Chief has a trident; he stabs that into the lioness, she leaps and swipes her claws across his neck. In the same deadly motion, she plunges her teeth into Naasir's arm and shoulder.

As I hurry Chica towards them, the lioness flops down, dragging my friend with her, and her chest sags one final time. I have to steel myself to slide down and grab the trident. It's a tough task, prising the jaws apart, and the pain in my leg's growing as it loses blood.

I've freed Naasir, although he can hardly stand. Quickly I put my back to his, looking round the arena for new opponents. There are none; the augur engaged Kiral to save Naasir, but he's lost a whole arm and is falling. With his body he pushes Kiral into the dying flames.

I have a grain of energy left; while Secundus holds Naasir upright, I stagger to Kiral's outstretched hand and pull him out of the fire, as anyone would. He's tinged with soot, and his body's a strange shape. "May God help you," is my hurried prayer for him. The editor's calling for Secundus, but he won't go without me.

Supporting Naasir between us, we walk quietly away from the lion cub, who's crept up behind us to sniff at its mother. It's afraid of us, and leaves us to edge towards the royal box. Caesar's relaying a message to the editor. He shouts it out to Secundus; now we're off the elephant, he can look down on us again. "Play actor! You have set fire to our arena!"

"In the name of my Sabine Woman!" Secundus insists. "You asked for a show... O Caesar. Did you all enjoy the show?" He's impossible; the audience love him.

"Actually, I lit the fire," I observe. The soldiers in Ephesus didn't take me for a troublemaker and let Naasir go, but I'm certainly trouble now, so just maybe they'll let Secundus off.

"See?" he's laughing, more sure of his audience than I am. "I don't need the others, I got the best woman! Hail Aysel Pulchra!" Screams fill my ears, I begin to see why Secundus loves the stage. Everyone's watching me, and I think the pain's making me delirious. My mind projects strange visitors into the crowd, my mistress and the Abram's friend Gaius- as if he'd set foot in such a crowd after his nightmare in the Ephesian theatre! The screams of praise are intoxicating, although it's a pathetic reward for whipping and bloodied arms and legs.

One scream hits me with its hopeless desperation, heightening my memory of home; "We make the gods!" It's Kiral. He has one more parting shot. He's grabbed half of the youngest veles' spear, and with a last effort he throws it. On the temple roof he missed me; not this time.

The blade bites into my shoulder, where Corinthus had my plate armour removed. I'm thrown to the ground. This is pain I can't possibly ignore. I refuse to delight the crowd by squealing; my teeth grit together so tightly my sweating cheeks ache. The shaft falls, pulling the tip, stretching the wound, I can feel every movement.

Someone's pulled the spear out, blood flows with it. My head's lighter than ever. There's a huge sigh of sympathy from the crowd. I can see through the people, through the seats and the circus wall and the mountain to a beautiful, distant light.

A movement nearby distracts me; a referee's coming, his sword ready in his hand. He's decided it'll be kinder to finish me off quickly than to let me suffer. No doubt he's right. As I drift out of consciousness I hear a man's voice shouting; "Stop!" Gaius, I imagine. "She's a Roman citizen!" Oh, yes? Me? I've lived and died a common slave. That's definitely a hallucination caused by this awful pain.

"This is Aysel Claudia Celera, daughter of Panaius Celerus of Ephesus. You had no right..." Daughter of Panaius Celerus? That's a laugh, obviously my sick mind's playing a sick joke. That *would* make me a Roman citizen, and *they* don't get condemned to fight in the arena! Wow, Corinthus would be in trouble if that were true!

Gaius' unbelievable protest is drowned by a whisper close to my ear.

"Please don't take her; take me, not Aysel!"

Naasir kneels beside me, trying vainly to staunch the blood from my shoulder. I wish he wouldn't touch it, and that the referee would get a move on. Naasir's actually crying, I can feel his tears on the back of my hand.

"In Jesus' name, save her, please! In Jesus' name, please!" He whispers it without stopping; it's a more comforting sound to me than the false sympathy of the crowd.

I'm losing the light, and the pain, and that vision of the Heavenly gates. It's all fading. What's wrong with me? I suppose I may as well stand up and find out.

For some reason the crowd's gasping in amazement; what a herd of sheep they are! I step up to Secundus' side; he looks surprised too, funny man. The editor passes Gaius a scroll, which he waves at me excitedly. Seriously, I can't recall what the commotion's about.

When Secundus puts his arm on my shoulder, he's shocked again. It's all right, it doesn't hurt. The pain's in my arm and leg. The editor's the same, he stares at me as if he's just witnessed a wonder; it beats me. But there's blood on my hand, I realise it's my own, and there's a matching red patch on the sand behind me.

I reach a hand to my back, as I start to remember Kiral's spear throw. There's nothing there, that's what the editor's staring at in total awe. He throws a heavy purse onto the sand, yelling at Secundus;

"Take your money, and your bride, and get out of here!"

The gladiator grabs the purse, and reaches out to Naasir.

"I said, get out!" the editor screeches. All right, we're going. Naasir's strong enough to stand alone now.

As we cross the sand, the editor calls Naasir, by his gladiator name.

"Naasir Bestia, the gladiator who doesn't kill! Do you want to live?" Naasir stands in front of the royal box and nods. "And be free?" That fires the slave with enough strength to nod again.

The editor appeals to the crowd; they've enjoyed the show, and Secundus is hyping them all up as we walk. They chant Naasir's name, including the 'Bestia' bit. The editor holds out a wooden sword, the symbol of a gladiator's freedom. He asks much more than he asked us, I don't know why he words it that way;

"Then bow to Caesar, your god!"

A brilliant light flashes briefly in my mind, the light of Heaven. Naasir looks up at Caesar and answers;

"I serve Jesus Christ, the Son of the Living God."

As he begins to explain what that means, he lifts up his head as a gladiator should, and the referee slits his throat.

* * * * *

254

Sword against Flame.

Junia's missing finger means she'll never be a Vestal Virgin, only a servant to one. When her mistress Mafuane falls in love with the mysterious, guilt-ridden Naasir, Junia tries to warn her of the horrors they face, like being buried alive.

While Naasir searches for light and forgiveness, the Vestal house is caught between Junia's uncle Cassius and the Emperor who hates him.

Junia needs to watch her back as Caesar attacks her family, but her care for her friend plunges her deeper and deeper into the dark world of the Roman Forum.

Prologue.

His master screams as the trembling slave runs with a golden goblet of wine.

"Who brought me this stupid letter? Cassius Chaerea has put down another rebellion? How nice! I don't care! Why would anyone in Rome rebel against me, heh?"

A purple-cloaked soldier steps in front of the slave, deflects the goblet thrown by his master, and dares to point out;

"Caesar, excuse me, but Chaerea is a war hero, the people love him."

Caligula's hand trembles at the thought of being challenged. The soldier backs away.

"He's a Nancy-boy who makes my flesh crawl! I want rid of him and his whole rotten family. Start with that niece of his, down at Vesta's place, the nine-fingered freak."